FIEFDOM

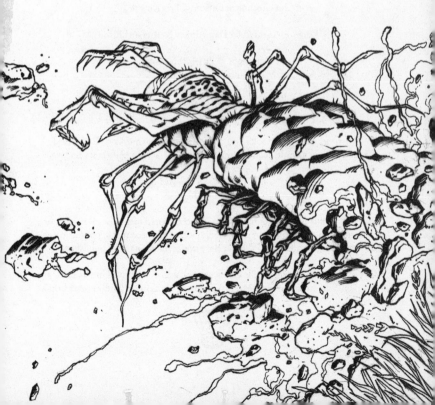

An Abaddon Books™ Publication
www.abaddonbooks.com
abaddon@rebellion.co.uk

Published in 2014 by Abaddon Books™,
Rebellion Intellectual Property Limited,
Riverside House, Osney Mead, Oxford, OX2 0ES, UK.

10 9 8 7 6 5 4 3 2 1

Editor-in Chief: Jonathan Oliver
Commissioning Editor: David Moore
Cover Art: Clint Langley
Internal Art: Richard Elson
Design: Pye Parr & Sam Gretton
Marketing and PR: Michael Molcher
Publishing Manager: Ben Smith
Creative Director and CEO: Jason Kingsley
Chief Technical Officer: Chris Kingsley

Kingdom created by Dan Abnett & Richard Elson

ISBN: 978-1-78108-235-5
Printed in the US

DAN ABNETT & NIK VINCENT
FIEFDOM
A KINGDOM NOVEL

ABADDON
BOOKS

WWW.ABADDONBOOKS.COM

"In the animal kingdom,
the rule is, eat or be eaten;
in the human kingdom,
define or be defined."

– Thomas Szasz

CHAPTER ONE
DOG TALES

"GENE THE HACKMAN, top dog, him done the great Walk Around," the old male intoned, chilly in the forsaken tunnel.

"Not for him the darkness, not for him the cold, not for him the Time of Ice that we know today. This is a tale of ages long gone, of the Old War. You of the Pack, you huddle in close and hear me tell it now. Hear me tell the old legend, so that you can better know the crafts of war handed down in the words."

The tale-teller was Edward Leer. Aged, he hunched by the fire on the U-Bahn platform and cleared his throat. He looked out at the attentive faces of the young pack members sitting around him.

It was by hearing the ancient fables of the Old

War over and again that the Pack preserved its knowledge of fighting craft. The tales were just dumb old myths, and no one was mad enough to believe that there had ever been any monsters. But the techniques of scrapping and warfare that the stories recorded were a precious resource that had to be preserved.

"Gene the Hackman, him Alpha dog," said Edward Leer. "Gene the Hackman, him got whet. Gene the Hackman, him got whet and walked the Earth and killed *Them*."

Leer's voice fell.

The fire crackled.

Flame shadows danced up the dirty tiled walls of Old Zoo. The tiles had been laid in the shapes of animals, and the light-flicker revealed them, quick and gone again, like eyes in a forest at night, lurking in shadows.

The Pack listened.

Evelyn War listened too. She sat away from the rest, down on the rails beside the platform.

That was her usual place. She was a loner, a virtual omega, and few in the pack liked to mix with her. They thought she was mad, as mad as her dead father. They thought she was mad because she had believed the things her father had said.

Edward Leer had been the Pack's tale-teller for as long as Evelyn War had been alive.

He had been whelped the same season as her father. Now that Oberon War was gone, Leer the tale-teller was her only ally in the Zoo Pack. He had been one of the few pack members who had considered Oberon War a friend and tolerated his mad pronouncements, even though he didn't believe them.

Now that Evelyn's father was dead, Leer kept an eye on her. The Zoo Pack had a brutal hierarchy. It had to be so in order to survive in the Time of Ice. Evelyn had no other protection.

She listened to the words of the story, coming from Leer's lips in the same precise order that they'd always come, in the same flowing, sing-song tones.

When Leer paused, which he did often to add suspense and drama to the telling, the pack youngsters waited, their breaths filling the cold air with spirals of steam. They huddled closer to the crackling fire.

Like Evelyn, they knew the words of the tale and the exact order in which they came, but they listened anyway. The fighting skills described in the stories would help them all become fine scrappers one day, maybe even Alpha dog. Besides, the talk of monsters and beasts kept them amused.

"Gene the Hackman," Leer continued, "him bared his teeth back to his gums. His spit flowed freely, foaming his tongue, dripping from his lips as his jaw tightened with the growl rising in his throat. Gene the Hackman, him stood firm, ears flat, eyes tight and hard, chest huge and heaving. Tougher and tough."

The Pack nodded, approving.

"Gene the Hackman, him top dog, Alpha male. Him fought fearless. Gene the Hackman, him fought with the double-blades, one in each fist, so that him could bite with them to either side, or draw them together in front of him. Him could swing them, double-strike across his body to sever and shear. Gene, him was quick. Only the quickest can fight well with the double blades. So Gene him come, and there was a Rak before him."

A murmur ran through the pack. Monster-talk always delighted them.

"Gene, him went at the Rak," said Leer, "thrusting them double-blades truer and true through the hard-shell of the Rak's thorax as it reared up high, high up over him."

Leer raised his skinny arms and made them dance like the monstrous bristly limbs of a mythical Rak. The Pack mock-shivered gleefully.

"Twice more Gene the Hackman him swung, swung hard, cracking the Rak's body and breaking its legs. Them was everywhere. Everywhere Them was. Them was screaming and dying. Gene the Hackman, top dog, him was making Them scream and making Them die."

Leer's voice dropped to a mournful whisper, like the sigh of the wind along the empty U-Bahn tunnels.

"Them killed, too. The Raks, them swarmed an old dog soldier. Friend of Gene. True friend, good friend. Pack friend."

The pack nodded again. There was always some

noble rumination in the tales on the theme of loss and the cost of fighting. It was an expected part of each story.

"The Raks, them chittered and clawed. Them bit and sucked, until Them killed the old male. Gene the Hackman, him saw the kill, and him saw red. Gene the Hackman, him howled. Gene the Hackman, him threw up his arms and him threw out his chest. The sky, it filled with his cry and with the hum of his blades through the air."

Younger members of the Pack nodded vigorously, and slapped the ground with their palms. Vengeance for loss was a principle of war.

"Gene the Hackman, him got whet with the old male's blood and him got whet with the Raks' gore. Gene the Hackman, him got whet with the sweat of his brow. Gene the Hackman, him got whet and him walked the Earth and killed Them. And that was the scrapping of that day."

The Pack approved the telling with cheers and howling.

"When Gene the Hackman, him was done and Them was dead, Gene the Hackman, him mourned the passing of the old male, just as us, we mourn the ending of all legends."

The tale was done. Old Zoo fell silent for a moment, but for the spit of the burning logs.

No matter the length of the fable – and many of the tales were short, bloody battle reports – the ending was always the same, always a tribute to the myth that was Gene the Hackman.

He was the legendary Aux sire from which all the packs descended.

A cocky young scrapper, Richard Dadd, new-called into the service of Zoo Pack, and several other pups, shouted eagerly for another tale. But Evelyn War knew that Leer was finished tale-telling for the night, and that he would not be persuaded to continue. The entertainment was done. It was time for work to resume.

About a third of the Pack, close to twenty of the young adults, had gathered to listen. Gradually, the group dispersed, some singly, some in pairs, taking their little clouds of breath with them deeper into the surrounding tunnels.

There were always duties to perform as night came in. Most of the adults were tending to the infants, running maintenance, taking their turns at sentry duties, or walking the perimeters of Old Zoo. The rest retired alone or with a mate, so they would wake in time for the early watch.

Evelyn lingered. She had duties of her own to attend to, and the first was to clear up the fire on the platform. But she also hoped to be able to speak to Edward Leer alone.

She hesitated. She knew he was often tired after a recitation, and she hated to bother him.

Edward Leer rose wearily from where he had been left sitting against the ancient tiled wall of the old underground station, adjusting a heavy felt blanket around his hard, bony shoulders.

The last log on the fire collapsed with a bitter spit

and a flurry of orange embers. Most of its heat was gone, but a final rush of sparks made the shadowy images on the grimy wall behind the old male dance one last time.

The tale-teller limped into the dark tunnel before she had the courage to step forwards. Evelyn sighed and watched for several seconds as Edward Leer's stooped frame receded into the gloom.

Silence. She savoured the rare moment when the platform, one of the Zoo Pack's main communal spaces, was utterly empty and quiet. That was when her father had liked to listen most, in the silence.

Evelyn was left alone. She was used to that. She walked towards the mouth of the nearest service tunnel to find the tools to clear the fire. Though she was considered omega, she was still a useful dog soldier, loyal to her pack. But she was also a Believer, and because she was a Believer, no one had anything to do with her.

She wished she had someone to talk to. A friend, a mate, a confidant. The things her father had said to her in the weeks before his death had made her uneasy.

She mourned him, of course, but it was his absence in the pack that made her truly anxious. There was no Hearer left in the Pack, and she was the only Believer. Her father had said... he had said that change was coming, and so the Pack would have to change too. No one had wanted to hear that.

She tried to put aside her unease. She had night duties to perform. Stopping for an hour to hear the fables recited was the high point of each day for her, even though she had heard Leer tell them a hundred-hundred times before. She knew every word of every legend so well she could tell them back herself.

Tale-telling was a responsibility. The duty often fell to the oldest member of a pack, the Aux with the longest memory. A gift of the gab helped too. In Zoo Pack, it was Edward Leer's duty to remember the words, so that they could be re-said.

A tale-teller needed to remember the order in which the words had to be spoken, the tone that must be used, where the pauses fell and how long they should last. He had to know in what order the stories ought to be performed, when the time was right to tell a particular fable, and when it was time to stop the tale-telling. It was a craft just as important as scrapping.

Evelyn's father, Oberon War, had talked about the legends often. But to him, they had been much more than a primer for martial skills.

"Leer tells the tales," said Oberon War, "over and again, so that we do not forget. But Zoo Pack must remember *Them*, in case *Them* ever come back."

She could hear his voice, telling her that. The legends were principally instructional, intended to educate the pack about fighting skills, loyalty, and solidarity. But Oberon War had said there were other stories, stories Leer never told. Oberon had known this because he and he alone had heard the Voice.

Oberon War had been a Hearer, the last of that kind in the Old Zoo Pack. Hearers were regarded as touched by madness. Evelyn always consoled herself with the thought that, in the legends, Gene the Hackman, Alpha dog, had been a Hearer too.

According to the stories, back in the days of the legends, all dog soldiers had been Hearers, and all their whelps had been Hearers too. Alpha males and beta males, the old and the young, and the dams, even the omega dogs, they had all been Hearers. They had all heard the Master's Voice, and they had all followed its Urgings.

The Voice had told them to fight to keep Them back, to kill Them deader and dead. The Voice had commanded the Aux in the Old War.

Oberon War, whelped to the Zoo Pack in the Endless Winter, had been the last Aux who claimed to be able to hear the Master's Voice. It was a talent that set him apart from the others, a dying skill. The rest of the Pack feared him and mocked him. No one ever befriended him. They were relieved when he died and they no longer had to listen to his madness.

To them, his mouth had too often been full of wrong.

Evelyn War had tried to Hear the Voice like her father. She had tried *hard*. She *wanted* to Hear, she wanted to be able to Hear the Voice the way her sire had, but she could not. But Evelyn War *Believed*. She believed the tales that Edward Leer told not as fables of a long-dead age, or as parable myths from which fighting skills could be learned, but as her father had: as the absolute truth, as a truth that was going to come full circle.

It was the one thing her father had insisted upon, even though the Pack mocked him for it.

Evelyn believed that one day, after the long, Endless Winter, Them would return. Them would come back and the pack would have to get whet again.

That was what the Master's Voice had told her father. She cleaved to it as a truth.

With every day that passed, that truth seemed to be bearing down on her, like an avalanche toppling towards her, threatening to carry her off. She could not explain the feeling. The truth had not faded with the memory of her father, as perhaps it might have, but grew stronger every day in her heart and mind.

Duties, *duties*. She found a rusty shovel and an old sack and was about to make her way back to the platform when she heard a sound.

A *ping*. A *ping* and a crack. Then another. Her head darted back and forth, following the noise.

She heard another crack, more like smashing this time. It had come from the platform.

It was almost completely dark, but – like all the Aux who lived underground – Evelyn could distinguish one shade of darkness from another. She saw all the tones of grey in almost any conditions.

She ducked, squatting low in her knees, so that her head was below the height of the platform. She took a breath and she waited, watching the tiled wall intently. She did not exhale, so as not to allow the steam of her breath to give away her position.

She heard another *ping* and a crack, and this time she saw the source. A hard projectile hit the tiles. She saw a whizzing stone crack a tile depicting the snout of some magical creature.

Evelyn knew where the missile had been launched from. The fables had taught her about trajectories and angles.

She sprang from her crouch, and bolted a dozen metres to her right. She could see the figure that had been firing the projectiles: it was on her level, on the tracks. It appeared to be doubled over, reaching for something between its feet.

She hurled her entire weight into it.

They wrestled, crashing over. Evelyn felt teeth sinking into the muscle at the base of her neck. She seized her attacker's ears, wrenching them hard, and banged the back of the head against the cold, dead rail that the trains had once run on.

"Bitch!" snarled a voice.

Evelyn War thought for a moment that she had decked another dam, until she realised how young the pup was. Still sitting on his chest, she gripped his jaw firmly in her right hand and tilted his head.

Fierce yellow eyes glared out from beneath a brow ridge that was hairless and still forming.

"Tougher and tough, eh?" said Evelyn. "Or just another piece of Zoo shit?"

"Tougher'n *you*," the pup replied.

Evelyn's grip lowered and tightened against his throat.

"Tough enough to choke a pup?" growled the young Aux, kicking at Evelyn's back to no effect.

"Don't tempt me," said Evelyn, "and you, don't run like some hairless-belly when I let you go."

Her hand still firmly locked around the pup's throat, Evelyn did a quick scan around his body, but couldn't see what she was looking for. He'd hidden the weapon, or his body had fallen on top of it when she'd dropped him. No matter. Her knees were pinning his arms, and there was nothing in his hands, so the worst he could do was run.

Evelyn let go of the pup's neck and stepped off him. By the time he had clambered to his feet, she had located the scattered pile of stones that he'd collected, and she'd scooped up the handmade sling he'd used to launch them at the tiled wall.

The pup rubbed his neck and watched Evelyn as she examined the sling. It was beautifully made. A well-worn piece of soft leather had been sewn into a pouch for a stone, and fixed to the middle of a length of firm, supple sinew, looped at one end.

Evelyn took the ends of the sinew in her hands and pulled hard, stretching the cord to check its strength. It made a sharp sound in the air as she twanged it.

She bent to pick up a small, oval stone and fit it into the pouch. She hooked the middle finger of her right hand through the loop and took the other end of the sinew firmly between her thumb and forefinger. Facing away from the pup, aiming down the tunnel,

Evelyn swung the sling, whipped it once around her head and let go with her finger and thumb as her muscular arm reached full extension.

The pup's eyes widened, and he craned his neck to peer down the tunnel. He counted off the time before they finally heard the stone land, skittering to a rest in the darkness.

Evelyn tucked the sling into her waistband at her hip, close to her right hand.

"That's *mine*!" said the pup.

"You can have it when you can *take* it," said Evelyn.

The pup eyed her up and down, and Evelyn returned the favour. He was a full head shorter than she was, but his face was serious. She snickered.

Evelyn shoved the pup in the shoulder with the flexed ends of three of her fingers, jabbing him in the direction of the platform.

"You, get up there, 'tougher and tough'," she said. "You, look at what you did."

The pup vaulted onto the dark platform and then turned to look down on Evelyn, his hands on his hips.

"Ben Gun is my name," he said. He offered her his hand.

Evelyn ignored it. She placed her hands flat on the platform concourse and sprang onto the walkway with one easy movement. Clapping the accumulated dust and ash from her hands, she pointed to the wall.

"You, show me," she said. "Breaker of things. Vandal."

Ben shrugged and began to trace the marks his missiles had made on the tiles with his fingers.

"Here, see? And here?" he said.

He looked at her.

"Me, I hit well," he said, proudly. "Good aim."

In some places the stones had cracked the tiles, leaving dark veins. In others, they had chipped the surface, exposing the hard, white clay beneath. In some places the stones had only glanced off, leaving dirty smudges

All the missiles had hit the old shadowy forms of ancient creatures, the sort of beasts that might have lived before... Before the Time of Ice, before Gene the Hackman, before there were any dog soldiers, even before the Masters had bred the Aux.

Before *Them*.

Evelyn ran a hand over one of the creatures. She didn't know what it was, but it was about the same height as a fully grown male, although its body was oddly shaped and its head was small.

One of Ben's stones had hit the beast in the head, and cracks radiated out in all directions. Evelyn couldn't bear to touch the tile for fear that pieces of it would fall away.

"You, see what you did!" said Evelyn, scowling hard into Ben's face. "This is old stuff! *Old time stuff!* And you smashed it for *target practice*?"

Ben frowned, bewildered, ears hard back against the sides of his head.

"Me, I hit what I was shooting at," he said. "Me, I'm going to be a dog soldier. It's what the Pack wants."

"These things were here first," said Evelyn. "They walked here before us, before the Masters, before the Aux. They are us and we are them."

Ben Gun looked at Evelyn and frowned. He reached his fingers out and touched the shadow on the wall, puzzled. He rubbed his hand against the shadow, the better to see it, but the wall was dirty and his hand was filthy. He obscured more of the strange creature than he uncovered.

"Me, I was just shooting at myths," he said.

Evelyn strode the half-dozen metres to the tale-teller's fire, reached in for a handful of the warm ashes and spat on them until she had made a paste between her palms.

She rubbed the paste into the shadow beast on the tiled wall, and the greys began to separate. She spat on the paste again as it dried in her hands. Ben joined in, and they cleaned the beast on the tiles until it was clearly visible in the grime that had built up over scores – hundreds – of years below ground.

Ben Gun stood away from the wall and glared in disgust at what they had uncovered.

It was a strange creature, standing upright on large, muscular rear legs, with an arched back and a strong, tapering tail spread on the ground behind it. Its short forelegs, more like arms, were held in front of its torso, almost as if it was boxing. Its head was small, with pointed ears on the top, and it had a snouted face.

"Me, I am *not* the same as that thing," he said in disgust. "The tales, them are for fools. Them are all lies and make-believe. There are no Masters. There is no Voice, and there certainly wasn't *never* no beasts." Then Ben squinted at Evelyn as if he was seeing her for the first time.

"You's *her!*" he said. "You's *Evelyn War*. You's mad and your father, him was *mad too*! If him said he heard the Master's Voice, him was a *liar*, and you's a fool for *believing* him!"

Ben Gun cleared his throat loudly and spat on the ground with a wet splat. Evelyn opened her mouth to say something, but he cut her off.

"Tougher 'n' tough... Me, I *am* tougher 'n' tough," said Ben, backing away from Evelyn, but never taking his eyes off the dam. "*You'll* see."

At the end of the platform, Ben squatted, placed his hands next to his feet, and dropped down onto the rails. Then he turned and ran off down the tracks and out of sight of Zoologischer Garten U-Bahn station, Berlin.

CHAPTER TWO
GROUND-SOUND

ALONE AGAIN, EVELYN War set to work clearing away Edward Leer's fire. After a few minutes, she heard another *ping*.

At first she thought Ben Gun had returned.

There was another *ping* and then several more at short intervals. It wasn't a slingshot missile; it was a new sound, one Evelyn had never heard before. It was almost like water dripping from a flask.

After a pause, there came a long, slow whistle that echoed out of the deep tunnels. That was *definitely* a sound that she had never heard before.

"What *is* that?" she murmured.

Evelyn held her breath, and turned her head slowly as the pings and eerie whistles continued to echo through the empty space and the surrounding tunnels. She tracked them for several moments, but then she lost them as the tunnels suddenly filled with the sound of rushing feet.

The dogs of Zoo did not need an alarm. They were permanently on guard. Ground-sound had alerted them. A patrol of dog soldiers rushed out along the platform, armed and ready.

"War?" called Thomas Hardy. "You, did you see anything?"

"Not a thing," she replied."

"What was that sound?" asked another. "That whistling sound?"

"Me, I know not," she replied.

Evelyn realised she was worried about the pup. Ben Gun had run off into the tunnels, directly towards the source of the uncanny sound.

She looked up at the dog-pack on the platform. They were armed and ready. Times were tough... tougher and tough. No one could remember a time before the Time of Ice. The Pack, like all of the Berlin packs, protected its territory fiercely.

"It must be Uhland Gang," said Ward Cleaver, an old scrapper.

The pack agreed.

"Uhland Gang, it is trying to sneak up the tunnels."

The pack snarled.

"Well, then, us, we'll bite 'em off, tougher and tough!" shouted Ward Cleaver.

Evelyn hesitated. Why would a sneak-pack attack from the Uhland give itself away like that?

"It's *not* the Uhland," she said.

The dog soldiers gathering in the tunnel looked to one another. No one seemed to know where the sounds came from or what they meant, but no one wanted to respond to the pariah Evelyn War. She might have *Heard* something, like her crazy sire.

"You, as you were, War," said Ward Cleaver. "You, get back to your duties,"

A fight suddenly broke out between two of the young beta males in the patrol.

They growled at each other. They swung fists, butted heads and cracked jaws. They wrestled each other to the ground, and the males and dams around them were distracted for several moments, drawn into the squabble.

"Enough of that!" a voice cried.

Hard wood struck marble. Edward Leer had appeared on the platform behind them, and smacked the ground with the staff of office that he always carried. He was not alone. The gathered pack saw that their leader was standing beside the old tale-teller, and fell silent.

Ezra Pound was a vast Alpha male of middle age. He had led Zoo Pack successfully for over a decade, and none had seen fit to challenge him. None had got the bone for it.

Ezra Pound's reign would not continue for very much longer; Evelyn War's father had told her so shortly before he had died. Sometimes the thought frightened her, sometimes it felt like a relief.

"Zoo Pack stands firm," began Ezra Pound, "tougher and tough! Me, I'm told there's ground-sound. Must be a gang, sneaking onto our lawn. Track Two, it belongs to Zoo Pack. This is our fiefdom. Us, let's find them, and make sure them don't forget it!"

Evelyn War had heard speeches like this too many times before. Another exhortation to scrap and to deepen the divisions between packs. It was a philosophy that her father had come to utterly despise.

The face of every male and dam was turned to Ezra Pound, intent on his message. But Evelyn had heard enough.

No pack had made the sounds she had heard.

She slipped away. No one cared about her, so no one noticed her leaving. She wanted to find Ben Gun and make sure he was safe. Behind her, Ezra Pound and the dog soldiers debated the origin of the noises and the tactics they should employ.

Evelyn War moved fast and almost silently, jogging east along the tunnel, dangerously close to the limits of Zoo Pack territory.

In the darkest reaches of the tunnel, Evelyn stopped and flattened her back against the ancient, greasy wall. She caught her breath.

In the airless silence, she listened, tilting her head, the better to hear what was happening ahead and behind.

A *ping* echoed down the tunnel. It was close, and sounded as if it was coming from above Evelyn's position.

It was forever cold in the Time of Ice. The

warmest places were to be found below ground. The Zoo Pack was one of the richest and toughest of Berlin's Aux tribes, so it controlled one of the best territories, a well-sheltered stretch of the central Berlin underground. Evelyn had been on an empty platform at Zoologischer Garten because, at night, anyone who wasn't on sentry duty went deeper into the service tunnels where the cells and communal dorms were situated. The service tunnels were the warmest, safest areas of Zoo Pack turf; there were fewer points of ingress, so they were easier to defend.

Had that idiot pup gone outside? Evelyn gathered her snug fur tighter around her shoulders and pulled the layers of her sleeves closer around her wrists. If she dared to venture above ground, it would be more than just cold.

She had to do her weather checks.

Evelyn pulled a long section of cloth from beneath the collar of her jacket. She secured it around her neck and head, wrapping it carefully so that she could still listen.

She paused. She thought she heard something, so she pressed her body against the tunnel wall and caught her breath again. When no new sound came, she continued her checks. She pushed her fingers down into the tops of her boots to check for the slender hilts of her long stiletto blades.

She would have liked a projectile weapon. Had she been on patrol, Evelyn would have been carrying a neat crossbow on her back. A pair of bandoliers for handmade bolts would have tightly criss-crossed her body, so that they didn't clatter when she ran and alert her prey. She missed the bandoliers. They had hugged her torso, making her aware of her every breath and, somehow, making her feel secure.

The blades would have to do.

Evelyn ran her hands over her boot clasps and elbow pads, and around the toggles and laces on her jacket. She needed to make sure that she was sealed from the weather and that her clothes wouldn't catch or be ripped. She couldn't risk getting ice-burn.

Before fastening her gloves back in place, she also checked her waist seal. Her finger caught on something. She hooked out the slingshot that she'd taken from Ben Gun.

Evelyn smiled. She had a projectile weapon, after all.

She tucked the sling into the double cuff of her jacket, where it would be easy to hook out, and she wouldn't have to hunt for it. Then, not relaxing her vigilance, she bent and picked up a handful of the small, smooth stones that could be found all over the U-Bahn tunnels. She couldn't pocket them; they'd cause a bulge, and they'd clink together when she moved.

She tucked them one at a time into the tight double cuff of her other sleeve, leaving a few millimetres between each stone so that they wouldn't touch. She could only carry half a dozen stones, but she'd only need them in an emergency, and if six wouldn't get her out of trouble, more wouldn't help.

As she tucked the last stone into the thick cloth, she heard the *ping* again.

The sound was definitely coming from above.

Without a second glance behind her, Evelyn War jogged hard down the tunnel for thirty or forty seconds, her thick, soft-soled boots making almost no sound.

She made her way beyond the edges of the Zoo Pack's fiefdom to the long-abandoned station at Wittenbergplatz.

The tunnel narrowed alarmingly as she approached the station. Rubble from the destruction of the old Track Three tunnel decades before, when the Krumme Pack had been defeated and buried alive, all but filled the space, almost blocking her way.

Evelyn had to climb over shattered slabs of concrete, and crawl through impossibly small gaps in the heaped debris in almost pitch darkness before she emerged on the other side.

She stopped again and listened. Behind her, she heard a call and then a chant. Zoo Pack was gathering for war, sending up a battle cry in preparation. She would be missed, and she would have to answer for that. But she would not go back without the idiot pup.

She was squatting on the tracks, below the platform level. Her back against the wall, she slowly straightened her legs, and her eyes rose above the height of the platform. In the deep gloom of the abandoned station, she could see the rusting girders holding up the arched roof, and the banks of broken-down machinery that had once carried passengers to the surface.

Evelyn War inhaled deeply. She froze, mid-breath, one hand on the platform's cold lip, when she heard the *ping* again. The station was anonymous, its sign obliterated by time and decay, living on only in the legends.

Evelyn swallowed hard. The pinging sound came again, echoing down the broken remains of the escalators just metres from her position. It was much louder now. She could taste the bite of the freezing cold surface air. She gently exhaled a cloud of moist steam, and hurriedly clambered onto the platform. There, her well-learned skills of hunting and stealth took over. She lay flat on her stomach on the impossibly cold surface for a couple of seconds. One move at a time, nothing too hasty. She braced herself for her next action.

"Tougher and tough," she said to herself, her breath curling around the words as she climbed to her feet. "Do your father proud, dam, or die trying. He was a Hearer and you's a Believer, and that's tougher and tough."

Evelyn War had not been to the surface for weeks. No one went outside alone. Her father had died above ground. Outside was the most dangerous place of all. All of the legends were about outside.

In the fables, the Masters had lived in the World above ground. Now, nobody but Evelyn believed the fables.

Evelyn knew that the Masters had been real, as an article of faith. Her father had Heard the Voice. He had died trying to follow their Urgings. He had died trying to save not only the Pack, but all Aux.

There is strength in numbers, that's what her father had said the Voice told him. *There is strength in numbers and we need strength to survive. A change is coming. An Age is ending. The Master wants us to form alliances.*

Evelyn War would never forget those words, and she would never forgive Ezra Pound for ignoring them.

Zoo Pack traded and bartered with other packs when it had to, but Ezra Pound was proud. He believed Zoo Pack needed to stand alone. In his mind, it was weakness to rely on the comfort of other packs, and weaker still to rely on their weapons.

"Tougher and tough," Evelyn said, climbing the old machinery of the unmoving moving staircase. There were no tread-plates left, just exposed machine guts. She climbed the handrail instead, going hand-over-hand and step-by-step up a narrow strip of metal that had once been covered by a thick sheath of rubber, long since perished.

Evelyn wished she had back-up as she scaled the skeletal remains of the escalators.

She reached what had once been the grand entrance hall of the Wittenbergplatz station.

She could not imagine what it must once have looked like. It had long ago been stripped of anything that could be looted or used to build with, or to burn, although most of the marble floor was intact, impossible to dig up without shattering the tiles. Everything not torn out in the old time was almost exactly as it had always been. The freezing temperatures of the Time of Ice had taken its toll on the glass, so there was little screening from the elements.

The next *ping* almost made Evelyn jump.

She swung around to get a full view of the entrance hall, something she had been avoiding.

The last time she had been in Wittenbergplatz station, she had been there with her father. The last time she had seen the grand hall, her father had been lying on the cold marble floor with blood oozing from the wound in his chest. The blood had congealed as it hit the air, freezing solid before it could spread across the bitterly cold tiles.

Evelyn looked at the spot on the floor where her father's body had lain. There was no mark of him, no stain. The only trace was in her memory.

CHAPTER THREE
HOW OBERON
WAR DIED

WEEKS BEFORE, ON the way to Wittenbergplatz station...

"There is strength in numbers," Oberon War said. "There is strength in numbers, and when Them return. We must needs strength. The Master's Voice, it demands it."

His whisper was low and guttural, but Evelyn could hear him well enough. If she could not hear him, she could have guessed what he was saying, because his words had become a mantra over the past weeks, and an urgent one in recent days.

"Strength in numbers," Oberon said again, and then, "Zoo Pack heard me once upon a time, before Ezra Pound, before the end of the Believers."

Evelyn knew that he was talking too much, that he

was too old to fight. She knew that she should have come alone, but he had insisted they come together. He had insisted that he must talk to the leaders of the other packs if Ezra could not be persuaded to meet with them himself.

"Aux heard me once. Aux heard me speak the Master's Voice and they Believed," he said. She knew that it was the truth.

Evelyn War could remember the strangers that visited the Zoo Pack when she was a pup. They came to hear her father talk, and to learn what the Masters had to say. Aux had been proud to be Believers, proud to follow Hearers, like her father, and to listen to their words.

"The Age of Ice, it has killed the Hearers and it has killed the Believers, but it has not killed the Master's Voice and it has not killed Them. Soon it will begin again," Oberon said.

Oberon War stopped in the tunnel. He stopped and he stood tall. Evelyn heard his sharp intake of breath. She turned to look at her father.

Oberon War's eyes glazed over and he appeared not to be breathing. He lifted his arms wide in front of his body, broadening his chest. He straightened his neck, making him taller and more upright than usual. Evelyn knew what was happening, and she knew that as much as she wanted to, she could not prevent what would come next. The Voice was in him.

"The Age of Ice will be done!" proclaimed Oberon War. "The Aux, them will get whet!"

His pronouncement boomed down the tunnel in both directions and echoed back at Evelyn.

She wanted to stop him, but there was nothing to be done. She wanted to drag her father down and away, but his feet were firmly fixed between the rails, knees locked, back straight, shoulders thrown back. He was old, but he was solidly made, heavy, and he was carrying the full weight of conviction of the Master's Voice.

She was young. So young.

Evelyn had tucked herself low under the arching wall of the tunnel while she waited for the last of the echoes to dissipate. She thought she felt a rush of air, as if something was moving down the track.

She knew that her father could be heard for hundreds of metres in two directions, and possibly along other branches of the underground system. She wondered whether he could even be heard on other levels. She wondered whether he could be heard above ground, outside. She was sure that he could.

Evelyn War wondered whether the Aux listening to Oberon's words knew that they were hearing their Master's Voice. If any of them suspected it, they would dismiss the idea at once as superstitious nonsense.

The echoes dispersed around them.

Oberon War dropped his shoulders, his chest collapsing, shrinking by several centimetres.

"Get whet," said the Hearer, but this time it was in his own weaker, more vulnerable old voice.

"Not yet," said Evelyn. "Us, we must talk to the pack leaders. Strength in numbers, remember?"

Oberon hadn't been talking to his daughter. As she shuffled out of her hiding place, Oberon looked around to see where and from whom her words were coming. He looked confused.

Evelyn took her father's arm and led him down the tunnel towards Wittenbergplatz station and their first meeting.

"Strength in numbers," he whispered back to her.

There was strength in silence and stealth, too, thought Evelyn War. Her father had robbed her of both, even though she believed in and trusted him. She was trying to fulfill his last and most urgent wish, and this was how he repaid her.

They had made it up to the grand entrance of Wittenbergplatz station and across the marble floor of the vast, deserted space. There had been no point taking their time silently skirting the hall, trying to cross it without being seen or heard.

They had been heard while they were still in the tunnels, and Evelyn knew it. She was surprised not to be greeted by armed dog soldiers from the Kade Pack. Wittenbergplatz was neutral territory, but it was on the boundary of Kade Pack land, and she had sent word that the famous Hearer, Oberon War, wished to meet with their leader. She expected to be intercepted by a war band, and she expected it sooner rather than later.

"Outside," said Oberon War.

"Checks first," said Evelyn, resigned to venturing

outside when she would rather have kept her aging father close to a route back below ground. He was vulnerable, made more so by his outburst in the tunnel.

"Strength in numbers," said Oberon, walking purposefully towards the station exit.

"Checks first," said Evelyn, again, taking her father by his arm and beginning to run his weather checks for him. She had insisted they put on eyeshades before making their way up to the station entrance, so she began by checking his boots, making sure that they were properly fastened and weather-tight.

As she worked her way over his outer clothing, Oberon began to check the fit of his cuffs and collar. Then he began to wrap his head.

"Good," said Evelyn, patting Oberon firmly on the chest before beginning her own checks. "Good."

Outside was as cold and dry and still as ever.

Exit from the station was up a ramp and through what had once been a window high above the concourse. Then out and down onto the hard-packed surface outside.

The old street level had not been seen in anyone's lifetime. It was buried under a metre and a half of ice that was as hard as concrete and almost as black. Once in a while it was covered with centimetres – or sometimes metres – of dry, drifting snow. But the snow blew away on the lightest of winds, or was collected for use as fresh water. Nothing ever tasted so good as clean water melted from virgin snow.

The ground that Oberon and Evelyn War dropped onto was black and slick. It was colder than freezing cold.

The temperature was already showing indigo on Evelyn's cuff gauge. Without extra thermal layers, she couldn't stay outside for more than an hour, and Oberon would start to suffer in half that time.

Evelyn grasped her father's arm and led him around the still-impressive shell of the station, which looked like a temple rising out of the square it stood in.

The extreme cold of the Time of Ice had caused the destruction of some of the older, smaller buildings in Berlin, and most of the glass in the city was gone. Almost all of the metal structures had survived, though. This part of Berlin was still crowded with some of the biggest, most impressive buildings that had once been the pride of the city, including the Kade Pack headquarters. Most of the buildings were abandoned shells, long since looted, now used as rat-runs through their territories by various Aux packs.

Evelyn looked west to the distinctive dirty orange roof of the Kade building, one of very few still inhabited. It was the only building she could see that did not have a thick layer of ice on its roof. It had been covered in the graffiti by the most intrepid young members of its pack.

Time was precious, so she did her risk assessment as they started to walk. It was only a few hundred metres, but if they stayed outside it could take as much as twenty minutes to get to the Kade building. And if they were turned away, her father could be in serious trouble before they made it back to shelter. Worse, if she had to fight, twenty minutes outside would put her at a disadvantage.

On the other hand, if she decided to try to navigate the unfamiliar rat-runs, she'd be out of her depth and she could be attacked at any time from any direction. If she got lost in the rat-runs, she'd be in real trouble. Better twenty minutes in the open... fifteen, if she could keep her father moving.

The moist warmth within her head wrappings was growing cold, and soon the moisture would turn to ice. Evelyn clutched her father's arm a little tighter, and he responded by walking a little faster.

They made their way south and then west, their thick, soft-soled boots making no noise on the hard, black ice that was the only street surface she had ever trodden.

They both saw the shadow at the same time.

Oberon jerked his elbow away from his daughter's grasp. He reached for the double-bladed weapon he still kept strapped to his side, despite his age and frailty.

The shadow was faster.

Evelyn drew the twin knives from their sheaths beneath her boot cuffs, and lunged to block the shadow.

The attacker was a lean, wiry male of indeterminate age, but strong and fast. His own short, narrow blade was at Oberon's throat even as the dagger in

Evelyn's right hand stopped millimetres from his chest.

The dog soldier wore no armour and carried no projectile weapon, suggesting that he was a scout or pathfinder for his pack, and that he was a Kade of some considerable status.

"You's the Hearer?" he asked, turning his head to speak into Oberon's ear.

"Oberon War," said Evelyn's father, sheathing his blade, useless to him in the stand-off. "I Hear the Master's Voice."

"Me, I am Evelyn War," said Evelyn. She kept her eyes firmly on the scout as he turned to look at her. Her right hand still extended, the point of her blade close to his chest, she slowly returned her left blade to her boot. Then, her gaze never wavering, she offered their assailant her closed left fist in salute.

The scout looked at Evelyn.

"Sheath the other blade," he said.

Evelyn's eyes flickered to her father for a moment. She could only see his back, but time was passing too fast, and she had to get him under cover as soon she could. She'd take her chances, but not now. She straightened and sheathed the weapon.

Without a second glance at Evelyn, and without acknowledging her salute, the scout turned and walked away down a narrow alley between two tall buildings.

"The Hearer, him goes with me," he said.

"Where him goes, I go," said Evelyn, pushing her

father after the scout and almost falling into him as she hurried into the alley behind them.

The narrow path was appreciably warmer than the outside. It led to a metal-shuttered first floor opening at the top of a ladder made from heavy iron staples driven into the wall of the building.

The scout mounted the rungs, but turned back when he realised that Oberon was less surefooted. Evelyn followed, but there was little room on the ladder, and she was in no position to help. The minutes ticked on.

Twenty-two minutes after leaving Wittenbergplatz station, Oberon War was finally inside, albeit not underground. He and his daughter were led into a large, warm space.

Evelyn had been through buildings often enough, using rat-runs in more familiar parts of the city, or when she had scouted for a Zoo Pack war band. But she had rarely been in an actual room before, and never in one like this.

It looked onto a great central atrium, which appeared to be filled with daylight; it was only then that Evelyn realised the Kade scout wasn't wearing eyeshades. She was grateful that she and Oberon hadn't yet removed theirs.

She began to unwrap her head, the cloth heavy and clinging as it thawed. She wanted to look up and see where the daylight was coming from, to see the glass, but it was more important to stay alert.

Evelyn War was outnumbered. It was obvious that she was no threat to the Kade dog soldiers – they'd even let her keep her blades – but that was no reason to let her guard down.

"You's the Hearer," said a new voice, deep and low.

Evelyn's eyes widened and she gasped.

He was a soldier like many others. He was exceptional, as every Alpha was exceptional. His hair and beard were dense and dark, with a smattering of steel grey to match his penetrating eyes. A deep scar cleaved the beard down one side of his face, across his jaw and diagonally across his throat. It was an old injury, but one he'd been lucky to survive.

This was John Done.

Evelyn knew his tale and his fearsome reputation. She had hoped for this meeting, had planned it. He was not the reason she'd gasped.

John Done sat in a large, square, leather chair, the skin grown dull and creased with age, the arms shiny from the caress of his hands. The chair stood in front of a wall of windows too wide and high for Evelyn to see the edges without moving her head. She wanted to maintain eye contact with him. She wanted to earn a little of his respect.

She did not gasp because of John Done, but because she had never seen so much glass.

"War," said John Done.

"Us, father and daughter," said Oberon.

"You, the famous Zoo Pack Hearer," said the Alpha dog.

"You mock?" asked Evelyn.

"You question?" asked John Done, glaring hard at Evelyn. She stood her ground and held the leader's gaze, despite the knot of fear in the pit of her gut.

Then he laughed, a wide, roaring laugh. His huge pink tongue lolled and Evelyn could see strings of spittle stretching between his gleaming teeth.

Oberon laughed too, and Evelyn took the time to look past the pack leader and sweep a glance over all that glass. It was three metres high and at least four wide, and it was flawless... utterly flawless, as far as she could tell.

Evelyn didn't need to answer the question and she wasn't asked another. John Done and her father fell into conversation, mostly about old times and old rivalries. It was a courtesy, nothing more.

When John Done was no longer amused by the company, he left Evelyn and Oberon in the care of one or two of the older Aux, veterans like her father.

It became clear that they were only interested in information, and that they would not advocate with their pack leader for the sort of alliance that Oberon insisted the Master's Voice called for. Evelyn grew impatient.

"Us, we've been gone too long, father," she said. "It's time us, we went home. It's cold and late. Ezra Pound, him will be missing us."

She turned to the scout, who had been a menacing presence at her side throughout the meeting. He nodded curtly as if in agreement with her. He gathered up a crossbow and prepared to lead them to the exit.

They had never removed their eyeshades, and they had no need to, even in the declining daylight. They were used to the murk below ground. Evelyn kept them on as she helped her father to run his weather checks. Then she wrapped her head and completed her own checks.

They ventured outside with the scout, who escorted father and daughter back to the Wittenbergplatz station, through the rat runs. That saved them time and limited their exposure; they arrived outside the station in a more comfortable state than she had expected.

Not wishing to linger, Evelyn nodded to the scout and offered her closed left fist in salute. Her father continued to trudge up the ice to the station entrance.

The first sign that something was wrong was a shift in her father's breathing. Evelyn saw the scout's pupils dilate and his brow furrow; he'd seen something. He raised his crossbow.

Evelyn spun violently. She heard the slap of a distant crossbow string, the whisper of a bolt in the air.

Suddenly Oberon War was in front of her.

Oberon's movement was clumsy and instinctive. His fall was lucky.

The bolt tore through the fur at his shoulder, missing his flesh by a hair's breadth. He fell heavily to the ground, winded.

There was a Zoo Pack crossbowman high above them.

The Zoo Packer's aim had been compromised, shooting while clambering through a window. The Kade scout's aim was true. His bolt hit the Zoo Packer and knocked him back into the station.

But there were more. A whole war band of Zoo Packers appeared at the station windows, shooting. Crossbow bolts whistled out across the ice.

Evelyn ducked.

"Cease! Cease fire!" she yelled. "It's us! Zoo Pack! Oberon War and Evelyn War! Cease fire!"

The Zoo Packers did not. Evelyn realised why when she looked over her shoulder and saw several Kade scrappers in the street behind her.

She had not known that they had a full escort on their return journey. The Kade Pack's stealth skills were extraordinary; she had been aware only of the presence of the scout. Now they were surrounded by half a dozen armed scrappers.

Squatting beside her father, she glanced up at the station and watched as another of her fellow pack members tumbled onto the hard-packed ice. She could see the dark patch on his chest where a Kade bolt had struck him.

Kade bolts cracked into the station frontage. Dust and chips of ice sprayed from the wall around the windows. A Zoo packer jumped clear of the station wall, and several crossbows withdrew from view back into the building as the Zoo packers wielding them ducked to safety from the Kade attack.

The air was full of the whistle of crossbow bolts and the cracks as they struck stone and ice. One of the Kade fighters, a couple of metres to Evelyn's left, fell towards her. He lay still in a mess of fast-freezing blood, his crossbow still in his hand.

Evelyn grabbed the crossbow from the Kade scrapper's dead hand. She seized the body by one of the bandoliers wrapped around its torso, and dragged it in front of her father to shield him from any stray missiles while he recovered.

"Father," she said, hastily unbuckling the bandoliers of bolts and pulling them from under the corpse. "Father, can you make it into the station?"

He didn't answer.

"It's cold. You should be underground."

"The alliance..." said Oberon.

"The Kade, them want no alliance, nor the Zoo Pack; and me, I want you alive."

Evelyn fastened the bandoliers around her body. They were too big and wouldn't buckle tightly around her torso. They would rattle when she moved and catch on things when she needed to climb or crawl, but all she had to do was keep her and her father safe. Safe from the Kade.

"You're on your own," yelled the Kade scout who had escorted them.

Evelyn turned on him, crossbow raised to his chest.

"We had orders to return you to Wittenbergplatz," he said. "Those men, they are your people. You, you're on your own."

The Kade stopped shooting and fled into the ruins. Their retreat was silent, and hardly took any time at all.

Evelyn and Oberon War were alone outside the Wittenbergplatz station, shielded by the corpse of a Kade fighter, facing down their own fellow Zoo Packers.

One last crossbow bolt chinked off the ice a couple of metres to the right of Evelyn's position.

Then there was silence.

She raised her borrowed crossbow above her head and waved it slowly from left to right. When the silence continued, she lifted her head into view of the apertures in the building in front of her so that she was sure she could be clearly seen by the Zoo Packers.

Cautiously, the men made themselves visible, gestured to her to follow them, and disappeared back into the station.

Evelyn War helped her father to his feet. He had been lying prone on the ice for several minutes, and the penetrating cold had added to the damage done to his old body by the fall. He was stiff and tired. Evelyn began to wish that they had never embarked on his foolish errand.

"There is strength in numbers," said her father, firmly, as if he were reading her mind.

"Not today," said Evelyn. "Today looking for strength in numbers almost got us killed."

It took several more minutes for Evelyn to guide her father back into the station building. He was staggering as they crossed the grand entrance hall. His footfalls were heavy and irregular on the marble tiles. Her borrowed bandoliers bounced and rattled.

She barely heard the bolt that brought him down.

She felt his body crumple beside her and heard the heavy thud as his dead weight sprawled on the cold floor.

Evelyn cried out in horror.

She unslung the Kade crossbow and tried to target the source of the shot. A Kade scrapper must have got inside the building.

But, one by one, Zoo packers stepped into view. There were five of them. She didn't recognise the pup on the far left, staring wide-eyed at her. She glared back.

"I thought you... him was Kade. I took the shot," said a voice to Evelyn's right.

She turned to face the male walking towards her. Robert Browning. She knew him. He'd known her father. She'd thought perhaps it had been the youngest Aux, the most naive. She thought he'd got nervous and made a mistake. She looked back at the pup for a moment, and then down at Robert Browning, bending over her father's body.

"You, don't touch him," she said. She pointed to Thomas Hardy, the biggest of them. "You, take him beneath."

She waited as Robert Browning walked slowly back to the rank. Thomas Hardy lifted Oberon War over one shoulder, ready to take him back below ground.

Her father was dead, a pathetic, stupid, pointless death, and he had accomplished nothing.

CHAPTER FOUR
NOW

EVELYN STOOD IN the grand entrance hall of the Wittenbergplatz station on the spot where her father had died.

It seemed like an eternity ago, though it was only a matter of weeks. But even if it had been an eternity, she would still be able to hear his voice in her head. The words he had spoken so often in his last days were still fresh in her mind: *There is strength in numbers*, that's what her father had said, and, *The Master wants us to form alliances.*

Evelyn shut out the words in her head and concentrated on the sounds around her instead. She could hear the pinging, but there were other sounds too: a low moaning and an odd creaking. These were new sounds to her, disconcerting, alien. She was used to silence, especially at Wittenbergplatz, one of the few places in Berlin that belonged to none of the Aux tribes, preserved as a sort of no man's land.

Wary, Evelyn did her weather checks and made her way up to the exit point.

The air smelled strange, even through the layers of her head cloth. Something wasn't right. There was another low moan from outside, and Evelyn ducked below the lip of the gaping window.

As she rose, she placed her gloved left hand on the lip, and then quickly lifted it away. It was slick; the ice there wasn't dry. That was what she could smell. She could smell water. Her glove was wet.

Careful not to touch the window frame or the wall, Evelyn looked out. What she saw frightened her. She didn't know exactly how or why it was different, only that it was.

Street level was still black ice, but it looked less flat somehow, the surface less like concrete. Everything was still a wasteland of old buildings, of endless frost. Then she heard the ping again, and thought she saw movement at the edge of her vision.

A drip. She'd seen a droplet of water falling.

"No!" she cried. "It can't be."

She remembered her father's words, and suddenly all of old Leer's tales were clamouring for space in her head, all the legends of Gene the Hackman. All the fables about the great Aux warrior getting whet. They filled her mind with vivid pictures.

Another drop of water fell.

"It's time to *get wet*," said Evelyn War. "When we *get wet* that is the time for the Aux to get whet!"

She heard soft footfalls on the marble floor behind her, and realised that she had been sitting at the exit for several minutes. She was cold, but not as cold as she should have been.

The footfalls stopped abruptly.

"Who's there?" called a voice.

Evelyn stood and turned around to look down on the entrance hall.

"Zoo Pack," she answered. "Evelyn War."

She hadn't been expecting them, but time had passed without her noticing, and Evelyn knew that her own hunting-pack members had finally caught up with her.

"It's just the useless omega bitch," said the leader of the war band, a rabble of six men and two dams.

"That's what they call me," said Evelyn, standing her ground.

"That's what Ezra Pound, him calls you," said the lieutenant, "so that's who you are."

"Not any more," said Evelyn, striding towards the war band. "Things will change. Things will change because my father, him said so, but things will change for me, too."

"Ezra Pound, him does not change," said someone in the war band, and the others snickered, one of them with a high-pitched cackle that echoed around the grand entrance hall.

"It's time to *get wet*," said Evelyn again.

The war band drew their weapons, took up combat stances and began to cast about, looking for an enemy.

"Who's out there?" asked the leader. "The Kade?"

"Not who," said Evelyn. "*What*."

After several seconds of bemused silence, the youngest scrapper's mouth dropped open. He was just a kid, relegated to the left flank of the pack formation, because he was fast and expendable.

"Wet," he said. He pointed at the dripping water.

The others looked from one to the other.

There was a long, shrill sound that could not have been made by any creature that the Aux had ever met.

All heads turned towards the exit of Wittenbergplatz, except for Evelyn's.

She thought she saw something, someone, beyond the pack, a head ducking back behind a corner, the familiar figure of a pup. She hooked her fingers into the waist of her jacket, feeling for the slingshot that was still there, and wondered if the young Aux had been following *her* all along.

She steadied her nerve and walked through the hunting-pack, who had lost all sense of what they were doing. They held their weapons too tightly, aiming into thin air, no longer looking for targets; or had let them drop, their senses confused, shocked by the sound.

As she made her way back to the broken skeletons of the escalators and her route below ground, the leader of the Zoo Pack war band finally turned and called after her.

"Where are you going?" he asked.

"To report to Ezra Pound," she said. "Us, we need to make alliances. There is strength in numbers."

CHAPTER FIVE
DEATH

Ward Cleaver paced.

He was edgy. He wasn't usually given to nerves. He'd been around. He wasn't the beta dog he'd been in his youth, but he'd scrapped with the best of them. He'd become a leader, pulled his weight, commanded Aux as well as any lieutenant in the Zoo Pack. He wasn't that much older than Ezra Pound, whelped only a couple of seasons before, but he was past his prime.

He was nervous, but it was his job and he was doing it.

The young and the old got the worst jobs, took the flanking positions in the war bands, were assigned the most far-flung sentry posts, the coldest and loneliest. He was old.

Ward Cleaver paced. He didn't like it. He was nervous.

He was twitchy.

His blade felt heavy in his hand, he'd been holding it for so long. He didn't dare sheath it. He didn't trust himself to be fast enough to draw it any more. The other fella might beat him to the draw, might get his blade in first.

"Tougher and tough," he said to himself.

He wasn't convinced.

The tunnel forked off in two directions. He didn't like it.

He couldn't see down the left hand fork if he walked the right, or vice versa, so he stayed on the main line. He couldn't stand still. He had to pace. He was filled with cold dread every time he turned his back on one of the forks. He turned often, so as not to have his back to either of the tunnels for too long at a time.

He moved awkwardly; an old injury had shortened his left leg, and the arthritis in his knee made it worse.

His ears were as good as ever though, and his eyes were keen. He could still swing a blade, too. Tougher and tough. He was still a good sentry.

He reminded himself that he could still do his job.

He'd heard about the noises. They'd all heard about the noises. Rumours were rife. It was the pinging he feared. He hadn't heard it himself, but it was like the tap of a sharp claw on hollow stone, they said. He could imagine it.

Other Aux had described the noise, and the description frightened him. If Ward heard the *tiktiktik* they described, he'd recognise it.

The pack didn't know what it was. The pack didn't know what it meant, but they knew it meant something. There was talk. There was talk of a *tiktiktik* and of another sound, a whistling sound. It was the ticking he was afraid of.

He shuddered. He turned his back on the forking tunnels for the final time, and walked back along the main track. He could see for hundreds of metres along Track Two ahead of him as it cut a straight line back to Old Zoo. Wade longed to be back on the platform in the warm fug of the pack with its cloud of breath hanging in the air around it. He wanted to be a pup again, sitting on the platform, listening to the tales of Gene the Hackman.

He looked down at the blade in his hand. He clenched his fist around it for reassurance. He glanced back into the deep below-ground darkness. He could see the great arching curves of the tunnel walls, fading into the distance into two black holes. He could see the pale tracks diverging as they swept away deep into the holes. And he could see many shades of grey in the thousands of stones that lay between him and the tunnel mouths, before they became a single, seamless carpet of another kind of grey.

The cold dread that filled him every time he turned his back on either fork was followed by a moment of reassurance as he looked back along Track Two and walked those two or three dozen steps towards home.

The *ping* brought him up short.

It made his heart stop, his foot in mid-air, unable to finish the step he was about to take. The sound. The sound the pack had been talking about.

Then he breathed out. Just water, dripping. He wasn't used to the water. It seemed to drip everywhere lately, from everything.

Four more steps, five... six. He was only two or three of his lopsided paces from the place where he should turn, marked by a long sooty streak down the tunnel wall to his left.

The whistle came from a distance, shrill and breathy, unlike anything Ward Cleaver had ever heard. His hand tightened on his blade, and the sinewy muscles of his biceps bunched as his fist closed. His hand came up level with his chest, blade ready.

Sweat gathered on his brow, despite the cold dread that had been filling him every minute for three long hours. The dread had suddenly grown sharply colder. His blood seemed to freeze in his arteries.

The whistle echoed down the tunnels behind him and he turned, slowly.

The tunnels.

The sound was coming from more than one place.

Ward Cleaver was sure that the sound was coming from both forks, from *both* tunnels.

It died away. He could hear the sigh of it long after the shrill tones had dissipated. The thing that had made the sounds was *breathing*.

It wasn't Aux. He knew no living Aux had ever made a sound like that, nor any that he had ever heard dying.

Ward Cleaver remembered his duty. He was Zoo Pack, and he was a chosen sentry. He had to protect the perimeter. He had to stand his ground.

Ward Cleaver took two tentative steps back towards the fork in the tunnel, his eyes unblinking, his blade raised.

It was the same. There was no shift in the grey patterns before him. The uneven surface of the old walls was the same, the shingle beneath his feet was the same, the diverging lines of the tracks were the same.

The only sounds were the crunch of Ward Cleaver's footfalls and the rasp of his breathing. He felt his fingers clenching and unclenching around the haft of his weapon. Stones shifted beneath his feet.

He thought he heard something right at the edge of his senses.

He stopped again, only a few metres from the fork, so close that his visibility down both of the tunnels was compromised. One of the larger stones shifted under his uneven stance and slid out from under his left foot. It grated against its neighbours, clattering impossibly loudly in the silence.

He was sure he would have heard something, but for that damned stone.

Ward Cleaver held his breath. The terrible sound came again.

tiktiktik tiktik tiktik tik tiktiktik tiktiktik

It was *the* sound, the sound he had heard the other packers talking about, the sound he had known he would recognise, should he ever hear it. He had not thought that it would be relentless.

tiktiktik tik tiktik tiktiktik tiktiktik tik

Ward Cleaver wanted to step back. He wanted a clearer view of both tunnels. He wanted to concentrate. He didn't know, not for sure, where the sound was coming from.

He only knew that it was getting louder... closer.

tiktik tik tiktiktik tik tiktiktik

Ward Cleaver had been holding his blade in his hand for more than three hours because he didn't dare sheath it. Ezra Pound, pack sire, always said that the other fella might be faster to draw his weapon, so Wade Cleaver was afraid. Something was changing.

Though his blade was already drawn, the other fella was still faster than him.

It came from the left. Ward Cleaver thought it was a shadow, but there was no light source to throw a shadow. Why was it so tall? So narrow? Why was its shape so wrong? It was full of wrong.

tiktiktik tiktiktik tik tiktik tiktiktik tik

Ward Cleaver took a lunging step and thrust with his weapon at shoulder height into the thing.

His blade made contact with something hard, more like bone than metal, and his left shoulder was pierced through. He pulled away, instinctively, feeling barbs tear through his muscle, disabling his arm.

He felt something in his side, but tried to ignore it. He jabbed his blade at full stretch, the second blow even less effective than the first, skittering off the bony surface.

Then he felt a burning sensation in his hip, and then another in his belly.

Ward Cleaver tried to defend himself. His sweating right hand tightened around the haft of his weapon. He swung it frantically back and forth, trying to connect with flesh, *any* flesh, trying to inflict a wound.

He felt the hot blood cooling on his clothes. He heard it pattering onto the stones at his feet, the thick liquid making a subtly different sound from the dripping water.

It was oddly reassuring. It was the first sound he had recognised since the whistling. Even his own footfalls had sounded wrong, too tentative, too fearful.

Ward Cleaver wouldn't look down.

He was dead and he knew it. Aux knew when they were beaten, though it didn't stop them fighting.

Ward Cleaver looked up.

He looked at the thing that was thrusting another barbed blade into him, forming a pattern of wounds down his left side and across his gut.

He could not find flesh to cut, because the creature had no flesh. It was a monster made of bone, of glossy chitin. Its blades were not weapons, but long, tapering, barbed limbs in matched pairs growing out of its barrel-shaped thorax, high above its abdomen.

The words of Edward Leer's tales tumbled through Ward Cleaver's mind.

He had heard them a hundred-hundred times. He had heard the legends of Gene the Hackman, of how he had used his blades. He had learned to fight with his own weapons by listening to them and by remembering them.

Wasn't that why they had a tale-teller? To teach them to be scrappers in Gene the Hackman's image? Weren't the legends a scrapper's manual?

Ward Cleaver looked up at the creature that was killing him. He heard his blade chink against the hard shell of its leg before his wrist gave way and his weapon fell from his hand.

He knew what it was.

He wanted to tell the Zoo Pack. He wanted to warn them all. He opened his mouth and, as loudly as he could, he said a single word.

"Them."

CHAPTER SIX
WARNING

"IT'S CHANGING," SAID Evelyn War. "It's wet."

"Ezra Pound, him won't listen to you," said Edward Leer.

"Him will have to," said Evelyn. "It's time to get whet. Us, we will all get whet."

"You believe it," said Edward Leer.

"You believe it, too," said Evelyn. "You knew my father and you know him was right. You know his time has come, the time to make alliances. There is strength in numbers.

"Ezra Pound, him won't see you. Him won't listen to you," said the tale-teller. He rose from his position, squatting on the tiled floor, his bony knees high and wide, raising himself on his staff in one slow, fluid motion. "But Alpha dog, him will listen to *me*."

He shrugged the heavy felt blanket higher around his shoulders and took several firm steps, passing Evelyn on his way out of the little cell that he shared with no one.

When she fell in behind him, he turned and stared at her, his eyes – green, with hard white edges – boring into hers.

"Me, I'm going with you," she said. "Me, I'll hear what Ezra Pound, him has to say. If you cannot make him listen, me, I will."

"If I cannot make Ezra Pound, him listen, you won't be 'the useless bitch', you'll be 'the dead bitch'," said Leer, turning away from Evelyn, but saying no more as she followed him out of his room.

"Me, I'm the tale-teller," said Leer as he and Evelyn made their way along the narrow, empty service tunnel that usually housed half a dozen of the more senior lieutenants of the pack. "Me, I'll weave a tale for Ezra Pound."

Small fires had been lit. The place was bright and warm, and one or two of the lieutenants' mates were performing their everyday chores. The temperature had risen by at least a degree in the last week, maybe two.

The walls of the tunnel were smooth and black from the grease and soot thrown up by the fires, giving them a glossy appearance that reflected too much light for Evelyn's comfort. She squinted against the glare as she listened to Leer.

"There are no more Hearers," said Leer as they

skirted a fire. "There are only scrappers. There are only hackmen."

"My father, him was a Hearer," said Evelyn. "It is his story you must tell."

Leer laughed, a sudden, musical sound that Evelyn didn't remember hearing before. It made him sound young. It startled her, but it was infectious, and she had to stop herself laughing along. She didn't want to laugh. She felt only pride for the memory of her father, and scorn that it should be treated with ridicule.

"My father, him was the last Hearer."

"And now the Hearer, him dead," said Leer, his laughter ending as abruptly as it had begun. "Ezra Pound, him hated your father, and him hates Hearers. Him hates Believers even more than him hated your father, and more than him hates Hearers. You're a Believer."

"Ezra Pound, him needs to know the truth. Him needs to make alliances," said Evelyn, almost in desperation. "My father, him knew about alliances. Him met with the Kade –"

"And now your father, him dead," said Leer, cutting Evelyn off.

They had reached the end of the service tunnel, with its fires and its reflective surfaces. They were walking into darkness, crossing back onto the main Track Two tunnel.

Evelyn stopped in her tracks, eyes wide.

"My father, him dead," she said, realisation in her voice. "Him dead after meeting with the Kade. Him dead looking for alliances, looking for strength in numbers. Him dead answering the Master's Voice."

"Yes," said Leer. "Oberon War, the Hearer, him was killed answering the Master's Voice. Him was killed because him was a Hearer."

"Him dead because of the Kade, because him tried to make an alliance," said Evelyn.

Edward Leer regarded Evelyn's silhouetted form.

"But Oberon War, him not killed by the Kade," he said.

The two Aux stood facing each other for several seconds. Evelyn War could plainly see Edward Leer's face, but he was a tale-teller and he knew how to control a tale. He knew when to disclose a detail or reveal a plot twist, and he knew when to hold back.

Leer's face gave nothing away that he did not want to give away.

She didn't need to see anything there. She had heard it all in his words. What if it hadn't been an accident? What if it had just been convenient?

Oberon War, him not killed by the Kade.

Finally, Leer turned from Evelyn and continued to walk down Track Two towards the Zoologischer Garten station platform. Ezra Pound's den, where he was surrounded by his lieutenants and lackeys and by his mates, lay just beyond. Evelyn had been there only twice before, and she had hated it both times.

Pound was a blunt Aux, all fight and no thought. He was Alpha and he smelled of it. She did not know how the dams could stand it. She did not know how

Leer could stand it, except that he was the tale-teller and clever, cleverer than anyone except her father.

Evelyn War trusted Edward Leer, because her father had. As much as two Aux could be friends, more than comrades in arms, Oberon War and Edward Leer had been friends. They had talked to each other for the sake of talking. They had shared stories together not just for their own sakes, but for their meanings.

Ezra Pound shared nothing. He was sullen when there was nothing to fight or mate, except there was always something to fight or mate, so he was sullen for the sake of it. His speeches, the same speeches that roused the other members of the Pack, left Evelyn cold.

They were base and isolationist and mean. The Alpha dog was a belligerent leader, hostile to his own pack when it suited him, and hostile to the world because he did not understand it.

This was not the Pack's assessment of him; he was the top dog, and their leader. It was Evelyn's assessment of him, learned from her father, and borne out by her experience.

She wanted Leer to make him understand the world. She wanted it now more than ever because the Kade pack had not killed her father.

Evelyn got jeers and sneers from the Aux in the warren of narrow passages, anterooms and chambers that made up the pack leader's den. Evelyn was aware that she would not have gained access to Ezra Pound if she had not been with Edward Leer.

She had to step over more than one large boot to avoid being tripped. Several times, she felt jabs to her body and the backs of her legs as the more vicious Aux got in snide attacks with elbows or the hafts of weapons. One particularly painful dig in her ribs, from three rigid fingers driving hard into her side, came as one of Ezra Pound's mates casually sauntered past Evelyn. It was accompanied by a hiss so vicious that she felt the dam's warm spittle on her earlobe.

The males and dams of Pound's coterie stepped aside for the tale-teller, but closed, unheeding, around Evelyn, making her fight her way through them to follow him.

The big Aux, the Alpha male, with his huge flat head and his short corded neck, thick at its base to sit firmly on his impossibly wide shoulders, sat low in his chair, as if lounging in some great throne.

He was a head taller than all but two or three of the males, and bulky in his torso and limbs. Somehow, he also managed to look totally relaxed in a way that Evelyn thought she had never seen another Aux look. He looked as if he felt utterly secure, always safe in the knowledge that he was top dog.

"My tale-teller," he said by way of a greeting. Then he leaned forward a little from the chest, if nonchalantly. "And the useless omega bitch. Why have you brought her?"

"Edward Leer, him didn't bring me, I came," said Evelyn, but no one was listening.

"The tales," said Leer. "There are legends for this time."

"Time?" asked the pack leader.

"There is change," said Leer.

Pound had slumped back in his chair, but his expression didn't change. He raised one hand slightly and gestured. One of his lieutenants stepped forward.

Robert Browning. Her hackles rose. He was the *last* person she wanted to see. Her opinion of him had changed dramatically in the last few minutes. Her father's blood was on his hands, but until now she had thought that had just been a terrible accident.

"There is wet outside," said Browning. "The ice is slick."

"A little water," said Ezra Pound. "Warmth." There was no fear in his voice. Browning's face was impassive, and yet Evelyn War had seen fear there when he had heard the ice moan. They had all been scared by the terrible sounds it could make when it began to move in the thaw.

Browning was showing no fear because he didn't want to lose face in front of his pack leader.

"It is time to get whet," said Evelyn.

Leer twitched slightly, but didn't turn to look at her. One or two of Pound's lieutenants stared at her. Someone called out, "Shut the omega bitch up," and then snickered.

The chamber grew quieter and began to fill up. Aux from around the compound had heard that Edward Leer had come to confront Ezra Pound.

The Alpha dog said nothing. Soon, all that could be

heard was the shuffling of feet as more Aux entered, packing the room with bodies. They filled every corner with hard flesh, warming the room until Aux breath no longer showed as steam in cold air.

Ezra Pound leaned forward, resting his elbows on his spread knees and holding his huge hands loosely in front of him. He was a forbidding figure, even without a single muscle flexed. He raised his head slightly.

"If this is about the Hearer, him dead," he said, as if it was the final word on the subject.

It *was* the final word.

Evelyn wanted to speak, but even she couldn't find anything to say in the face of the Alpha dog in full command.

Leer did not try to look Ezra Pound in the eye as the pack leader's implacable gaze was clearly fixed on Evelyn.

"This, it is about the tales," said Leer.

Silence lingered for several more long seconds as the gathered Aux waited for their leader's response.

Finally, the great Aux shifted to one side so that he was facing the tale-teller. His left hand sat squarely on his left knee; his huge, flat head, with its heavy brow ridge and narrow eyes, was tilted on one side to look up at Leer.

"Then tell us your fable," he said. "Make it tougher and tough."

CHAPTER SEVEN
A NEW LEGEND

"GENE THE HACKMAN, top dog, him done the great walk around. Not for him the darkness, not for him the cold, not for him the Time of Ice. Gene the Hackman, him got whet. Gene the Hackman, him got whet and walked the Earth and him killed Them."

They were the most familiar words in the world, the words told by every tale-teller at the beginning of every story. Edward Leer had recited them more times than anyone could remember down the years.

But now, in Ezra Pound's den, they sounded different. They didn't sound like the start of a fable to Evelyn. They didn't sound like the beginning of another retelling. They sounded as though Edward

Leer was telling the Pack leader something new and real.

"The land, it was vast and dry and filled with rocks. The Pack, them were in the big hills, tougher and tough. Gene, him was worried that there were no Urgings. Him was worried that him could not hear the Master's Voice."

Some of the dams in the crowd gasped. This was not like the other tales. This was a new story, one they hadn't heard before. There were no legends about the Master's Voice, there never had been. The tales were about the legend that was Gene the Hackman, about the scrapping.

One or two of the younger males shuffled their feet in discomfort. Eyes flickered, seeking reassurance in Ezra Pound's face. His expression never changed, and his stance remained relaxed.

Edward Leer's expression reflected the story he was telling. It was serious now, as he stood tall, holding his staff firmly, but not leaning on it.

"It was the longest walk Gene the Hackman, him had ever taken. Eight months all-away round. Them were living off body fat. Tod of Much Slaughter, him had got the bone for it. Him wanted to go away home. Him had got the bone to challenge Gene the Hackman.

"Gene the Hackman, top dog, him stood firm, but Tod of Much Slaughter, tougher and tough, him stood against Gene. Him wanted to walk away the long walk home."

More gasps. Gene the Hackman was a legend. No

one challenged the legend. No one got the bone to challenge Gene the Hackman. Still, Ezra Pound's expression did not change as all eyes turned upon him. Edward Leer was Tod of Much Slaughter, now, an aggressive sneer on his face, challenging Gene the Hackman.

"Gene the Hackman, him stood firm. 'My pack, my rules', him said. But Tod of Much Slaughter, him and his mate, Maryann Faithful, them turned their backs on Gene the Hackman and them walked away home.

"Gene the Hackman's pack was Jack so Wild and Old Man Gary. Gene's pack, them was mostly dead or gone. Jack so Wild, him was young and him missed home, and him was scared. Old Man Gary, him was loyal to Gene the Hackman, but him was old in scrapping.

"Gene the Hackman, him could not hear the Master's Voice and him could not feel the Urgings, so him followed the light. The light of a falling star that blinked on and blinked off. Him lost the light and him kept walking the long walk in the big hills. Jack so Wild, him was scared and him followed Gene, and Old Man Gary him was loyal and him followed Gene, and it was dusk.

"Old Man Gary, him was the first to see the bodies. It was a pack like them, but deader and dead. Starved to the bone and dried up. Raw bones.

"Gene the Hackman, him could still hear with his two ears. Him could still hear the echo in the big hills. Him could still hear Them.

"'*RUN!*' said Gene the Hackman."

The gasp came from all the Aux, males and dams both, and they jostled closer to the tale-teller, protesting at his tale. Gene the Hackman didn't run. Gene the Hackman fought. Gene the Hackman scrapped. Gene the Hackman was the warrior legend. One large beta dog bared his teeth, and raised a clenched fist so tense that his knuckles showed white.

Ezra Pound waved them back. He still slouched in his chair, but the muscles of his maw were tight, sinews taut as he clenched his teeth and worked his jaw.

"The tale-teller, him must finish his tale. Leer, him tougher and tough. Tougher than a scrapper," said Ezra Pound. Then he laughed, a mean sound filled with danger.

"Them had changed. This was a new Them. Them was bigger and faster and tougher and all tough. Jack so Wild, him could not outrun Them. Old Man Gary, him could not outrun Them. Gene the Hackman, him could not outrun Them. Gene the Hackman, him turned to face Them. Him drew his blades. Him knew him could not outfight Them. Them with their chitin. Them with their limbs and claws and teeth. Them with their screaming and tearing and biting. Them, all of Them. Tougher and tough. Tougher than Gene the Hackman.

"'Jack! *RUN!*' Gene, him shouted, but Jack, him fell. Him broke his ankle. Jack so Wild, him could not run and him could not fight. Gene the Hackman, him got whet. Him swung his blades. Him tore at Them and him defended the pup, Jack. Jack so Wild, him was weak and him was scared. This time, Gene the Hackman, him was too slow. Them was skittle-scuttle fast. Them got Jack so Wild first and Them bit him, and Jack, him was dead.

"Gene the Hackman, all him had was his wrath. All him had was his vengeance. Him knew him could not outrun Them. Him knew him could not outfight Them. Him only knew him could get whet and scrap and have some revenge on Them before him died.

"Gene the Hackman, him scrapped with Them. Him swung his blades, fast and furious. Him hacked through bone and chitin. Him spread great sprays of ichor. Him attacked Them from all angles. Him thrust and lunged and swept his blades. Him maimed and him killed, and more Them came upon him.

"Them stood tall on their hind legs. Taller than the Alpha dog. Them had long torsos with four swinging limbs of chitin, clawed and grasping. Them had great, round maws of countless teeth, in their jagged bony heads. Them hungered. Them tore and Them bit.

"Gene the Hackman, top dog with no pack, him swung his left hand wide, him lunged his blade in the face of one of Them. Them, skittle-scuttle fast. Gene the Hackman, him got bit. His left arm, him got bit clean off. Gene the Hackman, tougher and tough, him got bit bad."

There was silence in the chamber. Some of the Aux looked pale and anxious, had gathered together for consolation. Dams stood close to their mates for reassurance.

Leer had been taking the story steadily. He acted out the most dramatic moments of the scrapping with his staff. He lowered his voice sombrely at the moment of Jack so Wild's death, and again when Gene got bitten.

He had never told the myth before. The tale had been passed down to him, as it had been passed to every tale-teller of every generation. As far as he knew, he was the first to tell it in all those generations.

The tale-teller in Edward Leer relished the task. The Aux in him did not.

The only person in the room who shared any of his confidence was Evelyn War. She had not heard the story before, either, but she had suspected that such tales existed; her father had always said as much.

"VABOOOM!"

The audience, rapt and intent, reeled from the sudden sound. There were moans and squeals from the dams and younger Aux.

Edward Leer had been preparing for the explosion since his last revelation, slowly filling his lungs with air. The effort took its toll on the tale-teller; it was another few seconds before he could continue.

"And that was the scrapping of that day," he finally said.

"Gene the Hackman, him had taken a bad hurting. Him didn't know anything. Him only knew that Them were dead.

"Him had lost blood, but him found a way to get to the place. Him found a way to get to a Master. The Master, him gave Gene a new arm. Gene the Hackman, him was impressed. The Master, him gave Gene a new death toy. Gene the Hackman, him was impressed.

"Them came. Them came to the place. Them came for the Master. Gene the Hackman, him took the new death toy. The death toy, him fired bolts, faster and fast. The death toy, him didn't need reloading. Gene the Hackman, him fired the death toy into Them. Them died. Them all died. Them were broken to pieces on the ground, splashed in their ichor. Deader and dead.

"Gene the Hackman, tougher and tough, him survived. Him survived because of the Master.

"Gene the Hackman, him could not protect his pack. Him could not save Old Man Gary. Him could not save Jack so Wild. Tod of Much Slaughter and Maryann Faithful, them had turned their backs on Gene.

"A top dog, him without no pack is no Alpha. Gene the Hackman without no pack, him was Omega dog."

Edward Leer was clever, cleverer even than Evelyn War had known.

For his entire life, Edward Leer had been telling the legends of Gene the Hackman that the Aux wanted to hear: as inspiration for the scrapping, as a fighting manual.

Now he had told a story they didn't want to hear.

"The tale... me, I have told, it needed to be told now," said Edward Leer, almost apologetically. "This is a time of change. Us, we must face it. Zoo Pack, we must remember the Masters and what them bred us to do. The Masters, them taught us strength in numbers.

"If Gene's pack, it had stayed together, it might have fared better, especially when it came to facing Them that had changed. Gene the Hackman, him needed Tod and Maryann. Alpha dog, him needed other Aux besides."

Edward Leer paused.

"Just like Zoo Pack, us, we need other packs to stand beside us in the time of change."

The Aux in the chamber stood in shocked silence. It disturbed them, but they all understood Leer's explanation of the fable. They waited for Ezra Pound's reaction.

There was a commotion in the passage outside the chamber, and the noise in the room began to build as a beta dog squeezed his way through the throng. He began to address one of the lieutenants close to where Pound was sitting, but the Alpha dog gestured to him.

"You, speak," he said, and the room fell silent, the Aux eager to listen.

The beta dog was one of the younger pack members. He'd been hurrying, and looked clammy in his tightly-fastened garments, his head cloth flapping around his shoulders. He hadn't yet loosened any of his clothing in the warmer space at the habitation.

"My turn for sentry duty at the fork," he said. "Ward Cleaver, him gone... disappeared. Only blood... and this." He held out Ward Cleaver's blade, dented and nicked from ferocious blows.

The young sentry's breathing was becoming a little steadier, but he still looked panicked.

"What else?" asked Leer.

"Me, I heard something," said the Aux. "Me, I heard a sound like whistling. Me, I ran."

"Them," said Evelyn.

This time, no one could fail to hear her.

CHAPTER EIGHT
FERAL AUX

LED BY EZRA Pound, eight males and dams made their way out of Zoologischer Garten station early the following day.

It had been a long night. Pound had spent most of it sleeping, retiring after a brief conversation with Leer and ordering the expedition to the Warschauer Pack for the following morning.

His lieutenants had spent hours comparing notes on the tale, talking in hushed whispers in Pound's den and adjoining passages.

Double sentries had been posted at all points on the perimeter of their territory.

They had talked of the sounds that had been heard and of the missing sentry, and they had examined the nicks and dents in Ward Cleaver's weapon to try to discover what must have made them. They'd had no answers that they liked.

Leer had stayed for an hour after Pound retired, listening to the other Aux. When he left, Evelyn had gone with him.

The sea of waiting Aux had parted for them both. No one had touched Evelyn as she left the chamber, and no one had attacked her in the passage outside. They had not spoken to her or made eye contact, but they had looked at her with something a little closer to respect. She was no longer 'the useless omega bitch'. She was something far more frightening.

Evelyn had never been so far from Old Zoo before. She had never been chosen for a major foray into Berlin, never outside, not like this.

She hadn't had to ask to be part of the war band that made the long walk around to visit the Warschauer Pack. Ezra Pound had insisted on it.

She was determined not to be afraid of him, or of his motivation in adding her to the war band. Zoo Pack made regular visits to trade and barter with the Warschauer Pack. One of the female scrappers was out injured, Evelyn was a good fit and Leer had advocated for her.

That should have been enough for her, but Pound didn't like Hearers and he liked Believers even less. Perhaps it was a simple case of 'keep your friends close and your enemies closer'. Pound was a pragmatic leader, after all, even if he wasn't a great thinker.

Evelyn War would be safe enough with Ezra Pound and the war band, assuming she could keep her mouth shut. She was eager to learn whatever she could about the change being wrought in the world. And, most importantly, she trusted Leer. She could tell him what she found on her return to Old Zoo. He would have a story to tell. He would always have a tale to tell.

Evelyn was dressed in borrowed clothes. All the outdoor clothes were shared; they were in limited supply. No one could survive in the sub-zero temperatures for long without layers of felt and fur, and both were hard to come by.

The felt great coat she had been given came below her knees, but should have been longer. It fit snugly over her jacket, however, adding warmth, and the funnel-shaped collar covered her face up to her eyes. She could smell the breath of a dozen other Aux in the dense wool of the collar, but it had been worn exclusively by dams and the smell was sweet.

The fur cap was rank, worn by too many terrified young beta dogs, and she was glad that she was able to squeeze it on over her own head cloth.

The pelt she wore around her shoulders, covering much of her chest and back, was also old and greasy, but the cold air kept most of its stench away from her nose, and the collar did the rest.

The entire Zoo Pack had gathered to see them off. Evelyn glanced over her shoulder at the crowded platform as she walked away with the war band. She saw troubled faces. Edward Leer stood prominently among the Pack. He nodded to Evelyn.

Evelyn caught sight of Ben Gun among the onlookers. She thought about how worried she'd been for him that night, worried enough to go looking for him. But she'd found other things instead. Ben Gun, it turned out, had snuck into a service tunnel and been perfectly safe.

Evelyn had wanted to beat him for causing her so much aggravation, but there was something disarmingly spirited about him that stayed her hand.

She knew that the pup had made a new slingshot for himself, because she'd heard him practising with it, although he'd stopped aiming at the tiles on the station walls. He hadn't stopped following her around, though.

Now he would have to. He wasn't part of the war band. He had to stay at Old Zoo.

The war band travelled along Track Two underground as far as Wittenbergplatz, and out over the wet lip of the opening where Evelyn had sat for so long. It seemed like an age since she had been there, though it was barely a couple of days.

She could hear nothing, except for the sounds the Pack made in their soft boots. Then she heard the intermittent ping of dripping water outside.

It was still cold, but the sun was bright, brighter than it had ever been, and the street surface was slick.

The rabble of Aux was constantly on guard, moving and covering each other in the open areas, and sidling along the narrowest streets. They hugged the buildings and kept to the shadows, following the course of Track Two as it wended its way across the city above ground. The track was invisible beneath its thick layer of black ice, but its route was clear from the shape the ice made over and around it.

There were no signs of habitation, and no trace of other pack activity nearby.

The slick streets were treacherous, the ice slippery beneath the soles of their boots, and the Aux cursed under their breath as they slipped and slid. This new form of ice was unfamiliar to them, and unwelcome.

The buildings looked different, too. They were patchy, showing too much of their own skins when they had previously always been covered in hard, dry frost. The areas most exposed to the bright new light of the sun were beginning to thaw.

Evelyn had been on the streets of Berlin for several minutes, but her head cloth and the collar of her great coat were still damp with her breath. They weighed heavy around her neck, pulling her head into an unnatural stoop. The moisture should have frozen by now, should have stiffened the felt, but it showed no signs of happening any time soon.

There was a sound. The eight Aux threw their backs against the wall of a high building on the shaded side of the narrow street.

The sound echoing around the empty city streets was more a boom than a moan, and it was followed by a creak that seemed to last for several seconds.

Something was moving. The ice was adjusting. Only Evelyn and one other member of the war band, who'd been in Wittenbergplatz with her a couple of days earlier, had ever heard anything like it before.

Two or three of the other packers looked to Evelyn, who nodded soberly, reassuring them that she knew what the sound was and that it couldn't hurt them. Not directly, at least.

Ezra Pound did not look in her direction, but as the sound diminished, he gestured for them to move on. He relinquished point to Thomas Meltdown, his second in command, and moved back through the advancing troop to make sure each member of his war band was in good cheer.

When he reached Evelyn, he seemed at a loss for something to say. Then the moment was gone. Ezra Pound's ears flattened and he turned warily.

This moan was feral.

This moan was Aux.

The creatures were stooped and ragged. Their clothes, if they could be called clothes, hung from their bodies in rags, stripped from their limbs, torn and bloody.

The feral Aux were on all fours like beasts, not like scrappers, not like Aux at all. They stalked at the edges of Track Two where it ran above ground through Kreuzberg. The creatures were skin and bone, starved and fierce with fright.

Ezra Pound stepped out of formation when he saw the wild dogs, a double-blade in each hand. He filled his chest, threw out his arms and bellowed a great roar.

"Get whet!"

It was a threat as much as an instruction to his war band, and one that would have dispersed most attacking forces.

But these Aux were too afraid to quit, too wild to surrender. These Aux were so terrified they had only two things on their minds: to kill or to die trying.

The first of the beasts threw itself forwards, lunging from the chest, using its arms as forelegs, a single blade strapped to its back.

The blade did not glint in the overpowering brightness of the sun, as a clean blade should. This weapon had not been tended to for far too long. It was dull and old, and had not been cleaned or oiled in days or weeks.

These Aux had lost their discipline.

These Aux were feral, and very dangerous.

As the lunging beast flexed its right arm, reaching back for its weapon, Ezra Pound took three long, bounding steps towards it.

He leapt, two double blades swinging, severing the shoulder joint across the beast's right armpit and the artery in its neck to the left. The Aux howled and died, falling limp onto the ice.

Another followed, and another, and then three more. Soon, the Zoo Pack war band was deep in the scrapping, swinging blades at close quarters.

The skirmish was all confusion as the feral Aux

fought low, on all fours, slicing as often into legs as they did into guts.

Evelyn's stilettos were tucked into her boots, and, for the first time, she was glad that the great coat was short. A blade in each hand, she crossed her wrists as a small, wiry beta dog found his way under her neighbour's guard and brought a blade up towards her.

She uncrossed her hands in one swift, decisive move, throwing her arms out wide. She made two diagonal cuts across the youth's throat, very nearly decapitating him. Hot blood flowed onto the ice at her feet, and spread alarmingly.

Evelyn stepped back as the blood made a rush for her boots. She had never seen blood flow like that before. Blood cooled fast outside. It congealed and the flow became sluggish. Pools of blood should be thick and dense and slow moving. Blood should not spread so fast, nor move so freely; it disgusted her.

The six feral Aux were killed in no more than a couple of minutes. Ezra Pound disposed of one more after the first, and Thomas Meltdown took two also.

The highest ranking dam made a messy kill, injuring her attacker, half-disembowelling him with a clumsy blade defence before finishing him off. There was too much viscera and a lot of blood and bile spreading together on the slippery ice.

The dam almost retched when she was done, splashed with a great wad of the muck from her opponent's stomach.

Evelyn had made the final kill.

Ezra Pound looked at her, but said nothing. One or two of the other packers nodded at her, and the oldest bared his teeth in a sort of smile, before fist bumping her upper arm a little too hard.

Far from a 'useless omega bitch', she'd become useful. Evelyn War had won her place in the pack. Evelyn War could scrap. Tougher and tough.

The war band moved on and descended into the tunnels of Track Twelve. They were all relieved to be below ground again, even though this was no man's land territory.

Built last, Track Twelve was among the smallest, deepest and darkest in the U-Bahn systems. There were no escape routes, as the unmanned service tunnels required only the space for small-scale machinery. They were useless for the Aux.

They disliked using the newest tracks, Twelve through Sixteen, which is why no packs had ever made their homes in them. All the packs travelled in them, however, when they had to.

Several of the war band loosened fastenings in the layers of their clothes to let the air circulate, unused to the warmth of the sun and the wet of their own breath and sweat. Evelyn's head cloth and collar were still heavy with moisture, but she preferred to leave them in place.

She welcomed the darkness, though, and the familiar echo of kilometres of empty tunnels threading away into the distance. She welcomed the layered tones of grey all around her, and she breathed more easily in the confined spaces below ground.

Threat could come from only two directions: ahead and behind. The *ping* of falling water droplets echoed as much as every sound they made. When Pound gave his orders – in the stentorian tones that he never wavered from – those, too, reverberated in the cramped space. The solid, curving walls clung almost too closely around the small group of Aux, as they walked two abreast down the track.

Pound's confidence grew quickly. He was Alpha, he was top dog, and soon the war band was jogging down the narrow tunnel, making good time on the journey to Warschauer. He never conjectured about the future. He never slowed his pace. As far as Ezra Pound, leader of the Zoo Pack, was concerned, every threat was behind them. That was the confidence of the Alpha dog.

Evelyn kept to the rear of the pack. She was exposed to any threat from behind, but they were moving quickly. It was what they were running *towards* that alarmed her.

Dorothy Barker called out and stopped. She had seen something.

The war band halted.

Ezra Pound and Thomas Meltdown came back to see what she'd found: a mangled Aux crossbow.

The lathes were bent double and the stirrup was buckled. Dorothy Barker held it in her hands, saying nothing, her mouth open, her face, free of its head cloth, pale.

"How?" she finally asked.

There was no answer.

The crossbows were virtually indestructible, handed down from one scrapper to another through the generations. It took great skill to forge new ones, and they were seldom made, not least because they rarely needed to be made. They needed to be looked after and strings had to be replaced from time to time, but the crossbow itself did not wear out and could not be destroyed.

This crossbow was warped and broken, and utterly useless.

"Not how... *what*?" said Evelyn, eventually. It was the only answer.

Eight heads rose as one as they all heard the whistle echo down the tunnel. It was a long way off, but no less threatening for that.

Evelyn looked to Pound.

"How far?" she asked.

"How far what?"

"To Warschauer Pack?"

"The tunnels take us –" began Pound.

"Outside," said Evelyn. "You heard it. We all heard it."

"How is the bow, him broken?" asked Dorothy, still holding the crossbow.

Ezra Pound took the bow roughly from the scrapper and turned it over in his hands for several seconds while Evelyn looked on. She could not keep the pleading out of her eyes.

"How far?" she asked.

"The tunnels," said Pound, his eyes still firmly on the weapon.

"It's warm," said Evelyn.

She did not expect Pound to hear her or listen to her. The other six Aux in the war band said nothing, either too stunned by the sight of the mangled crossbow or too in awe of their leader. Evelyn didn't know and didn't care which.

"How far?" she asked once more.

The whistle echoed again through the tunnels. It did not sound any closer, but the sound alone was enough to make the hairs rise on the backs of eight sturdy necks, despite head cloths, collars and pelts.

"It's warm," said Evelyn.

"We fought feral Aux," said Pound. "We fought our own."

"That's what you do," said Evelyn, unflinching. "You're Alpha."

She hated reminding Pound of his status in the Zoo Pack. She didn't believe in him, and she hated manipulating him, but she'd do it if she had to.

She had to. Track Twelve was narrow and there was no escape into service tunnels. There was only behind and ahead. Behind would lose them ground. Ahead... That was where the whistling sounds were coming from.

They had to make alliances. There was strength in numbers.

Zoo Pack had always traded with Warschauer Pack. It was the nearest thing they had to an alliance.

It was the first connection that Evelyn had a chance to exploit.

"Look at the crossbow. Be our leader, Alpha dog," she said.

Evelyn couldn't believe that she was flattering this slab of meat that the Zoo Pack followed. She couldn't believe that she was betraying her father and herself to further their cause. She wondered whether the ends could justify the means. She wondered whether it was clever or foolish. It felt foolish.

Ezra Pound looked down at the crossbow for two or three more seconds that felt to Evelyn like an eternity. Then he threw the Aux weapon aside with an echoing clang.

"Up," said Pound, and the single word echoed around the tunnel.

Evelyn War wished that he hadn't spoken so vehemently, so loudly, in such a firm tone. She hoped Them hadn't heard him.

CHAPTER NINE
THE HEARER

WALTER SICKERT WAILED and thrashed. His eyes were wide, but the orbs spun around and then high into his head, so that nothing of the black pupils showed.

He had been babbling for hours, for days. Babbling about the Voice, about the Voice in his head and about what it was telling him.

He had been this way, or something like it, for almost a week. He had been wide-eyed, sleepless and staring for upwards of a month, clutching and grasping at anyone who would stop for a moment to listen to his ramblings. Very soon, no one stopped.

They were afraid of him. They were afraid of what he was saying, of why he was saying it, of where the words were coming from.

Walter Sickert was a pup. He had been scrapping for a season or two, but poorly, getting himself into scraps that the betas had to save him from. He was lucky to be alive. He was given the dullest, safest sentry duties, and not trusted, even on the flanks of any war band. He was allowed only to forage close to Warschauer and not to hunt. He had no freedoms and no status in the Warschauer Pack.

But, now, he had the Voice.

He belonged to no familial group, except that his grandfather, Oswald was alive.

He was claiming to be a Hearer. There was a history. His grandfather's uncle had been the last Hearer in the pack that anyone could remember. Hearers were rare, deader and dead. Only the purest-blooded Aux packs had a Hearer, only the city packs, and they were pariahs all.

This was the Time of Ice and the Hearers belonged to the time of legends. They were not ragged, useless pups.

Oswald Sickert, faithful to the memory of his uncle, heard the things his grandson said. He listened to the pup's ramblings. He listened and he Believed.

He was old, and he had a pedigree. He had been a scrapper in his day, a lieutenant, tougher and tough. He had the ear of the Pack. He left the pup with the dam, mopping his brow and soothing him as best she could.

The old male made his way through the tunnels, fast and steady, towards... He stopped, watching the curls of his steaming breath rise straight up into the arch of the grey, dripping brickwork above his head. Droplets *pinged* all around him. It was wet. It was wrong.

He stopped, hand to his mouth, and he pondered.

He could not take this to the pack leader. He could not take this to the lieutenants. They were scrappers, tougher and tough. This was not about scrapping. This was about time and change.

This was about Hearing. Who would listen to him, who would be willing to listen to the Hearer? Who would Believe?

Oswald Sickert stood in the tunnel, alone for several minutes. The grey of the curving tunnel walls met the grey of the gravel beneath his feet, met the grey of the tracks that he did not understand the old use of. He only knew that this was his home. That the Aux lived underground because this was the Time of Ice.

He felt a drop of water land on his forehead and pour down his face. It ran over his brow ridge and dropped onto his cheek before finding a ragged path down past his mouth and onto the felt wrap he wore loosely around his body.

The Time of Ice was over. He was wet.

The old male looked down at the damp stain on his wrap, a dark grey patch spreading on the lighter cloth. He was reminded of some of the things his grandson had been babbling about. He remembered things about water. He remembered things about getting whet. He remembered Walter saying that all the Aux would get wet and then they would all have to get whet.

Oswald Sickert touched the damp patch on his wrap, and he understood. When the ice turned to water the Aux would *get wet*. And when the Aux got wet they would all have to *get whet*.

He came to a realisation.

"The tale-teller," he said, his voice bright and hard in the echoing tunnel. "The tale-teller, him will know the truth."

The tale-teller, Thomas Wolf, was duly brought to Walter Sickert.

He tried to reason with the pup. He tried to tell him a tale, an old familiar legend, told a hundred-hundred times before, something the pup would recognise, something to soothe him.

"Gene the Hackman, top dog, him done the great Walk Around," said the tale-teller. "Not for him the darkness, not for him the cold, not for him the Time of Ice. Gene the Hackman, him got whet. Gene the Hackman, him got whet and walked the Earth, and him killed Them."

Walter Sickert was not soothed.

His eyes rolled back into place and he stared at Thomas Wolf.

His face drained of the last vestiges of colour, and he began to shake all over. He pawed at the blankets and pelts the dam had spread over him, dragging and clawing at them. He thrashed his legs until the covers were dislodged and spread across the cot and into a heap on the floor.

He shrieked in the tale-teller's face and tore at his chest as the big male tried to reach out to him to calm the pup.

Then the pup bolted. He bolted so hard that he knocked the dam aside. He careened into his grandfather, throwing him against the wall and winding him so badly that the old male crumpled to the floor.

It was several seconds before Thomas Wolf had recovered himself enough to steady the dam. He tried to help Oswald Sickert to his feet, but he was pushed aside.

"Save Walter," the old male said, coughing for the breath to speak. "Him needs you."

The tale-teller hurried out of the cell that Oswald shared with Walter Sickert and followed the sounds along the passages and tunnels of Warschauer towards the communal chamber, towards the Pack's command centre.

There was no mistaking where Walter Sickert was heading. He left a wake of noise and confusion. He stammered and yelled his message at all who crossed his path. He attacked any who spoke back at him, confronted him, laughed at him.

He frightened the Aux. He frightened them into embarrassed laughter, or he frightened them into turning their backs on him.

He despised that more than anything. He struck out at their backs and clawed at their heads, trying to turn them, trying to make them face him, trying to make them listen to his words, to understand his meaning. No one understood.

His message was important; so important.

When Thomas Wolf reached the communal chamber, Walter Sickert was lying face-down on the hard, tiled floor with its chequerboard pattern. A splash of his blood smeared the white tiles. One of the biggest of the beta scrappers had a knee in the pup's back and was holding his arms by the wrists, pulling them hard towards his knees, making his head jerk.

Walter Sickert was unconscious.

He had stopped talking for the first time in days. He had stopped trying to make the Aux of the Warschauer Pack listen.

The tale-teller was followed into the chamber by the pup's grandfather.

"Him should be put out of his misery," said one of the lieutenants, standing over the pup as he lay inert on the tiles.

"Let him be," said Thomas Wolf. "Him sick. His grandfather, him is Oswald Sickert, him has good standing. Him and I, we will answer for the pup."

"Let him be," said the Warschauer Pack leader, rising from his chair at the far end of the chamber. "Let him be, but keep him quiet."

The lieutenant booted the pup in the ribs contemptuously and walked away.

Oswald Sickert stooped to lift his grandson into his arms, but the tale-teller, bigger, stronger and a dozen years younger, wouldn't allow it. He carried the pup back to his cell.

Once there, the dam cleaned Walter's wounds, and salved the bruise in his side.

Thomas Wolf then sent her away to find his pup, Reuben Blades, with instructions to bring back medicines to treat the invalid.

The self-proclaimed Hearer woke wide-eyed and frantic, and had to be held down while the dam administered the precious Corydalis tincture.

The medicinal plants that the Aux used were hard to grow below ground. They were used only sparingly.

The medication worked, and Walter Sickert rested somewhat peacefully for the first time in weeks.

"What will become of him?" his grandfather asked the tale-teller.

"Nothing, old one," said Thomas Wolf.

"But him tells the truth," said the old male. "Him tells the truth about Them."

CHAPTER TEN
WARSCHAUER

THE BUILDINGS GREW lower and more spread out as the Zoo Pack war band ventured further from the centre of Berlin. They had been pillaged more comprehensively, denuded of their materials, and the remains had been left to rot. The cold had wreaked more havoc on the shells of buildings, which had crumbled under the stress of the frost and ice. Many of them were ruins.

The Aux living at the edges of the city were poorer and fared less well than those who lived deep underground in the most protected areas. They had long ago taken everything that they could use out of the environment, including the tiles from roofs, anything made of wood or containing gypsum, everything that could be remade or burned.

Few Aux lived above ground, in the Time of Ice.

The Warschauer Pack had an old familial link with the Zoo Pack, going back so far that no one could remember exactly what it was. But Ezra Pound somehow knew that it mattered, and it was one of the few things that he respected.

It was a useful association, too. The Warschauer lived a wilder life. They still hunted and gathered. They provided new pelts, precious meat and weapons, and they bartered them for information. Their status was elevated too, by their association with a true city pack.

The old ties were the most reliable, and Pound would never give them up. He was a creature of habit, of habits formed long before he was top dog.

The going above ground was relentlessly tough. The ice was slick, and recent snowfalls made the going harder when the Aux suddenly found themselves up to their thighs in snow that was wet and heavy, instead of the dry powder they were accustomed to.

They had never been so wet.

Every surface was clammy and cold, in a way that the ice had never been. They were relieved, at first, when they were able to walk on solid ice. But it was too slick, they could not move confidently on it, and they were soon frustrated. The intermittent moaning below their feet disconcerted them. They had known nothing like it in their lifetimes, and had heard nothing of it in the tale-teller's tales.

This was a time of change.

The change would bring forth new legends for a new generation of tale-tellers, if there was anyone alive who knew how to craft a story.

Nothing had changed for as long as anyone knew anything about anything. Gene the Hackman had lived in a time of legends. Nothing was what it had been. They were not equipped for change. Ezra Pound was not equipped for change.

The long hard trudge to Warschauer left the war band tired and frustrated. It had taken longer than it should have, and the perils had been greater. But for Evelyn, even the smallest rewards were greater than anything she had expected.

They went below ground into the Warschauer Pack's main communal area.

Evelyn War had never seen anything like it. As she unwrapped her head cloth, she took in her surroundings. Ezra Pound and Thomas Meltdown were making their formal greetings in another room. The six remaining Zoo Packers were left in the vast underground space that Evelyn had only ever heard tell of.

Nothing like it existed anywhere else in the old U-Bahn system. The room was vast, and doors and openings led into a number of smaller chambers that she could not see into. She had never been in a room so huge, above ground or below.

The floor was tiled, black and white, old and worn. Clearly valued by the Pack, it was scrubbed clean so that it gleamed, with its stark, geometric pattern and its black edging. Evelyn was mesmerised.

Then someone said, "Look," and pointed. And she looked. Strange, glittering reflective orbs were suspended overhead. They too were clean, cleaner than anything she had seen underground, cleaner than the animals woven into the tiles of the walls at Zoologischer Garten. She was ashamed that her own pack did not take pride in their home, did not venerate their surroundings as the Warschauer clearly did.

She had heard descriptions of the place, but the pictures in her head did not live up to the reality. It was a place of magic and wonder.

As the six of them stood, heads tilted back to look up at the glistening globes suspended high above them, or looking around at the gleaming floor, heads were thrust out of the doors and openings and then retreated, sometimes reappearing.

Evelyn stopped looking around and began to concentrate on the faces of the Aux.

There was tension in the air, and the faces looked strained.

No one entered the chamber while Ezra Pound and his second were in conference with Saul Bellow, the leader of the Warschauer Pack. No one entered and no one left. When Pound returned to the main chamber with the local leader, they both looked serious. Only then did other Warschauer packers begin to emerge.

There was business to be done, information to be handed down in return for pelts, felt and two good crossbows. Evelyn couldn't help but think of the one they had found on Track Twelve only hours before.

The room seemed to become more lively, and the Aux more relaxed, so she said nothing. She kept to the periphery, still watching, but growing gradually less wary.

It was a long trek out to the Warschauer Pack, and the Zoo Pack, when it visited, never returned on the same day that it travelled out. There would be food and gossip. One or two of the Zoo Pack beta males might make liaisons with occasional mates among the Warschauer. Everything would become more festive.

There was no day and night underground, but the circadian rhythm of the Aux was fixed. Dawn and dusk were fixed. They did not need the sun to rise and set or the moon to be full in the sky above ground for them to feel the urge to wake or the need to sleep.

As the sun set above ground, Aux brought food and drink into the huge chamber. More of the Warschauer Pack began to gather, entering the room in twos and threes and small family groups, until the space was thronging with them. They were subdued at first, but they were excited by the Zoo Pack's visit and soon became animated.

The temperature of the vast space, as big as it was, soon rose with the heat of the dozens of bodies within it. The volume rose too as the Zoo Packers reacquainted themselves with old friends among the Warschauer Pack.

Evelyn was the outsider, but Evelyn War was the outsider wherever she ventured. She ate and drank what she was offered, but talked little, remaining at the edges, close enough to listen to what was being talked about, but not drawing attention to herself.

There was some talk of the sounds, of the moaning of the ice and the pinging of the water. There was some talk of the warmth of the sun and of the change that was coming. But it was all whispered and none of it reached the ears of the leaders.

Pound gave an account of the scrap with the Aux they had encountered on their long walk around to Warschauer, but only to boast of his prowess. He spoke loudly and gestured with his arms to re-enact his kills. He made no mention of the attackers' condition, nor speculated on the reasons for their wild behaviour.

Aux fought. They were tribal and territorial, but they were disciplined and organised; not feral, never bestial.

Several times, a young beta dog walked around the room towards Evelyn from her left and then back again. He seemed to slow down as he passed behind her, as if hesitating. But he said nothing, and Evelyn did not look at him. It was Reuben Blades, the tale-teller's pup.

While the meal was being cleared, Evelyn thought she saw him looking at her, but she glanced away before they made eye contact.

It was not unusual for a young male to seek the attention of a female as a mate, but Evelyn seemed an unlikely target for him. She clearly had little or no status in the war band, and she was not popular among the males of her own Pack. She saw no reason why a Warschauer male would show any interest in her. The Aux was young, though, and young males could be foolish when it came to choosing mates.

After the food, the Aux moved around, forming new groups. More pack members came into the chamber that Evelyn hadn't yet seen, removing wet clothes, returning from their duties. Others left to replace them, or to perform chores.

In the hubbub, Saul Bellow stood. He puffed out his chest, allowing the pelt he was wearing around his shoulders to slide off them and fall down his back. The vast expanse of his naked, gleaming chest was exposed, a pair of ragged parallel scars running diagonally across it.

Evelyn watched as he lifted his staff and bounced it hard off the tiled floor twice, making two resounding *cracks* reverberate around the space.

Silence fell.

"Ezra Pound, him Alpha dog, top dog, leader of Zoo Pack, him welcome friend, him true ally of Warschauer Pack," declared Saul Bellow. "Him eat at our table and him bring great joy to our house!"

Evelyn heard the same stentorian tones that she heard whenever Ezra Pound spoke, and she knew that the two males were brothers at heart. It dismayed her.

The Warschauer Pack roared their approval of

their leader's speech. Evelyn found herself joining in as she saw her own packmates cheering.

She had seen and heard nothing that might further her cause, however, and she was disappointed. Her small triumph earlier in the day meant little. It certainly did not give her the clout to raise the subject of alliances, or of Them, with Ezra Pound; not here, not now.

She glanced around as the cheer died away and chatter replaced it.

Reuben Blades, who was looking directly at her, lowered his gaze, and began talking quietly to two males, one middle-aged and one old and stooped.

Evelyn was convinced the youth had been staring at her. She was sure he was talking about her. She knew, now, he wasn't interested in her as a mate. He wouldn't discuss that with the two older males.

They looked almost like a family group.

She was alone, standing aimlessly. It didn't look right. She picked up her beaker and started to walk a little further into the room, as if towards a group of Warschauer dams; scrappers by the looks of them, about her age.

She walked at an angle to the young Aux and his group, not getting any closer, but keeping them in her line of sight. She nodded and smiled to one or two Aux as she passed them.

A sudden roar went up. Evelyn looked to her right to see Thomas Meltdown in an arm wrestling competition with an Aux a head shorter than he was, but almost half again as broad.

Meltdown would win. Evelyn raised her beaker in his direction, and then turned her head slowly back to glance at her targets, just as the middle-aged male looked up at her.

They were definitely talking about her.

Evelyn made eye contact and tilted her head fractionally, lifting it perhaps a centimetre. Then she walked purposefully across the room to a position beyond the group, hoping that one of them would join her. She deliberately chose a noisy part of the room, where a gaggle of Warschauer Packers, mostly dams, had gathered around one of the Zoo Aux, who was performing particularly athletic acrobatic tricks.

He had stripped down to his undergarment, and his admittedly impressive physique was a big hit with the dams, who were shouting and yelping to egg him on. The Warschauer beta dogs who were also gathered around were jeering at him, trying to break his concentration; or scoffing at the dams.

It was inevitable that a riot or a fight would break out some time soon, but Evelyn was in no doubt that the Zoo Aux would have his pick of mates before the night was over.

As she reached the back of the little throng, Evelyn was joined by the young Aux that had been watching her all evening. He looked a little startled, a little afraid.

"Me, I'm Reuben Blades," said the Aux. "Are you her?"

"Me, I'm Evelyn War," said Evelyn.

"The Hearer, him your father?"

Evelyn was surprised. She swung her head around and stared right into his eyes for the briefest moment, and then turned back to watch the scene playing out in front of her.

The Zoo packer was balancing himself on one hand, grasping one leg of an upturned stool, the seat of which was balanced on one leg of another upturned stool, his legs wide apart in mid-air. She whistled and clapped to show her appreciation of the stunt, and to cover her conversation with the youth.

"Thomas Wolf, our tale-teller, him wants to speak to you," said the young Aux, and then turned to walk away. Evelyn did not move for several seconds, watching the Zoo Packer perform a succession of flips, twists and somersaults in a tight circle as the cheering crowd made room for him.

She whistled and clapped as enthusiastically as she was able, not sure what she would be facing if she did as Blades had asked. She knew that she'd do it anyway. He knew who she was, and it mattered to him. It also mattered to the Warschauer tale-teller.

Tale-tellers were important. The only ally she had left in the Zoo Pack, her father's only ally, was Edward Leer.

It was a good omen.

As the acrobat puffed himself up for his crowd of adoring dams and jeering males, Evelyn backed away. She looked to her right, to where the young Aux had been standing with the old male who must have been the tale-teller. She could not see them, but, assuming they must be nearby and would make themselves known, she began to walk in that general direction.

Reaching a narrow doorway, its door half open, Evelyn glanced around to make sure she wasn't being watched, and looked inside. The interior was unlit, but she could see the shapes of three mingled grey shadows: Reuben Blades, the middle-aged male and the ancient Aux she assumed to be Thomas Wolf.

Evelyn glanced around once more and then slid into the dark room, pushing the door to behind her.

"Evelyn War?" asked the middle-aged male. His tone was breathy, melodious and low, and Evelyn knew, immediately, that she had been wrong.

"You, you're Thomas Wolf, the tale-teller," said Evelyn.

A roar went up from the great chamber, and four pairs of eyes looked towards the door. The tale-teller nodded at Reuben Blades, who moved to stand sentry, one ear to the chamber and the other to what was happening inside the room.

"The Time of Ice, it is coming to an end," said the tale-teller. "Everyone, them are afraid. No one, them don't listen."

"The Aux, them listen to the legends," said Evelyn. "Ezra Pound, him listened to the new tale."

Thomas Wolf looked long and hard at her.

"Edward Leer, him tell a new fable?" he asked, but he continued before Evelyn could answer. "Him tell a new fable, and Ezra Pound, him come to Warschauer and him eat and him trade and him not talk of the new tale."

The old male seemed to slump under the weight of the tale-teller's words. His head shook from side to side, slowly, mournfully, but he said nothing.

Evelyn War looked at him.

"Him, who is he?" asked Evelyn War, gesturing at the old man.

"Oswald Sickert," said the old man.

"There isn't time," said the tale-teller, his eyes flicking over to Reuben Blades at the doorway.

"The whistles, the echoes, them are heard here, too," said Evelyn.

"The sounds, them are heard," said Thomas Wolf. "Aux, them die, deader and dead. Them disappear. Them never come back from sentry duty. There is much talk, much whispering."

"There is strength in numbers," said Evelyn.

"Ezra Pound and Saul Bellow, them must talk," said the tale-teller. "Evelyn War must make them talk."

There was another roar from the crowd. Reuben Blades turned from door.

"Saul Bellow, him is calling for the tale-teller," he said.

Evelyn's expression hardened.

"Evelyn War and the Warschauer tale-teller, we must make them talk," said Evelyn. "Evelyn War and Thomas Wolf, we must make them listen and we must make them talk."

CHAPTER ELEVEN
THOMAS WOLF'S TALE

THOMAS WOLF WALKED out into the chamber, followed by Evelyn War. Walter Sickert's grandfather and Reuben Blades disappeared into the crowd behind them.

The throng of Warschauer Pack parted as they realised their tale-teller had come among them. They stared at Evelyn, following in his wake, and looked to one another for reassurance.

Thomas Wolf took up a position several metres in front of where the two pack leaders sat together. Evelyn noticed, for the first time, that he did not have a staff of office; that he did not need one.

The heavy-set Aux stretched his massive arms out on either side of his barrel chest and brought his meaty hands together in a resounding clap that echoed around the chamber. Any Aux that had not already fallen silent soon did so.

Then the tale-teller turned his head, casting his eyes around the room to make sure that he had everyone's attention. When he was satisfied, he began.

"Gene the Hackman, top dog, him done the great Walk Around. Not for him the darkness, not for him the cold, not for him the Time of Ice. Gene the Hackman, him got whet. Gene the Hackman, him got whet and walked the Earth, and him killed Them."

Evelyn was confused. This was not what she expected.

There followed a long silence.

"This is not that," Thomas Wolf said in a lower voice.

The gathered Warschauer, and the Zoo Packers among them, swayed and shuffled, waiting to hear the tale that they were expecting.

"The Time of Ice, him were long and him is old and tired, and him is dying, deader and dead," said the tale-teller. The words were new, never before spoken, not by him, not by anyone. Never before heard by the Warschauer Pack.

Evelyn had not moved from where she stood, slightly apart, in the front rank of listeners.

Thomas Wolf stopped again. He glanced at Evelyn, as if for confirmation. She did not know what to do, so she simply looked at him with firm eyes. She hoped that she could fill him with some of the intent that she felt, some of the intent that her father had passed on to her.

"There is strength in numbers," said the tale-teller. He stopped abruptly, and there were some low murmurs from several Aux in the crowd.

"The ice, him creaks and him moans. Him hurt bad. Him dying. The sun, him hot and bright. The sun, him new again. Him reborn in a new age. Him reborn in the age of wet. It is time to get whet."

The tale-teller breathed hard, mustering his confidence. He was speaking plainly, in his low, musical tones. Everyone in the huge chamber could hear him, but Evelyn was afraid.

Evelyn was afraid that without conviction, without phlegm, Thomas Wolf's words would carry no meaning. He would not speak with the confidence of a legend learned, of words deeply embedded in his consciousness.

"It is time to get whet," said the tale-teller again. "The Warschauer Packers, them walk the tunnels and them take blades and crossbows and them never return. Them scrap with blades and them scrap with crossbows, tougher and tough, and them never return. How many? Them get whet and them never return, deader and dead."

The tale-teller's voice was steady now, firm and strong as he remembered the scrappers the Pack had lost in the last days and weeks.

Evelyn could feel his mettle growing, and she could feel the Aux around her being drawn into the story. They knew he was right. They knew he was speaking the truth. They wanted answers.

"Raymond Carver, him tougher and tough. Him

much loved. Him strong and brave. Him gone, deader and dead. Him gone underground. Him never return," said Thomas Wolf.

"We know Raymond Carver, him not killed by an Aux. Him could scrap with any Aux and return. Him not killed by a beast. Him a killer of beasts. Him our best hunter. Him skittle-scuttle fast. Him tougher and tough.

"Raymond Carver, him killed by the times. Him killed by Them what whistle. Him killed by *THEM!* All Warschauer scrappers deader and dead, them all killed by the times. Them all killed by Them what whistle. *Them* kill the Aux, deader and dead. *Them* kill the Aux. *Them* take our brothers and sisters."

"Enough!" bellowed the Warschauer leader, and then in a quieter, resigned tone, "Enough. You sound like Walter Sickert. Walter Sickert, him mad, him shameful to the Warschauer."

The crowd, still reeling, fell silent once more as Thomas Wolf turned to face the pack leader.

"I am the tale-teller and my words are truth. Walter Sickert, him tell a truth, too."

The leader glared at Thomas Wolf, baring his teeth, a silent threat in his expression. "You should not hear this shame," he said to Ezra Pound. "The tale-teller, him will tell another tale. Him will tell a fable of Gene the Hackman."

Evelyn stepped forward.

"I will tell a tale," she said. "I will tell of Ezra Pound, him scrapping with the Aux on our long

Walk Around to the Warschauer. I will tell a story of my father, Oberon War, him meeting with the Kade Pack. I will tell a tale of Oberon War, the Hearer, him deader and dead, killed by the Zoo Pack."

Ezra Pound stood abruptly as Evelyn said her last words. He glared down at her, his expression no less threatening than Saul Bellow's. Then he smiled at the leader of the Warschauer Pack.

"Warschauer Pack, it bears no shame," he said. "The tale-teller, him will speak. You and I, we will speak." The Warschauer Pack leader nodded gratefully, unaware that Ezra Pound had been driven to his largesse by Evelyn.

"In private," said Saul Bellow, wheeling and striding off. Pound fell in beside him. The silent crowd parted, and Thomas Wolf waited for a moment, before walking out behind them.

"And bring the useless omega bitch," said Ezra Pound over his shoulder, loudly enough for the entire room to hear him.

Evelyn War was the *useless omega bitch* again. She'd taken a risk; name-calling was the least she might have expected. She didn't care.

She stepped into line several metres behind Thomas Wolf. She didn't want him to suffer by association with her.

The nearest of the Warschauer Packers drew a little closer to her, curious as to who this strange dam was and what she had done to turn the tide of events.

Reuben Blades caught Evelyn's eye very briefly as she walked past him, then quickly looked away. He soon disappeared into the crowd; his job was done.

Evelyn looked for Oswald Sickert, but she did not see him anywhere.

CHAPTER TWELVE
CONFRONTATION

As SOON AS the door to the side-room was closed and the two leaders were alone with the tale-teller and Evelyn War, Saul Bellow turned on Thomas Wolf.

"You shame me before our ally and friend. Why?" he roared, grabbing hold of Wolf by the front of his jacket with his huge hands. He almost looked as if he was going to lift the big Aux off the floor and shake him.

The tale-teller had no time to answer his leader.

"There is no shame," said Ezra Pound, clasping his friend firmly by the shoulder.

Saul Bellow let Thomas Wolf go. The tale-teller straightened his clothes, pale and clearly distressed.

"Who is Walter Sickert?" asked Evelyn War.

Thomas Wolf opened his mouth to answer, but, once again, was given no opportunity.

"Mad Aux," spat Saul Bellow. "Deluded pup, him says he can Hear. Him says him is a Hearer. Him mad. Him brings shame on the Warschuaer Pack. Think nothing of him."

"There is no shame," said Ezra Pound once more. "The ice, him moans and creaks. The ice, him wet. The Zoo Pack, we have lost sentries, too. We have lost scrappers, tougher and tough. You and I, we are old allies. You and I, we stand together against the whistling foe."

Ezra Pound and his spiritual brother clasped hands and embraced, their chests smacking together as if that was all that mattered.

"I want to meet your Walter Sickert," said Evelyn War. "Him claims to be a Hearer. Him might have some answers." Now she was sure that the tale-teller could help her. Oswald Sickert must be related to the Hearer, and that was why Thomas Wolf had wanted to meet her.

"Him mad. Him a blight on the Warschauer Pack," said the pack leader. Abruptly, he turned from Ezra Pound and took a long, threatening stride across the room towards Evelyn War. "The useless omega bitch, her is trouble?" he asked Pound, never taking his eyes off her.

"Evelyn War," growled Ezra Pound. "Her is a Believer. Oberon War, him was her father. Him was a Hearer."

Evelyn saw spittle fly, bright white, as her Pack leader spoke, although she never took her eyes off Saul Bellow's face as he loomed over her.

"Tell him about the Aux you killed, deader and dead," said Evelyn, defiant. She finally broke eye contact with the Warschauer Pack leader and looked over his shoulder at Ezra Pound. "Them was feral. Them was wild... no discipline, no organisation... Them was... desperate."

Pound slumped visibly.

"We have killed the wild Aux," said Saul Bellow. "We have always fought for territory. Them were never like the city packs, never like us, but them were tougher and tough, and true."

"Not them we fought. Them were wild and frantic. Them were deader and dead before we made them dead," said Ezra Pound. "Them attacked on four feet. Them were dogs, not Aux. Them were ragged. Them had not cleaned their weapons. Them were every scrapper for himself."

There was a long pause.

"I want to see Walter Sickert," said Evelyn War. "I want to listen to the Hearer speak."

"Walter Sickert, him no Hearer," said Saul Bellow. "Him a mad pup. Him dangerous."

Evelyn looked to the tale-teller, who still looked pale and frightened.

"Tell them," she demanded.

All eyes turned on Thomas Wolf, but faced with his Pack leader's gaze, he had nothing more to say. He was drained, from trying to craft a new fable that would have an impact. It had moved his leader to have this meeting, to talk more freely of what had come to pass in the last days and weeks.

He had done his job as well as he could, with only this low-ranking stranger for an ally. Besides, faced with justifying his claim to his angry Pack leader and to the intimidating figure of Ezra Pound, he was not at all sure that Walter Sickert *was* a Hearer. The pup had tossed and turned on his bed. He had rocked and sweated.

"Walter Sickert, him sick," said the tale-teller at last. "Him sad. Him sweats on his bed and him wails. Him does not know what him says."

"But you believe his words," said Evelyn, earnestly. "You are friends with Oswald Sickert."

"Useless omega bitch," said Ezra Pound. "You heard the tale-teller. Respect your betters. Me, I should have had you whipped. You should have died beside your father.

"Enough of this talk. We are done." The Alpha dog forced a smile onto his lips. "Entertain us, Saul Bellow. Tomorrow, we make a long Walk Around back to Old Zoo."

As the two leaders left the room, Evelyn War caught the eye of the tale-teller, who could manage nothing more than a sad shrug in her direction. The hierarchy of an Aux pack did not allow for outright insubordination, particularly not among the senior males, unless one got the bone to challenge a leader. And as powerful as his position was, a tale-teller never got the bone for that.

The party resumed in the chamber. A loud *whoop* went up from the Warschauer Pack as their leader entered, baring his teeth in a broad grin. He heartily encouraged the celebrations, including his friend and ally in the revelry long into the night.

Evelyn War walked the room, joining in at the periphery of various groups, searching for allies, looking out for Aux who might want to talk to her. They looked her up and down, but they all turned their backs on her, including her own Zoo Pack brothers and sisters, since Pound had demoted her once more.

It was clear from the whispers she overheard that the Warschauer Pack were afraid and that they hoped the alliance with the Zoo Pack was strong and sustainable. They hoped Ezra Pound was doing something about the lost Aux and the whistling monster.

It was a threat to them, a constant, nerve-wracking threat, and no one was addressing it. Fear had closed that door, but the dog soldiers' unease was evident in the face of every Warschauer scrapper.

No one was facing up to that. Ignorance was bliss, but ignorance was killing a Warschauer Aux a day, and the numbers were mounting.

Evelyn walked the room for an hour or two, moving from group to group, hoping to find a friendly or sympathetic face, hoping to find a way to make contact with Walter Sickert. Hoping to see Oswald Sickert.

The Warschauer Packers shunned her, turning

their backs whenever she came close to them. They did not speak to her, not even to hiss at or abuse her. They simply ignored her presence.

They had seen her speak up to her leader when it was not her place to do so, and they did not want to expose themselves to the dangers of associating with her. They had heard her called 'the useless omega bitch' by Ezra Pound and they did not want whatever status they had earned within their own pack to be compromised by this stranger from Zoo Pack with her insubordination.

She looked for Reuben Blades, but he was nowhere to be seen, and the tale-teller was kept close by his leader.

There would be more telling of myths before the night was out and the revelries were over. Tales of great legends. Tales of Gene the Hackman. Nothing that Evelyn War wanted to hear.

"Hold out your beaker," said a voice behind Evelyn's left shoulder.

She had been clasping her empty beaker in her hand for some time. She did not care to drink. There was no respite from her concerns and she had no desire to drown her sorrows. She did not feel sorry for herself; she felt sorry for the Zoo Pack and the Warschauer Pack, for every dog soldier and scrapper in the grand chamber at Warschauer.

Getting drunk on their half-fermented ale would only muddy her thinking and give her a thick head for the long Walk Around home, when she was sure she'd need a clear one.

Evelyn put her hand over her beaker and began to turn her head.

"Don't turn," said the voice. "You, hold out your beaker. I'll fill it."

"I don't –" began Evelyn, but she was cut off.

"You and I, we should talk," said the voice. "Let me pour you a drink, or I might go back to thinking you're a useless omega bitch."

Evelyn had heard enough to identify the speaker, so she took her hand from over the mouth of her beaker slowly. She expected ale to be poured into it, but she got water. She lifted the beaker to her lips, but before she drank, with the vessel in front of her mouth, covering her words, she said, "The room on the left."

She was grateful for the two or three long gulps of cool water that she drank, and made sure that her beaker was empty once more. It would look bad for her if she was caught drinking anything but the ale laid on especially for the Zoo Pack's visit.

Evelyn turned; there was no one behind her, as she anticipated. She waited a full minute before she began to make her way to the room furthest from her. It was the same room where she had first spoken to the tale-teller. She prayed that it would not be occupied.

When she entered the room, Evelyn saw a figure leaning with its back against the wall opposite the door, arms crossed, one knee bent, the corresponding foot flat against the wall. Evelyn marvelled at how relaxed the Aux looked.

"Close the door," said the familiar voice. "You know things. I want to know what you know. Ezra Pound, him not telling us anything."

Evelyn War closed the door and walked into the room. There was no furniture, nowhere to sit, so she took up a position on the wall opposite the Aux, slid down to her haunches and sat on the floor, her knees apart.

Finally she had found a potential ally among the Zoo Pack scrappers, and, however long it took, she was going to cement that alliance. There was strength in numbers, that was what her father had tried so hard to instill in her, and two was twice as many as one.

"The Aux, why were them wild?" asked Dorothy Barker. "Why did them bleed so much?"

Evelyn remembered how the dam had almost retched after making her kill in Kreuzberg. She remembered the feral Aux's blood and filth on the dam's clothes.

"I don't know," she said. "There are always wild Aux. Them live outside the city. Them scavenge and attack. Them always have."

"Not like that," said Dorothy Barker.

"No," said Evelyn. "Not like that. I've never seen the wild Aux, them not like that."

"The ice, why is it slick?" asked Dorothy. "Why is it wet? The sun, why is it bright?"

"I don't know," said Evelyn. "Everything is changing. Nothing is the same. The Time of Ice, it is dying."

"The tale-teller, him said that," said Dorothy. "Why does the ice moan?"

"I don't know," said Evelyn. "The ice, it is moaning and dying."

Dorothy Barker was becoming agitated. She flexed her back away from the wall and stood over Evelyn. Evelyn did not get up, but allowed the dam to loom over her. She looked up at her, meeting her angry gaze.

"I do not know," she said. "I only know what my father, Oberon War, the Hearer, him told me."

"And you Believed him?" asked Dorothy, spitting her contempt through the words. The question was rhetorical, but Evelyn answered it anyway.

"Ezra Pound, him gives us no answers. The sentry, him disappeared. The ice, it moans and dies. The wild Aux, them feral. Oberon War was my father. Him believed there was strength in numbers. Him tried to make an alliance with the Kade and him died trying... Him heard the Master's Voice. Yes, I Believed him."

"Strength in numbers?" asked Dorothy. "Against what?"

Evelyn War looked unblinking into Dorothy Barker's eyes.

"Against Them," she said.

CHAPTER THIRTEEN
NEW RECRUITS

"Then it was all for nothing," said Edward Leer when Evelyn War and Dorothy Barker reported back to him on their return from the visit to the Warschauer Pack.

"Ezra Pound, him did nothing," said Evelyn. "But the tale-teller, him sent his pup to find me. Him talked to me. Him brought Oswald Sickert to me. Him tried to reach out to his leader. We must talk to Walter Sickert if him is a Hearer. If him can tell us more."

"Evelyn and me, we can go back," said Dorothy Barker. "Tougher and tough."

Edward Leer looked from one dam to the other and sighed.

"Not alone," he said. "Two, you are not enough to get whet."

"My mate, him makes three," said Dorothy Barker.

"No," said Evelyn.

The two dams were glaring at each other. Leer looked from one to the other.

"Three, you are still not enough to get whet," said Edward Leer.

"My mate, him is Robert Browning," said Dorothy. "Tougher and tough. Him worth two scrappers. Him worth two Aux."

"Robert Browning, him not coming to Warschauer," said Evelyn. "Him not coming to find Walter Sickert. Him..." She trailed off.

"Him my mate," said Dorothy.

The stand-off seemed unshakeable.

"You meet with him," said Dorothy finally, turning to Edward Leer. "Tale-teller, you choose." Then she turned back to Evelyn and glared at her once more.

"And Ben Gun," said Evelyn. "Me, I want to take Ben Gun."

"The pup?" asked the tale-teller. "You can't take a pup."

"Ben Gun, him loyal," said Evelyn. She didn't know why she'd blurted out his name, and he *was* only a pup, untried as a scrapper, but she had seen his prowess with the sling. He was a loner, like her, and he had been following her around ever since their encounter on the platform.

He was fast, too, skittle-scuttle fast, and he was quiet. He'd been there wherever she was, and she'd never heard him coming. Besides, she was sure he could outrun anything he couldn't outfight.

The Aux dams left the tale-teller without another word, each to find her recruit.

Evelyn left Edward Leer's cell and trotted the length of the narrow service tunnel where it was located. She blinked hard against the glare off the reflective black walls, and dodged the small fires. She hated that tunnel.

She thought she saw Ben Gun's shadow where the service tunnel joined Track Two, but when she got there he was gone. She called his name, and her voice echoed down the track, but he did not answer.

She dropped down onto the track and jogged for a hundred metres or so east. Then she turned and jogged about the same distance west, calling for him. Still he did not answer. Finally, Evelyn returned to the platform and hoisted herself up to sit on the edge of the platform, her legs swinging above the tracks.

She took the slingshot she had confiscated from Ben out of her waistband and a stone out of her cuff, where she had taken to storing them.

She idly placed the stone in the sling. She took aim at the opposite curving wall, where a runnel of water was wending its way down the uneven surface. The missile hit with a *crack*, and a droplet of water fell to the ground, landing with a familiar *ping*.

She placed another stone in the slingshot and looked along the wall for another likely stream of water before running her eyes left and right down the tunnel.

There was something in the shadows to her right.

She picked out her target, whipped her arm and propelled the stone at the wall. Another *crack*, and another *ping*.

And again.

The shadow to her right had got closer. It had ducked under the lip of the platform and was only a few metres away, crouching among the stones. Evelyn wondered, not for the first time, how he had moved without her hearing. Loose stones were abundant between and around the tracks; it was impossible to walk on them without disturbing them, without making them grate or skip or slide. Ben Gun seemed able to do it.

The third stone did not raise a *ping*.

"Missed," said a voice.

"You, show me," said Evelyn, not moving from her seat on the edge of the platform.

Ben Gun stood up. He was too short to hoist himself onto the platform the way that Evelyn had, so he faced it and clambered onto his knees before turning to sit next to her, about a metre away.

He put a handful of stones on the platform between them, ten or a dozen in all, and took out the new slingshot he had made for himself. All the while, he instructed her in the proper use of the weapon.

Evelyn and Ben spent the next half an hour shooting stones at the tunnel wall, hitting drops of water, clumps of moss, stains, scratches, anything they could identify as a target. Ben Gun missed nothing. Evelyn missed maybe one shot in half a dozen.

"You, watch this," said Ben Gun. "You, put a stone in the air."

Evelyn whipped her loaded sling, and a stone flew high into the apex of the tunnel. As it began to fall, there was a *crack*, and it was smacked off its trajectory by the stone from Ben's slingshot.

Evelyn squealed with laughter and clapped in delight.

"Ben, you want to be a warrior?" she asked him after the echoes of her laughter had died away. "A scrapper?"

"Me, I *will* be a scrapper," said Ben. "Me, I'll be a lieutenant one day, tougher and tough."

"Ben Gun could be a scrapper tomorrow," said Evelyn War.

Ben looked at Evelyn wide-eyed.

"Me, I have not been called," said Ben. "Me, I have not been chosen. Others, them are bigger and stronger. Me, I am fast and I have this" – he twirled his slingshot through the air on the end of one finger – "but some pups are bigger and stronger. The lieutenants, them are fools for not calling me. You, can you make them call me?"

"Me," said Evelyn. "*I* am calling you."

Ben's face fell.

"You are not a lieutenant," said Ben.

"The times, them change," said Evelyn. "This, it is a secret war band."

"You are not a lieutenant," said Ben, again, not looking at her. "You cannot call me."

"Then Edward Leer, him will call you," said

Evelyn dropping down onto the tracks and taking a step towards the pup.

"Him the tale-teller," said Ben, lifting his head to look into Evelyn's face.

He had not looked at her eye-to-eye since their first meeting on the track. He had known she was always serious, but he had never seen her like this and never so close, except for that first time. He had heard about her. He had followed her. He was curious. Now he could see that she was more serious than any Aux.

"The tale-teller, him not a lieutenant," he finally said.

"This war band, it is more important than anything," said Evelyn. "And him more powerful than a lieutenant. Him more powerful than anyone."

"Except Ezra Pound," said Ben Gun.

"Pfftt," said Evelyn War.

Ben Gun's eyes opened wide and his mouth opened wider, and the tunnel of Track Two filled with the echoes of Evelyn War's laughter for several seconds.

"If me, I'm going to make the tale-teller, him call you," she said, "you will have to understand many things."

"What things?" asked Ben Gun, deadly serious.

"The first thing you will have to understand," she said, "is that there are many things – many, many things – them more powerful than Ezra Pound."

CHAPTER FOURTEEN
MORE FERAL AUX

THEY WOULD BE faster outside than in the tunnels.

It was easier to leave the Zoo Pack fiefdom by one of the stations at the periphery, so the four Aux gathered during the night, careful not to coincide with the change of sentry duty.

The tracks were quiet, apart from the pinging water droplets that never seemed to stop.

Edward Leer had decided that Robert Browning was an asset. Dorothy Barker held sway over him, and, despite his loyalty to the Zoo Pack, had easily persuaded him that the mission back to Warschauer was worthwhile. He was a fierce scrapper and no challenge was beyond him. He was also a lieutenant with access to outside clothes and to arms. They needed him.

Evelyn War, Dorothy Barker, Robert Browning and Ben Gun came above ground at Deutsche Oper on track two. It added a few kilometres to their journey, but there were only four of them, a smaller group, so they could move faster.

"Us, we don't move like a war band," said Robert Browning as they came up into the station. The moon was high and visibility was good. "Us, we move fast, together."

"Who put Robert Browning, him in charge?" asked Ben Gun.

Browning turned on the pup and glared at him, a deep furrow line appearing on his brow ridge.

"Only asking," said Ben, shrugging. "Me, I thought Evelyn War, her idea, Evelyn War, her war band."

"Robert Browning, him hold rank," said Evelyn War.

And then, "What are you doing?" she asked after pausing to watch Ben take several lengths of rusted wire springs and begin to weave them into the treads of his boots.

"Here," said Ben, handing a bundle of the springs to Evelyn. "You too."

The constant pinging from outside was interrupted by a long low moan and a creak. Silence fell among the group.

"Us, we need to get moving," said Robert Browning.

"Yes, us must go," said Dorothy. "Us, we'll be safer in the dark."

"Will we?" asked Evelyn. And then, "Why are you doing that?"

"For the ice," said Ben. "So us, we don't fall on the ice."

It took only a few minutes, and with all their boots modified, the four Aux left the station and headed east. They didn't want to risk being seen, so they avoided the rat runs through the buildings that Browning was familiar with and stayed outside, keeping to the main streets where nobody ventured.

It was a risk. They felt exposed, but they could also move fast.

They stepped cautiously onto the ice, but the wire springs gave them a good grip on the slick surface. After a few tentative steps, they started to jog down the slippery streets.

The going was good, and the first two or three kilometres were uneventful. The four Aux set up a steady rhythm, slowing at corners to check and cover and to knock the accumulated ice from the springs in their boots. Then they moved on again at their steady jog.

Suddenly Ben Gun stopped and squatted low in the middle of the street. He gestured to the others as a deep rumble vibrated the air all around them.

Robert Browning pulled the crossbow off his back with one swift movement of his right arm and made a gesture with his left, lurching towards the shaded side of the street to take cover.

"No!" shouted Ben.

Too late.

The rumble was followed by a loud *WHOMP*.

Evelyn and Dorothy were thrown off their feet in a cloud of snow and ice.

Ben stood up almost immediately from his crouched position, and began to make his way through the cloud of ice debris and snowflakes towards where he had last seen Browning.

Behind him Dorothy groaned, and Evelyn coughed.

"What – What just happened?" asked Evelyn.

"Uhn... Are we under attack?" asked Dorothy.

"The ice," said Ben over his shoulder, "it falls."

Dorothy staggered to her feet and peered through the clearing mist.

"Robert?" she asked, still bewildered.

"Robert Browning, him under there," said Ben Gun, pointing to a mound of ice and snow banked up against the side of the street, newly fallen from the roofs of the adjacent buildings.

"You, help," said Dorothy striding towards Ben, shrugging off her confusion to come to her mate's aid.

Evelyn was beside her in a moment, and the three of them started lifting slabs of ice off the heap, heaving them into the street.

"Robert," said Dorothy, over and over, "Robert, you say something."

"Wait," said Ben, stopping abruptly and taking a step back from the rescue.

"You, keep digging," said Dorothy.

"You, listen," said Ben.

Evelyn put a hand on Dorothy's arm to stop her scrabbling around in the wet, freezing detritus of the ice fall to prevent her making more noise.

They all heard another rumble. Ben was moving already, but Evelyn had to half-drag Dorothy back into the middle of the wide street to pull her out of danger. This time they were all low to the ground when another roof gave up its heavy load of ice and snow. All they felt was the scattering of ice shards as the spray from the impact hit their backs.

Dorothy called out, "Robert!" but the fall had happened two buildings over and the weight of debris at the site of Robert Browning's accident had not been added to.

Dorothy Barker was the first on her feet, striding back to continue to dig for her mate.

"Aaargh!"

They all heard it: the pained, angry cry as Robert Browning punched and clawed his way out of his live burial.

As Dorothy reached him, he turned his head hard to the right, and clenched and unclenched his left fist. His neck made a cracking, crunching sound, and Browning let out a satisfied grunt. Then he looked at his left hand and squeezed it again, apparently satisfied that it had sustained no permanent injury.

"You, help me get out of here," he said.

In a matter of moments, with all four working together, the big Aux's legs were free of the avalanche. He was cold and wet, and he would have some bruising, but he appeared to be otherwise unharmed. He limped back into the middle of the street.

"Ben Gun, you, how do you know so much?" he asked. "You, how do you know about the outside? You knew about boots, and now you know about this." He gestured at the piled ice.

"Me, sometimes I go outside," said Ben. "Me, I like to see things, hear things. Me, I like to do things. The Pack, nobody cares about me. The Pack, nobody watches me. Me, I do what I like."

"Good!" said Robert Browning. "You, keep doing that. Just you tell me everything."

"We keep to the wide streets, and tracks, move fast, listen. Every sound, it means something. Me, I know sounds."

"You, how much of the city do you know?" asked Dorothy Barker.

"Me, not much. Half an hour from Zoo. No outside clothes," said Ben Gun, looking down at himself. He was wearing the outside clothes that Robert Browning was able to take from the stores without them being noticed, whatever was left.

Ben's clothes were the smallest, generally assigned to the smaller dams, and had been adapted by them for their use. If he looked ridiculous, he didn't care. He had been called. He was a scrapper. He was with a war band on a long Walk Around.

"Doesn't matter *where* I know," said Ben Gun. "*Sounds* matter. Me, I know sounds."

Ben looked at Evelyn, who had been quiet for some time. They were in the area of Kreuzberg where the feral Aux had attacked on their last visit to Warschauer, and she was on her guard.

She liked to be underground among the tunnels. She didn't like the light. She could feel her body reacting to the day, becoming more alert. Dawn would not be long. She reached between the rough toggles of her coat, drew out her eyeshades and put them on.

"South," said Ben Gun, almost under his breath. "Us, we should travel south."

The group slowed slightly as they approached another junction.

"There are no sounds," said Robert Browning. "Us, why should we change direction? Warschauer is east."

"The sun, him will rise soon," said Ben. "Him bright. Better we should not walk into his face. Better we weave a path across him."

He glanced at Evelyn War and was glad to see relief on her face. Robert Browning only nodded. They checked and covered at the next intersection, knocked the ice out of the springs in their boots, and took the road to the right, despite it being narrower.

They continued for three or four kilometres, as the sun began to rise, tacking back and forth across the sun's face, finding a new route to Warschauer.

They encountered nothing but the *ping*, *ping* of dripping water as the sun continued to do its work on the ice of ages, and the changing hues of the world. The greys of the night gave way to the colours of the day, more colours than any Aux had ever seen as the shroud of ice, frost and snow continued to rise. What had lain beneath, unseen for lifetimes, little by little, emerged.

Evelyn had feared hearing the cries all the way across Kreuzberg, but she was not surprised when they came.

The howl reminded her vividly of the gushing of blood and the splash of viscera on Dorothy Barker's coat. She spun sharply in Dorothy's direction, and the two exchanged a nod. The feral Aux were still at a distance, probably a kilometre away.

"Ambush," said Robert Browning. "The dogs, if them come our way, us, we should take them by surprise."

"Us, we could take them in the open," said Ben Gun. "Where we can see them. The dogs, them hunters. Them follow sounds, too."

"How?" asked Evelyn.

"Slingshots," said Ben, "Us, you and me." He pointed to their right where the street gave way to a large piece of open ground with scrappy trees and a couple of derelict buildings.

Another howl came at them from the south and east, closer this time.

"Quickly," said Ben.

"You and Evelyn, you set them up," said Dorothy.

"Me and Dorothy, we pick them off," said Robert Browning, drawing the crossbow from his back with a wince, his shoulder complaining.

They took up positions as the howls and grunts grew closer, louder.

Ben held up three fingers to indicate how many feral Aux he anticipated. Then he began to loose missiles from his position on top of a tall stone monument, about two metres above ground level.

He somehow managed to simulate the gait of some of the small, densely furred rodents that survived in Berlin. They scratched an existence out of the tough vegetation that managed to find its way through the frost, or lived off the bark and needles of the trees. He skittered stones off the trunks of the trees, too, making sounds like claws and teeth scratching at them.

Evelyn tried to do the same, but her first few stones fell too heavily or landed too hard on their targets. It didn't take her long to adjust, however, and she had a good stock of missiles. She'd been astounded by the number of perfect stones of various sizes that Ben Gun had produced from the many places in his clothes where he'd managed to secrete them without them clicking and banging and tumbling together. She marvelled at how clever he was.

Evelyn War suddenly heard a long, low growl to her right and then the *plink plink plink* of small stones falling rhythmically on ice, sounding just like the swift footfalls of a fleeing rodent. As she turned her head to look at the feral Aux, it was lunging in the direction of its supposed prey.

The first crossbow bolt struck its leg, and the second went straight into the top of its lowered head. It slumped flat onto its belly on the ice.

More of Ben's stones hit their targets. This time

the bark of a tree *thokked* hollowly as another howl filled the air.

Evelyn remembered that she was supposed to be half of the set-up team and reloaded her slingshot, looking from left to right for her next target. She saw an Aux coming in from the left, skulking silently, bewildered by the corpse of its comrade lying flat out on the ice.

Another crossbow bolt whistled through the air, but Evelyn ignored it. She did not see it sink into the torso of a second beast. She whipped her slingshot fast and firmly. Her target wasn't the ice, or the trunk of some sickly conifer, her target was the bright, hard eye of the feral Aux.

Letting loose, Evelyn watched her projectile dart through the air almost as fast as a crossbow bolt. The Aux didn't move, and it didn't seem to see its death coming.

Her aim was true, the impact explosive. The Aux's eye was shot through into its skull, and the beast reeled. It clawed at its face, but its jaw had already slackened, and it could not even howl. Its legs buckled beneath it and it folded at the waist, even as it tried to pluck the stone out of its head.

Finally, the Aux dropped, heavily, onto its back, arms falling away to either side.

A final bolt from Dorothy's crossbow finished off the second feral Aux, who did not see fit to die from one chest wound.

Ben Gun dropped down from his vantage point and Evelyn stepped out from cover behind her little building. Robert Browning had his crossbow raised above his head in triumph, despite his sore shoulder, and Dorothy Barker was baring her teeth in a grin that spread wide across her face.

Not one of them had suffered a single scratch or had even expended an ounce of energy in hand-to-hand combat. Not one had needed to unsheathe a blade. It had all been accomplished with a few stones and four crossbow bolts. They weren't even breathing hard.

"Fine scrapping," said Robert Browning, his expression grave. "What the tale-teller, him say. It is true."

"The time, it is changing," said Dorothy Barker equally seriously.

"Us, we must find Walter Sickert," said Evelyn War. "We must find the Hearer and listen to all of the truth."

CHAPTER FIFTEEN
DEADER AND DEAD

THEY HAD NO plan for their arrival.

They were Zoo Pack, and they were allies. They would be welcome at Warschauer.

"Robert, you a lieutenant, you know Warschauer Packers. Who can you speak to?" asked Dorothy Barker as they approached the station.

"You've been before?" asked Ben Gun. He did not wait for an answer. "You Robert Browning, beta-dog, lieutenant; you, of course you've been before."

"The problem, it is me, I have been before," said Evelyn War.

Evelyn slowed on the long approach to the old station at Warschauer. It stood among low derelict buildings on open ground, and now that she was there she was loath to go near it. She was fearful of the reception she could expect now that she didn't have Ezra Pound's protection and there were only four of them.

"You, them didn't look at you," said Dorothy. The bigger dam was suddenly taking off her heavy felt cap, folding down the collar of her coat and unwrapping her head cloth.

"You wear mine," she said.

They exchanged head cloths, and Dorothy looked Evelyn up and down.

"Ben Gun, you give Evelyn your eyeshades," she said.

The two Aux swapped eyeshades, Evelyn keeping her eyes tightly shut against the glare of the sun.

"You, them won't see you," said Dorothy Barker, appraising Evelyn's appearance once more. "You, them won't smell you."

Evelyn hoped it was true. The outside clothes Robert Browning had borrowed for them were among the oldest, and the scents of the many Aux who had worn them before masked her odours.

Most of the Warschauer Packers had also turned their backs on her at every opportunity, and would probably prefer to forget her. They had chosen not to associate with her and perceived her as a danger.

If she stayed behind Robert Browning and Dorothy Barker, if she kept her mouth shut, she might get in and out of Warschauer without being noticed.

"Us, how do we get in?" asked Dorothy Barker.

"Us, we're Zoo Pack," said Ben Gun. "We walk in." He bared his teeth in a smile.

They couldn't help admiring the simplicity of his plan. They couldn't help admiring his confidence, and he was probably right. It was an old alliance, and Zoo Pack had always been the senior partner over Warschauer Pack.

"Us, we walk in," agreed Robert Browning.

The ice creaked and moaned, and water droplets pinged from every surface. Everything was more exposed, further from the centre of the city. Everything everywhere was getting warmer and wetter.

It was quieter underground.

Water droplets still pinged, but not so often and the echoes somehow softened the sounds.

The four Aux made their way down onto the platform that led to the communal area that had so impressed Evelyn. It was Dorothy who stopped first.

"Here, it is too quiet," she said.

They all stopped for a moment in the tunnel to listen, turning their heads to take in every sound. All they could hear was the *ping* of water, no footfalls, no distant voices, nothing but the *ping* of dripping water and their echoes.

Three of the Aux unsheathed blades. Robert Browning drew one hefty double-blade; Dorothy and Evelyn drew stilettos, Evelyn from her boot and Dorothy from a sheath in her sleeve. Ben Gun readied his slingshot.

They regrouped, checking and covering all the way along the tunnel. They stopped twice more to listen, but heard nothing.

The carnage was total.

The wrecked bodies of more than a dozen Aux littered the huge communal room, and the blood of dozens more covered the floor and walls.

Dorothy turned at the threshold, pushing past Evelyn to get away from the sight. Her skin bleached of all its colour, her pupils dilated, Dorothy dashed back along the tunnel and then stopped, breathing hard.

Evelyn took Dorothy's place at Robert Browning's shoulder for a moment, before following the other dam back down the tunnel. They both needed consoling.

Robert Browning stood in the entranceway to the great chamber, taking in the full extent of the horror. The tiled floor was awash with blood, a solid, swimming red where once had been bright squares of black and white. The walls were covered in great splash marks of arterial spray, too, litres of it.

He looked up at the ceiling, at the glittering balls, for relief, but even they had blood on them, dripping into the pools of blood on the floor, not with the all-pervasive ping, but with a dull wet sound.

Ben Gun saw it all, head turning this way and that. He did not stare and he did not think. He looked and he listened.

"Us, we have to get out of here," said Evelyn. "Us, we were right, and we were too late."

Robert Browning turned, head lowered, and he and Ben Gun joined the others, making their way back the way they had come.

As they reached the platform and their exit route back outside, Ben Gun stopped once more.

"Us, we have to go," said Robert Browning. "Us, we have to go skittle-scuttle fast. Whatever him did this... We have to go fast."

"You, wait," said Ben.

Still listening, his head turning, he began to walk silently along the track beyond the platform. When he had walked fifteen or twenty metres, he beckoned to the others.

Robert Browning glared at Dorothy, but when Evelyn followed Ben without hesitation, Dorothy soon joined her, and, eventually Browning came, too. He drew his second blade, and strode down the tunnel, a weapon in each hand held wide from his body.

When they reached him, Ben Gun was stooped over at the waist, listening intently. He held out a hand, and they stopped still. Then he stalked forward another five or six metres before standing tall.

"There," he said, pointing towards the entrance to a service tunnel nearby. "Someone, him is chattering. Him is babbling. Him is talking wildly... the same words, the same sounds him is saying over and over. There!"

Evelyn War jogged forward, Ben Gun getting in step with her as she passed him. She waved him away with a flick of her hand.

"Walter Sickert," she said. "It must be him."

It proved to be a young Aux, wide-eyed, babbling incessantly, his brow ridge glistening with sweat and dripping. He was sitting tight to the tunnel wall, his knees drawn to his chest, his hands clenched around them, knuckles white. He was rocking vigorously, his sweat-drenched hair swinging in long strands.

She did not dare to reach out to touch him. She tried to catch his eye, but he looked first down at his knees and then thrust his head back so that he was looking high into the arched ceiling of the tunnel.

He never stopped talking, but she struggled to make sense of what he was saying. Some of it was words, but some of it seemed to be sounds, and it was all coming too fast and repeating too maniacally.

She heard the phrases 'deader and dead' and 'tougher and tough' several times. The pup was clearly traumatised, but as far as Evelyn could tell there wasn't a mark on him.

Where his skin was visible, there were no scratches, bruises or contusions, and his clothes seemed to be intact, including the blanket wrapped around his skinny, hunched shoulders.

The massacre at Warschauer was so complete, she had no idea how he had survived it.

"You Walter?" she asked.

The pup did not respond. Evelyn asked again, and again.

"You, Walter Sickert?" she asked. "Walter Sickert, you the Hearer?"

The pup blinked.

"You the Hearer?" Evelyn War asked again. "Walter Sickert, you the Hearer?"

The pup's eyes closed very slowly and then opened again. His gaze did not return to the ceiling. He did not look at Evelyn, but past her, over her shoulder.

Perhaps his hands were gripping his knees a little less tightly. He was still talking fast and the words he spoke were still incomprehensible, but Evelyn thought she was getting through to him.

"You, Walter Sickert, the Hearer," she said, more a statement than a question now. "Me, I'm Evelyn War, the Believer. Me, I believe you, Walter Sickert, the Hearer."

Then everything in the tunnel stopped.

Everything except for the faint echo of a long, low, distant whistle.

Walter Sickert's eyes glazed over and he said one more word before his head dropped onto his chest and he fell unconscious.

"Them."

CHAPTER SIXTEEN
SOLE SURVIVOR

THE WALK BACK to Zoologischer Garten was long and hard, with Robert Browning doing most of the heavy lifting when it came to transporting Walter Sickert. Dorothy Barker took several stints, lifting the pup over her shoulder, one limp leg wrapped around her ample forearm and his two slender wrists held in her other hand. But as light as he was, she could not carry Walter Sickert at speed over extended distances.

Evelyn insisted that Ben Gun guide the war band home. Following his lead, they made it back to Old Zoo without incident.

Without fanfare, too, sneaking back in the way they had left, via Deutsche Oper and the less-used tunnels, they arrived back on their home territory after nightfall, tired and hungry.

Ben Gun was sent for Edward Leer immediately.

Walter Sickert was still out cold.

There was hardly room in Evelyn's tiny cell for the six of them. It had been her father's and she should not have taken it, but no one wanted to live where the Hearer had lived. No one of rank or status who had the right to a single cell when it became available wanted to be infected by the memory of the Hearer. No one wanted to be associated with him.

Evelyn had neither rank nor status, and should have continued to live communally. But the others were relieved to be rid of her, and she wanted to be near her father's memory, to his words and ideas.

Walter Sickert lay inert on her cot. The others stood huddled in the remaining space.

"The Warschauer Pack, them are all dead," said Robert Browning, speaking as the ranking pack member. "There was a massacre."

"Not him," said Edward Leer pointing to the figure on the cot. "The pup, him Warschauer?"

"Evelyn War, she thinks him Walter Sickert, him the Hearer," said Robert Browning.

"Him *is* Walter Sickert," said Evelyn War. "Him knows what happened. Him knows why it happened."

"Him, how long has him been... like that?" asked Edward Leer.

"The pup, him mad," said Robert Browning. "Him babbling mad words. Him makes no sense."

There was silence in the room. Evelyn could not

dispute what Robert Browning said, but she still believed.

"Walter Sickert, him survived," said Ben Gun.

"Ben Gun, you what do you mean?" asked Edward Leer.

"Walter Sickert, him must know something," said Ben Gun. "Him the only Warschauer that survived."

Edward Leer shuffled around Dorothy Barker and Evelyn War and perched on the edge of the cot, peering down at Walter Sickert's face. It was unbearably pale and there was still sweat on his brow, but all the tension had gone out of it. The young Aux seemed to be sleeping, albeit very soundly.

"If the Warschauer Pack, them are dead, deader and dead, Ezra Pound, him must know," he said, finally. "If this pup hears the Master's Voice, Ezra Pound, tougher and tough, him must know what it says."

"Walter Sickert, him can't speak. Him can't tell what the Master's Voice it says," said Dorothy Barker quietly. She was faithful to Evelyn War and their cause, but Robert Browning was right. Walter Sickert was useless; Ezra Pound would never listen to the deluded pup.

He was a scrapper, an Alpha dog, a leader. He was a pragmatist. He understood brutal words with a simple message. He understood the words that he spoke, the speeches he made.

And they had all heard enough of them.

"Him looks peaceful," said Edward Leer. "Hearers, when them are pups, them suffer and them struggle. Them learn to Hear and them learn to understand and them learn to speak. Him will learn. This, it takes time."

"There is no time," said Evelyn War. "Me, I know there is no time, and you, tale-teller, you know it too."

"Then me, I will make time," said Edward Leer.

"How?" asked Dorothy Barker.

"By helping Walter Sickert, him to make a better mind, him to make a better Hearer," said the tale-teller. "First you, tell me everything you saw at Warschauer."

"Blood," said Dorothy. "There was blood, it was everywhere."

"Arterial blood, it was," said Robert Browning. "Too much blood for the number of bodies."

"The bodies, them were too broken," said Ben Gun.

"Too broken?" asked Edward Leer.

Dorothy's eyes widened, and she said, "Like them had no bones in them."

"Too few?" asked Edward Leer.

"Like many more Warschauer, them were taken," said Ben Gun.

"Weapons?" asked Edward Leer.

"Them left none," said Robert Browning.

"Blades," said Ben Gun. "Them used blades with barbs. Them ripped, to make so much blood. Them made gouges and scratches in the walls, too. Me, I saw them, fresher and fresh, in the walls."

"The Warschaur, did them kill?" asked Leer.

"All the dead, them were Warschauer," said Robert Browning.

"Them killed no one," said Dorothy Barker. "Them only died."

"Walter Sickert, him did say something," said Evelyn War. "Him said what my father, him said, too. Him said what me, I have said."

"What did him say, Evelyn War?" asked Edward Leer. "What did the Hearer, him say?"

"Him said, 'Them'," said Evelyn. "Him said it was Them. Us, we could tell Ezra Pound that. Us could say Walter Sickert, him said it was Them that killed the Warschauer deader and dead. We could tell Ezra Pound, him needs to make alliances. We could tell Ezra Pound, him needs to know that there is strength in numbers. That Them are tougher and tough; that Them kill deader and dead. We could tell Ezra Pound, him needs to know that the ice is dying. We could tell Ezra Pound, him needs to know that it is time to get whet... Us, we will all get whet."

Evelyn War was becoming agitated. She was speaking too fast, breathlessly. There was not room for her to drop down onto the cot beside Edward Leer, but her knees buckled anyway, and it was Dorothy Barker who caught her and held her steady.

"Evelyn War, her started this, and her was right. Evelyn War, her is still right," said Dorothy Barker. "You, tell a tale, Edward Leer, or make Walter Sickert, him talk."

"You, do it fast," said Robert Browning.

"Me, I'll tell a fable," said Edward Leer. "You, you must all do your share, too. You must spread the word among the Aux. Robert Browning, you must gather the lieutenants. Them have heard the sounds in the tunnels, them have lost scrappers. You, tell them what you saw in Warschauer, and you, Dorothy Barker, you spread the word, too."

"Me, what will I do?" asked Ben Gun.

"Ben, you will go to my cell and bring the medicine, to help Walter Sickert. Then you will become his friend."

CHAPTER SEVENTEEN
GETTING THE BONE FOR IT

Zoo Pack had lost five Aux, including two during the time that the secret war band was away from the fiefdom: one moments after they had emerged outside at Deutsche Oper and one two hours before their return.

Two sentries had not returned from their duties. No bodies were found. There was blood and one broken blade, but no other evidence that they had ever existed.

Robert Browning had little trouble gathering a large number of his fellow lieutenants together. He was a popular Aux, reliable in the scrapping, strong and true. They did not know why he would call a meeting. It was the exclusive right of the Alpha dog to summon them together, but something was wrong and they were ready to talk.

"Me, I have been to Warschauer," began Robert Browning.

One or two of the lieutenants looked at one another, bewildered.

"No," said one of them hesitantly. "Me, I was there."

"Me, I took a small war band, just three others. Us, we went without being sent," said Browning. "Me, I took Evelyn War."

"The useless omega bitch," said the Aux who had spoken.

"Her not so useless, Oscar so Wild," answered Browning. Then, "Warschauer Pack all dead. Deader and dead."

There was a single gasp from one of the gathered lieutenants, but several of them started or shook their heads in horror.

"Us, we will be next if we don't listen, if we don't change," said Robert Browning.

"Us, we listen," said Oscar so Wild. "Us, we listen to Ezra Pound."

A cheer went up from about half of the lieutenants, but it soon died away.

"The Warschauer, them all dead. Our sentries, three of them are gone, deader and dead," said Browning.

"Five," said a voice from the crowd. "Robert Browning, you speak true. You were gone two nights. Those two nights, two more sentries, them gone, deader and dead."

"Us, we must listen to Evelyn War. Us, we must

listen to Edward Leer. Us, we must listen to the Warschauer Pack Hearer. Him knows the truth," said Browning.

"Robert Browning, you killed Oberon War, the Zoo Pack Hearer, deader and dead," said Oscar so Wild. "You killed him because Ezra Pound, him ordered it. Now you speak of a new Hearer, an outsider."

"I was wrong to kill Oberon War. Ezra Pound, him was wrong," said Robert Browning. "The Warschauer Pack Hearer, him knew the Pack was in peril. Him survived, tougher and tough. Zoo Pack, we must hear him. Zoo Pack, we must listen to him."

"Us, we must listen to Ezra Pound," said Oscar so Wild. "Ezra Pound, him Alpha dog."

Another half-hearted cheer, from Oscar so Wild's cronies. He held great sway with many of them, was the most senior, the strongest of them, second only to Ezra Pound, and the most likely to succeed him. He had not yet got the bone to challenge the Alpha dog, but one day he would.

Oscar so Wild stepped out of the crowd and took two long, determined strides towards Robert Browning.

"Robert Browning, you got the bone to challenge Ezra Pound. You look for allies among the lieutenants. You dare to stand against the Alpha dog," said Oscar so Wild. The big Aux's torso and shoulders tensed, and he snarled at Robert Browning. "You got the bone to challenge me."

Robert Browning blocked the huge fist that Oscar so Wild drove at his chest and threw a punch of his own, which landed, but seemed to have no effect on the big lieutenant.

The punches came faster after that.

Oscar so Wild landed a good swing on Robert Browning's jaw, and Robert's head jerked with the impact. He struck back with a solid jab to Wild's throat, which should have winded the Aux, but he didn't stop punching. He sank half a dozen blows into Browning's gut, as the smaller Aux began to snake his arms around his attacker's neck.

The scrapping was brutal and inelegant, but not serious. There was no deadly intent in the wrestling match. It was a show, for Aux of equal rank: that there was a pecking order, and it must be maintained.

Robert Browning jerked his legs and twisted his body as Oscar so Wild pinned him to the floor, grappling to sink his teeth into the back of his neck.

Browning would not be bitten. He forced the senior lieutenant off his chest and rolled him, claiming the advantage himself.

With the big Aux pinned on his side, Robert Browning kneed him hard in the back, yanking down on the wrist he was holding in both of his hands. Wild snarled and bucked, and then rolled onto his belly and was back on his feet.

More punching followed, and the two Aux were soon back in a clinch. Robert Browning's teeth made contact with Oscar so Wild's bicep, drawing blood. He got a heavy cuff around the ear in payment.

The blows were hard and heavy, and bruises were already beginning to show. Oscar so Wild had a cut above his brow ridge to the left, and his ears were ringing from repeated blows to his head. Robert Browning's jaw was bruised and swollen, and Wild had cracked at least one of his ribs.

Robert Browning backed away and swung again, an uppercut that took Oscar so Wild by surprise. The bigger Aux's hands dropped and his head snapped back.

Robert Browning dropped his shoulder and lunged for Wild's sternum, winding him and sending him crashing to the floor. Oscar so Wild's head hit hard and bounced. His mouth slackened for a moment, and he was out cold for just a second before he lifted his head and shook it. His mouth drooped and his pupils were dilated.

Robert Browning was standing over him.

"Me, I haven't got the bone to challenge Oscar so Wild, *nor* Ezra Pound," said Robert Browning. He leaned in and offered the big Aux his hand. Oscar so Wild took it and allowed Browning to help him to his feet. Dignity was satisfied.

"Me, I've got the bone for it, to scrap whatever them's out there, to fight whatever them's killing Aux, deader and dead," said Robert Browning.

Someone in the crowd started to clap. Another pair of hands joined in with the applause, and then another.

Oscar so Wild's cronies kept quiet.

"Ezra Pound, him Alpha dog," said Oscar so Wild. "Him will do the right thing. Him will lead the right way. You, don't tell us. You tell him. You tell Ezra Pound."

"Me, I will tell Ezra Pound," said Robert Browning. "Me, I wanted you to hear it first. Us, we must stand together. Us, we must be ready for what is to come."

"Us, we are Aux," said Oscar so Wild. "Us, we are Zoo Pack. Us, we are always ready. When Ezra Pound, him orders it, us, we will all get whet."

When the cheer went up in the room, all the Aux lieutenants joined in. No one was in any doubt that they were in peril, no one was in any doubt that Robert Browning had spoken the truth. They were scrappers – they were Aux warriors – and the fear of the whispers they had shared about their dead sentries was gone, because someone had finally spoken.

CHAPTER EIGHTEEN
WALTER SICKERT WAKES

WALTER SICKERT'S HEAD rolled slowly from side to side as he lay on his cot. He had been unconscious for hours: spent, exhausted by his mental exertions and by his fear.

Edward Leer took the rag – soaked in aromatic oils – from Walter's forehead and gestured for Ben Gun to take the pup's hand.

Ben did not hesitate. He perched on the cot and loosely clasped the clammy hand in both of his.

Walter Sickert's eyes opened slowly and then closed again. He sighed, groaned and frowned.

When he opened his eyes again, he fixed for a moment on the ceiling before looking first at his hand, held in Ben Gun's, and then at Ben's face.

There was a look of mild shock on Walter Sickert's

face, but not of panic.

"Walter Sickert, Hearer of Warschauer Pack, me, I am Ben Gun of Zoo Pack," said Ben, squeezing the pup's hand slightly. Walter Sickert returned the squeeze. Ben Gun glanced at Edward Leer, a smile flashing across his face. The tale-teller nodded back at him.

"Hearer, you are safe," said Ben Gun. "You are at Old Zoo, safer and safe. Us, we found you and we brought you here."

Walter Sickert opened his eyes again, and looked at Ben Gun. He parted his lips, but no words came out. He sighed and closed his eyes once more.

"The Hearer, he is calm," said Edward Leer.

Walter Sickert's eyes opened suddenly wide at the new voice. Ben Gun squeezed his hand again, and this time the Hearer clenched his hand hard in answer.

"Hearer, that voice, him Edward Leer. Him Zoo Pack tale-teller. Him will help you. Walter Sickert, you are safe. Safer and safe."

Walter Sickert's grip on Ben's hand did not loosen. His lips parted, and a single word spilled out.

"Them," he said.

Edward Leer placed the rag back on Walter Sickert's forehead, newly moistened with warm oil to soothe him. Then he sat on the small stool next to the cot and began to speak.

"Gene the Hackman, top dog, him done the great Walk Around. Not for him the darkness, not for him the cold, not for him the Time of Ice. Gene the Hackman, him got whet. Gene the Hackman, him got whet and walked the Earth, and him killed Them," he began.

Both Walter Sickert and Ben Gun visibly relaxed.

"Two-Feet-Walk-on-the-Ground, him ran the World. Him big fella. Them hated him very much. Two-Feet-Walk-on-the-Ground, him make Gene the Hackman to keep Them off his lawn and him sleep long time. Two-Feet-Walk-on-the-Ground, him the Master. Gene the Hackman, him keep Them off the lawn while the Master sleep long time.

"Them got together, tighter and tight. And Gene the Hackman, him Heard his Master's Voice and him got whet and him killed Them. Him clever. Him had muscles in his head. Him knew the one thing always drew Them quickest. Him built fires, and Them come. Him pulled his two great blades and him swung and him hacked and him scrapped, and him killed Them, deader and dead.

"Gene the Hackman, him heard the Master's Voice and him felt the Urgings. Gene the Hackman, him led the pack on the Walk Around, and him kept the lawn clean of Them."

Walter Sickert looked at Edward Leer.

"Me, I hear the Master's Voice," he said.

"Me, I know," said Edward Leer.

There was silence in the tiny cell for several seconds before Ben Gun found the courage to speak up.

"You, why don't you tell that tale before?" he asked. "Why don't you ever tell that legend if you are the tale-teller?"

"That, it is an old story," said Edward Leer. "That, it is a frightening tale, too old to tell. For us, most of us, there is no Master. There is no Master's Voice. There is no Them. There is only Aux, now. There is only us."

"Why is it frightening?" asked Ben Gun.

"Us, we are afraid of the things we do not understand," said Edward Leer. "Us, we are afraid of old things, of dead things, of forgotten things. Us, we are afraid of dying things."

"Of Hearers?" asked Ben Gun.

"If we do not Hear," said Edward Lear.

"Us, we heard the whistles in the tunnels at Warschauer," said Ben Gun.

"Them," said Walter Sickert, as if in agreement.

"Us, we hear the moans and the creaks of the dying ice," said Ben Gun, "and the water falling. Me, I hear everything. Me, I listen to everything. Me, because I listened, we did the long Walk Around safe back to Zoo Pack."

"Then that is what we must tell Ezra Pound," said the tale-teller. "That is what *you* must tell Ezra Pound."

CHAPTER NINETEEN
PACK MEETING

HOURS PASSED IN preparation. Preparation that brought Dorothy Barker and Robert Browning back to the cell, battered and bruised.

Evelyn could not rest. She returned tired and gaunt from her exertions.

Ben Gun was a pup and needed little rest. He seemed to thrive on the adventure and on the responsibility that Edward Leer had handed to him. The tale-teller showed no outward change. If he was tired or hungry, if he was anxious, he did not show it.

They made a strange group as they walked Track Two towards Ezra Pound's den, six Aux who until two days ago had nothing in common, except for the mates, Dorothy Barker and Robert Browning.

The useless omega bitch was an outsider, never seen with anyone, and the pup was just a pup.

The oddest sight was Robert Browning carrying the second pup, wrapped in the blanket, his hand reaching out to hold Ben Gun's. He was a stranger to Zoo Pack, and everyone they passed stopped to watch them as they made their way along the track.

Some of the Aux sensed that something was afoot, and began to follow the disparate little band. They whispered to each other about the bruises on Robert Browning's and Dorothy Barker's faces, and about why these six Aux should be together in one group.

The tale-teller brought up the rear. He said nothing, despite one or two of the Aux calling out to him. He listened to them, though, the whispers they spoke to one another.

As they reached the command centre, word began to spread, and several of the lieutenants that had been in Robert Browning's meeting began to appear. The dams had set up a whispering campaign too, after Dorothy Barker had spoken to them and spread the word among them.

Her mate gave her status. She had ended up scrapping with three of them, nevertheless, but had come out on top. The meeting had ended badly for her, but dams are more cynical, more competitive, with more to lose. They take longer to make decisions, are less likely to embrace change or challenge the status quo.

The dams, too, knew that change was coming, and that their lives were under threat. They sensed that Dorothy Barker might be giving them a useful warning. They, too, watched the procession. Soon, a substantial crowd began to gather behind the little group, following them down to the Alpha dog's den.

The narrow passage allowed for only one Aux to enter the command room at a time, and Thomas Meltdown at the entrance baulked at the sight of Robert Browning carrying the pup.

"You, why have you come?" he asked.

"You know why," said Robert Browning. "It is time."

The Aux looked nervous, and Robert Browning was about to reason with him when Oscar so Wild stepped into the entrance. He had been in the command room with Ezra Pound. As one of his senior lieutenants, Wild was often in the command room with the Alpha dog.

"You, let him pass," said Oscar so Wild. The two Aux, bruised and battered by each other's fists, nodded to one another. Oscar so Wild stood aside for Robert Browning to enter the room with his burden, and for Evelyn, Dorothy, Ben and Edward Leer to follow.

Ezra Pound sat in his chair at the far end of the room, with several of his lieutenants in attendance, the same Aux who had been in Robert Browning's meeting only a few hours before.

"What is this?" asked Ezra Pound. "Who is this?" He gestured at the pup. He seemed irked by the intrusion.

"This, him Walter Sickert," said Evelyn War over Robert Browning's shoulder.

"Walter Sickert?" spat Ezra Pound, as if the name meant nothing to him. Then he remembered. "Saul Bellow, him shunned the pup as mad." He gestured with a hand as if to wave Robert Browning away.

"Saul Bellow, him dead," said Robert Browning. "Deader and dead, and all the Warschauer Pack with him."

"Me, I was there," said Ezra Pound, his anger rising. "Me, I saw him, I spoke to him, I ate and drank with him. Saul Bellow, him not dead."

"Us, we went back," said Evelyn War. "Me, I wanted to talk to a Hearer. Alpha dog, you denied me... Me, I went back."

"Me, I went with her. Me, I took her back to Warschauer," said Robert Browning, defiant.

"And me! I went to Warschauer!" said Ben Gun, loudly from behind Evelyn.

There was laughter from one or two of the beta dogs in the room. The pup didn't know what he was saying, didn't know what he was doing speaking up in front of Ezra Pound.

"Him, shut him up," spat Ezra Pound, glaring at Robert Browning. Browning only glanced over his shoulder at the young Aux. But Ben Gun didn't notice. All he knew was that Walter Sickert was squeezing his hand, encouraging him.

"Deader than dead," said Ben Gun, "the Warschauer, all of them."

"The pup, get him out of here," growled Ezra Pound.

Evelyn stood close to Ben Gun, one arm around his shoulder, as Thomas Meltdown drew close. If Robert Browning wouldn't do Ezra Pound's bidding, there were still plenty of Aux in Zoo Pack who would.

Then Edward Leer stepped forward.

"Ezra Pound, Alpha dog, leave the pup, him alone. Him is foolish, him is eager. Him brought your scrappers home safer and safe. Him is true to the Zoo Pack."

"You defend him?" roared Ezra Pound, sitting upright in his chair, his hands squarely on his knees.

"Us, we all defend him," said Robert Browning, "and each other. The Warschauer Pack is deader and dead. Them didn't get whet. Them didn't kill. Them died."

"Us, we're dying," said Oscar so Wild, quietly.

"You!" shouted Ezra Pound. "You! What do you know?"

"Me, I know what we all know," said Oscar so Wild. "I know what you know."

Ezra Pound thought for a moment.

"What do I know?" he asked.

The meeting was long and slow, and there was much arguing. No one challenged Ezra Pound. No one got the bone to challenge the Alpha dog. There was too much change in the world for change in Zoo Pack.

They talked of the ice dying and of the sentries disappearing, and finally they talked of Them.

Edward Leer soothed the Aux with his legends of Zoo Pack's founding, of them finding their home, staking out their fiefdom and keeping peace within it.

He frightened them with tales of the Masters, of the Master's Voice, of the Urgings and of Them.

Finally, he roused them with his myths of Gene the Hackman, of the legend's prowess and his bravery, of him getting whet and killing Them, deader and dead. He gave them hope.

"We will mourn the Warschauer Pack, but we must make alliances, tougher and tough. There is strength in numbers," said Edward Leer as he finished his final tale.

"The ice, it dies," said a melodic voice in the silence after Edward Leer's tale-telling.

Walter Sickert's voice had gained strength since Ben Gun and the tale-teller had last heard it in Evelyn War's cell. It seemed to resonate around the room, filling it with warm, musical sound. Everyone listened.

"Them come back, because the ice dies," he continued. "The Voice, it tells me so."

The silence continued as the Aux waited for more.

"I do not want to Hear, but the Voice, it is there. Them whistle and Them kill. The Aux, we must stand together, tougher and tough, to kill Them, deader and dead."

The silence continued for a long time after Walter Sickert had made his short speech.

Then someone standing in the entrance to the command room finally coughed and said, "Sentry rotation."

Ezra Pound was deep in thought.

"How many sentries have we lost on this duty?" asked Robert Browning. "When will us, we know? How many?"

"There is strength in numbers," said Evelyn War. "Robert Browning, him killed my father, and yet us, we stand together."

Ezra Pound, his head still down, gestured with his hand, and several Aux moved to leave the room to take up their sentry duties.

"Sentries, double up," said Ezra Pound. "This, it is the last rotation at Old Zoo. Us, we pack what we can carry. Every Aux, him carries four cycles of rations. Every Aux, him carries all arms. Leave no weapons. Every Aux, him wears his bedding. Every Aux, him ready to leave Zoologischer Garten in one rotation. Every Aux, him ready to get whet. Me, I call every Aux to scrap, male and dam, every Aux who can hold a blade or carry a crossbow will get whet."

There was a hubbub in the room for the short minutes that it took the Aux to organise double sentries and for them to leave.

As the noise died down, Ezra Pound looked at the little group of scrappers that had defied him and made the long Walk Around to Warschauer. His gaze landed on Ben Gun, still holding Walter Sickert's hand. The pup's eyes were alight and he was smiling.

"Pup, you are proud to be called," said Ezra Pound, amused.

"No," said Ben Gun. "Me, I am proud that Evelyn War was right. Me, I am proud to be Walter Sickert's friend."

Ezra Pound frowned at Ben Gun and his hands tightened around his knees, where they were resting as he leaned forward a little further.

"Every Aux, him proud to be called," he said. "Every Aux him proud to be a scrapper."

"Me, I was already called," said Ben Gun. "Evelyn War, her called me, but I refused." He hesitated for a moment, a frown of regret flashing across his face. Then he smiled again. "Then Edward Leer, him called me to take Evelyn War to Warschauer. Me, I was called twice."

A hush fell over the command room. The Aux pup had made another misstep. A terrible misstep at a crucial moment.

But Ezra Pound was a simple Aux, a pragmatic leader. He had been shown an enemy, and he had been shown a solution. If Them were killing Aux, he would stand against Them, and if it would take many Aux to kill Them, he would ally with many Aux Packs.

Ezra Pound lifted one meaty paw from his knee and brought it down with a resounding slap. He bellowed a great roar of laughter that washed through the command room. The tension in the room broke and a wave of laughter followed in the wake of the leader's roar.

CHAPTER TWENTY
LEAVING THE FIEFDOM

IT HAD BEEN their home for generations, and now it was deserted.

Every member of the Zoo Pack left Old Zoo. Some emerged at Deutsche Oper, some at Wittenbergplatz and some at Zoologischer Garten itself. But they all left the familiar tunnels that made up their fiefdom at the end of the sentry rotation. They'd had only scant hours to prepare, and were ordered only to take what they could carry and still be able to scrap.

Two Aux did not return from sentry duty.

The very young and very old were parcelled out among the newly called pups, and all were kept at the centres of the three groups, for their own safety. They were not allowed to stay in family groups for the safety of the Pack.

If sacrifices had to made, if there was to be collateral damage, it would go easier on all of them.

Injuries among the Aux had been very light recently. Sentries didn't come back injured from their duties. They simply didn't come back at all.

The least able Aux were among the oldest, slowed down by long-healed injuries. They were arthritic, and rheumatic. It didn't matter. All big groups move slowly.

Ezra Pound led the group emerging from Zoologischer Garten, insisting that if he was going to abandon his fiefdom he would at least do it with some dignity.

Oscar so Wild took a group through Wittenberg. He had a large proportion of the youngest Aux, since the route along Track Two was partially blocked and required agility.

Robert Browning led the Deutsche Oper group. He saw it as a good omen, even though he was separated from Dorothy Barker. Mates never scrapped together. Loyalties must never be divided.

This had played on Ezra Pound's mind when he had ordered the evacuation. He had decided that the best way, the only way to ensure Robert Browning's loyalty, was to flatter him by making him the leader of a group. Then he had given him Ben Gun. The pup was a liability and would get Robert Browning into trouble. Then he could be rid of both of them, if need be.

He kept the tale-teller in his own group, and the Hearer, too. He was Alpha dog. The tale-teller would hold too much power away from Ezra Pound. He was too clever, and the Alpha dog knew it.

Dorothy Barker and Evelyn War he sent with Oscar so Wild. He trusted the beta dog. He had not got the bone to challenge his leader. He had spoken up, but he had kept some respect.

Ezra Pound knew that it was safer to repay that respect than to embarrass the Aux by putting him under the leadership of another lieutenant. He also knew that no dam had ever influenced Wild, and these two wouldn't either.

The Aux stepped outside into a world that many had not seen for a very long time, and some had never seen at all.

Everything was a haze of grey in the predawn, and the great buildings seemed to loom over them like vast, lumbering beasts. The Aux were too used to curving walls and low ceilings, narrow spaces and darkness. The straight lines and flat surfaces of the outside world confused and disturbed them.

The youngest looked around wide-eyed, or cried into the shoulders of the surrogate parents and siblings who accompanied them. The oldest shook or tried not to look at all, or they reminded themselves of when they had been scrappers, tougher and tough, and tried to find some courage.

As the sun began to rise and the grey landscape began to resolve into colour, there were more shocks and more wonder and fear. The pups began to grow curious, adapting more quickly than the ancients. The oldest began to see how fast the world was changing.

Half an hour into the long trek, Killian Hook, an old Aux in Robert Browning's group, took a pelt from around his shoulders and handed it to the dam next to him. Then he took off his fur cap and gave it to a beta dog to replace his worn felt one. After that, his thick felt blanket came off. He handed it to a pup, who wrapped it around himself and the infant he was carrying. His head cloth came off next, but he let that rest around his wrinkled neck as he unfastened the front and cuffs of his jacket. Last of all, he took off his boots and handed them to another Aux.

He had been gradually working his way to the rear of the group, falling behind as he disrobed. No one tried to stop him, at first, but those around him began to watch him, baffled.

The ice was moaning and creaking, and sliding away under their feet, but the air was still full of the steam of their breath. It was still cold, too cold for an Aux to walk naked through Berlin.

A beta dog who had been a scrapper for only two or three seasons was the first to try to help the old male. He took hold of his jacket and tried to fasten it back around his chest, but Killian Hook batted his hands away and snarled at him.

When a dam asked him what he was doing, he simply looked at her with disdain. Everyone knew who he was, who he had been.

Killian Hook was famous among the veterans, famous for being a scrapper, for being a lieutenant. He could have been Alpha dog. He could have got the bone to challenge the last leader, but Ezra Pound had been younger, keener and more arrogant. The Aux had lost his chance, missed his moment.

Zoo Pack respected him, and no one in his group would tackle him further. Word of his strange behaviour got back to Robert Browning.

"Killian Hook, let the old scrapper be," he said.

As the sun rose higher in the sky, those who had eyeshades put them on. The youngest didn't have them, had never needed them.

The Aux of Zoo Pack lived their entire lives underground until they were called, until they were old enough to be useful. Many of the old Aux lacked eyeshades, too. Some pulled peaked caps low over their eyes and squinted, looking only at the ground beneath their feet. Others improvised with their head cloths, wrapping thin layers around their eyes. Some of the smallest infants, those being carried, were covered in blankets and bedding from around the shoulders of those carrying them.

The constant ping of dripping water was lost in the rumble and scrape of footfalls on ice.

One of the preparations that had been considered necessary was adapting boots to the wet surface of the ice. All footwear had been fitted with whatever was available to give them more grip; some had springs or washers threaded into their treads, others had chains wrapped around them, but all had been made safer than they would otherwise have been.

The city was big and quiet. All three groups made slow, steady progress using the broadest thoroughfares. There was ice debris everywhere, in great heaps against the buildings and in fallen shards, scattered by the force of impact right across the streets.

Many of the roofs had lost their coverings of ice. The threat of more falls from above had diminished since Robert Browning had been buried in ice only days before; nevertheless, the Aux looked and listened and had drills for staying safe when there was any threat of an ice fall.

The hard lines and edges of the newly exposed roofs looked alien to all the Aux, whether they were used to being outside or not, and the colours were extraordinary. The only building in the centre of Berlin that had remained exposed through the Time of Ice was the Kade building, with its orange roof. Now, everywhere they looked, there were orange roofs, and red brick walls were beginning to show, too.

The changing landscape made navigation difficult. The Aux traditionally used rat-runs through buildings or travelled along the narrowest streets and alleys. They used the tunnels as much as possible for long journeys, but it was no longer safe underground.

They were above ground in an increasingly alien city, using unfamiliar streets. Landmarks had to be checked and double-checked against the group leaders' compasses. Progress was slow.

It was two hours before the three groups expected to come together.

Killian Hook could no longer walk in a straight line. He could hardly walk at all. He stumbled around aimlessly, but would not allow anyone to help him.

His speech was irritable and incoherent, and he would swing his fists wildly at any one who tried to help him. He would not be covered. His skin went from startling red to a bluish grey, and the muscle he had left after too many long years of retirement seemed to shrink in his skin. His only concession to the outside world was to use eyeshades.

Everyone knew that he was dying and no one could do anything about it.

Robert Browning hoped that they would meet up with Ezra Pound before Killian Hook finally collapsed. He hoped that the Alpha dog might command the old male to wrap himself back in his clothes, to take some sustenance, to die with some dignity. It was too late to save him. The cold would kill him. The Time of Ice would take one of its last victims.

Then Browning realised what Killian Hook was doing, and why. He understood it. There was a rightness in it.

The old male couldn't fight Them and wouldn't die a coward's death or a fool's death. He wouldn't put another Aux scrapper's life in danger defending a useless old Aux, either. He'd go now, on his own terms, one less mouth to feed, one less dependent to worry about.

Robert Browning slowed the group to Killian

Hook's pace, allowing the old scrapper some peace and privacy a few metres behind them.

When the old male fell to his knees, Browning went to him. He did not carry him, but he helped him to the shady side of the street. There was no fight left in the old Aux.

Browning propped Killian Hook up in the doorway of a building, making sure that he would not fall over when the time finally came. He sat down a few metres away from him and waited. He watched the curls of steam coming from the old scrapper's nose and mouth.

The rest of the group kept at a distance. Ben Gun kept them entertained, talking to them about listening and scouting, giving them all a lesson, showing them how to cope outside. He made some of the beta dogs laugh and some of them shake their heads and scowl.

Robert Browning thought every soft wisp that left Killian Hook's mouth was his final breath. Then, after several seconds, another would come, or his chest would heave a little or shudder, and the younger male would see a new stirring of life. He began to wonder whether he wanted it to be over more than Killian Hook did.

A minute passed without movement, and another minute, and another.

Killian Hook had been a great Aux. Tales would be told of his scrapping, if there was a tale-teller left in Berlin to tell them after the ice was gone. He should have died with a blade in his hand. A peaceful death was no death for an Aux who could have been Alpha, but peace was all he had.

Robert Browning stood and walked away.

"You, Patrick Bateman," he said as he joined the group, "you know where to take Killian Hook underground. Do it fast."

Patrick Bateman was the biggest Aux in Browning's group and the strongest. He could manage the corpse alone. Time was short and staying in one place was dangerous, but Robert Browning would not leave Killian Hook outside.

The old Aux must go back where he belonged, back to the tunnels. They had passed a Track Fourteen station only minutes before they had stopped. Bateman turned back so that he would not have to carry the body past the group. He was gone for only fifteen minutes. He did not talk about where he had taken the old Aux or how he had left the body, and no one asked him.

CHAPTER TWENTY-ONE
THE DAMMED

TWO HOURS TURNED into three. Ezra Pound's group and Oscar so Wild's went underground at a Track Fourteen station northeast of Wittenbergplatz. They were cold and exposed, and fear and indecision drove them to seek shelter.

They posted a sentry outside to look out for Robert Browning's party, but hope of their safe arrival dwindled over the next half-hour.

Dorothy Barker became restless.

"Them, where are they?" she asked Evelyn War.

"Ben Gun, him is with them," said Evelyn. "Them will be here."

Dorothy jumped off the platform where the rest were huddled, some of them dipping into their rations. She paced up and down a hundred metres or so on the track.

"Them are safe," said Walter Sickert in his melodic tones. "Them are outside."

Dorothy stopped in her tracks and glared up at the platform. She could not see the Hearer, but she was aghast at his words.

"The outside isn't –" she began, but stopped abruptly.

They all heard it... the echoes of it, at least.

No one stopped to pack away rations, or to adjust the clothes that they had loosened, or to rewrap their head cloths. They stood, as one, and quickly made their way back to the surface.

They had all heard the rumours and they had all heard the tales. They had all been present when Walter Sickert had spoken of the whistling sounds Them made.

Now, they all heard the echoes of those sounds for themselves. Them were far away. Echoes travelled long distances in the tunnels and the sounds were faint, even to sensitive Aux ears, but the threat was real and mounting.

The Zoo Pack finally met three hours after its departure from Old Zoo. There were many hours of travel still ahead, and already they were dying.

The fastest stretch of the day's journey took Zoo Pack along the old Landwehr Canal. It was unfamiliar territory, but it offered the best opportunity for the Pack to walk in the most compact group, to help each other and move more quickly.

Faster was safer. The ice was deeper, the canal

forming a ridge more than a metre higher than the land around it. The ice seemed colder, too, less slick and easier to walk on.

The youngest pups were handed from one surrogate to another for carrying, but the Hearer was borne along by the same four Aux.

He was calmer, much calmer than he had been at Warschauer, but he was weak. The balance of his mind was still delicate, and he was still being treated by the tale-teller.

He was carried in a sling by two Aux, one on either side of him. They changed sides regularly and swapped out for another pair of Aux every half-hour or so. They got into a rhythm with their burden, who was still and light, but a burden nevertheless.

Ben Gun and several of the other Aux remained on the flanks of the large party, scouting the buildings they passed, watching the shadows and listening.

They heard nothing but the moan and creak of the ice and the occasional WHOMP as it fell from roofs, sometimes close by, sometimes at a distance. Once or twice they heard the skitter of rodents on the ice or the tapping of bark in the trees lining one side of their route. But Zoo Pack passed several peaceful hours on the march without incident.

Then they turned south, away from the canal, and the territory changed. They were back in the streets.

No Aux from any pack used the city centre Track Seven, not ever, not for anything. Track Seven belonged to the Mehringdamm Pack. It had always been that way. They had cut off and sealed a portion of Track Six, too, where it intersected with Track Seven between the Hacker fiefdom to the north and the Tempelhof fiefdom to the south. But Track Seven, from Richard Wagner Platz to Karl Marx Strasse, was their fiefdom.

As they approached Mehringdamm, tired from hours outside and from hours on their feet, on alert, every Aux scrapper reached for a weapon.

The *Dammed* were full of wrong. They were solitary, always had been. They did not barter or trade. They did not mate with members of other packs. They did not communicate or negotiate. They did not talk the same language, or any language that the other packs recognised. Something had gone wrong with them a long time ago.

No Aux crossed their territory underground. Outside, in daylight, had never been a problem before. The Dammed hunted at night; they liked the dark, and the darker the better. They were even known to avoid the nights of the full moon. They liked the ice black and the sky blacker. They thrived underground and in the winter.

Oscar so Wild was the first to see movement.

He was too late. The Aux was upon them before the lieutenant even had time to signal. It was big. Bigger than Ezra Pound, by half.

It was a great slab of hard flesh with a small head and no discernible neck. It heaved into the flank of the group, throwing its weight around. Its eyes were white pinpricks, apparently sightless, although that didn't stop it taking down two Aux with its huge fists before it tripped over the dam it had felled in its scrapping.

It didn't try to get up. Its body so swollen that it could only roll, it preferred to remain on its back and fight off its enemy with fists and feet.

The dam it had taken down plunged a stiletto into the place where its neck should have been, penetrating eight or ten centimetres, but when she pulled the blade out, expecting a gush of blood to follow, there was barely a trickle.

The injury was enough to anger the beast, however, and it roared as it swung out. The dam's head was staved in, crushing her skull and killing her outright. Blood trickled from her nose and both of her ears as she crashed to the ice.

"Step away!" shouted Oscar so Wild, and the Zoo Pack instinctively followed his order. The other fallen Aux, a young male, scuttled across the ice on his hands and knees.

Suddenly, the Dammed had no targets within reach and no eyes to locate them.

Silence fell on Zoo Pack. All that could be heard was the slabby Aux's grunting, and the shifting of his immense weight on the ice beneath his body.

Ezra Pound put a bolt into the beast's chest from four metres away.

The Dammed Aux howled. He beat the curled thumb and forefinger of his fist against the wound, driving the bolt in still further. He howled again, and then a second bolt sank into his chest a few centimetres to the left of the first.

The Aux roared and thrashed, but did not thump his chest a second time.

It took four bolts to kill the beast. By then, more of the Dammed Aux were lurching out from between the buildings, blindly sliding on the slick ice, following the cries of their pack mate.

The air was filled with their odd grunts and rumbles and their roars of rage and frustration.

Their hearing was intact, but they were slow and fumbling. It was clear that they were all sightless.

Ben Gun had found his way quickly to Evelyn when the first Dammed Aux had appeared.

"Us, we can beat them," he told her. "Us, we can escape them. Us, we must scatter, evade. We are many and they are few. Them cannot follow all of us. Them have only their hands to kill with."

Evelyn ducked towards Robert Browning.

"Tell Ezra Pound, him to scatter the pups and the ancients. Tell Ezra Pound, him to make noise. The scrappers, us to make noise. Us, we must lead them in and pick them off."

"Us, we're exposed," said Robert Browning. "Us, we should take cover."

"The Dammed, them cannot see us," said Evelyn. "Them are slow. Them cannot understand what us say, the orders us give. Us, we can fight them. Us, we can win."

Ben Gun had already begun to spread the word and organise the pups and the oldest of the pack. They rallied.

Old Aux took the burdens of the very young. The

pups big enough to run turned the threat into a game, looking for the best gaps between the Dammed Aux, and the likeliest hiding places between the buildings.

"Us, we fight!" ordered Ezra Pound, his voice ringing out over the heads of Zoo Pack. "Aux, you with crossbows prepare, tougher and tough! Zoo Pack, you others scatter, faster and fast!"

He took a breath and cast an eye around the pack at the stumbling Dammed.

"You, on my count –" the Alpha dog began, but he was interrupted by Robert Browning.

"Scrappers, you shout and holler. You make noise!" he ordered.

"One... two... three!" bellowed Ezra Pound.

As soon as he had opened his mouth on the word 'three', every Aux without a missile weapon began to scatter, zigzagging out of the group. They ran for the buildings and the passages between them, giving the Dammed Aux a wide berth at every touch and turn. It didn't stop the huge Aux swinging at the air, trying to make sense of a battle they could not engage in.

At the same time, the cry went up from the Zoo Packers left standing to fight. They shouted and bellowed, and some whistled and growled. They brought their crossbows up and began to aim at the huge, lumbering targets.

The Dammed Aux were drawn to the sounds, too relieved to have a target to aim for, and too stupid to realise that they were walking into a trap.

Then the bolts started to fly.

One Dammed Aux came lurching at the scrappers with three bolts embedded in his body; the last one, loosed at point blank range, had disappeared deep into his flesh, and yet still it came.

When he finally fell, he fell forwards, knocking over one of the dams while she was reloading. He landed on top of her, his dead weight breaking her leg as they crashed onto the ice. Her scream pierced the air, but she was out cold before the corpse had settled across her chest, finally smothering her.

The Zoo Pack was using up its bolts fast. The Dammed took three or four bolts each to kill, and the dams were as big as the males and just as intent on slaughter.

"You, aim for their eyes!" shouted one of the lieutenants.

Their targets were close and slow moving, and many of the Zoo Pack were good shots. The Dammed were big and strong. Their hides were tough and their muscles as dense and hard as wood. It was proving difficult to penetrate to their organs to kill them. Head shots, if they were accurate, would be faster and more efficient.

In the side streets off Mehringdamm, the old and young of Zoo Pack were hiding in the shadows and in doorways. They kept still and quiet, listening to the battle raging. They could hear their packmates hollering and stamping, making any noise they could to draw the attention of the Dammed Aux away from them. They were grateful for it. They were scared, too.

They had given the Aux they could see a wide berth, but there were others still in the area. The Zoo Packers could hear the footfalls of the Dammed and the sounds their bodies made blundering into the buildings they could not see as they made their way towards the noise.

They could hear the Dammed Aux communicating with one another, but could not understand their grunts and howls.

Randall Flogg, a small child strapped to his body with a blanket, gasped when he came face to face with a huge, Dammed Aux. They met where an alleyway opened into a patch of wasteland behind a big old building.

At the change in Flogg's heart rate, or perhaps the smell of fear in his sweat, the child he was carrying began to cry. The old Aux was crippled with arthritis and too slow to get out of the way as the Dammed Aux wildly swung out with a paw the size of Flogg's head.

One lucky punch to the jaw broke Flogg's neck, and the old Aux landed on his back on the ground. The infant's crying did not stop.

The Dammed Aux struck out again, hitting nothing but air. Realising his opponent was down, he kicked, and when that didn't stop the wailing, he stamped.

The crying stopped abruptly.

The Dammed Aux moved on, following the sounds of his dying brothers and the cacophony their enemies were making.

Ben Gunn did not have a crossbow. All he had was his trusty slingshot and the two blades he'd been given, one by Evelyn and one by Edward Leer. The blades were useless, but he trusted his slingshot more than he trusted anything. He was also determined that he wasn't going to run with the pups and the ancients. He was going to stand with the scrappers.

He didn't expect to kill a Dammed Aux with his slingshot, so he didn't try.

He loaded his slingshot with the biggest, heaviest stone in his cache. Then he looked around at the roofs of the buildings along the street, and at the trees among them.

One of the roofs had the perfect pitch; the ice covering it was hanging low and heavy. Ben Gun whipped his arm, aimed and loosed. The stone hit the ice on the roof with a hard *crack*. Two of the Dammed Aux milling beneath it turned their heads this way and that, listening for the sounds, distracted.

He let another shot loose, and another. Then he aimed high up the trunk of a tree, ten metres to the left of the roof. He shot three more stones at it, hitting it with a string of resounding *THOKK*s. The Dammed Aux turned their heads again, this time in the direction of the tree. They were confused, weaving this way and that, not knowing which sounds to follow.

Ben Gun continued his campaign of confusion, careful to keep his targets away from any routes the fleeing Zoo Packers were taking.

He slowed down more than half a dozen of the Dammed Aux, and even saw two turn against each other. He had never seen brawling like it. One of them would be dead by the end of the scrap. The other would get a bolt through the eye or three through the chest. Ben Gun was sure of it.

Two or three minutes later, the roof that Ben Gun had aimed his first volley of shots at shed its load onto the street below.

A Dammed Aux standing beneath it was buried in tons of ice. Ben Gun kept an eye on the debris from time to time while distracting three more Dammed on the other side of the street. But the avalanche had been much more dramatic than the one that had buried Robert Browning. The angle of the roof had been steep, the fall had been almost vertical and there had been many more tonnes of ice.

Ben Gun suspected that the Aux wasn't going anywhere. He had no friends to dig him out.

The battle raged for long minutes and bandoliers were emptied of bolts. When a Zoo Pack Aux ran out of ammunition he regrouped to the centre of the pack and concentrated on making noise, or took more bolts from those who still had supplies.

None of the Aux with crossbows left the street. No one else tried to make it past the few remaining Dammed. No one wanted to run.

Then, as suddenly as it had begun, the fight was over. The last Dammed Aux was taken out with a bolt to his right eye. He clutched and clawed at his face. Silence fell among the Zoo Pack as they watched the sightless beast die. It was a pathetic business.

There was worse to come.

Within minutes, the old and young Aux began to emerge from their hiding places to return to the Zoo Pack. The pups had all seen their own dead before, but they had not seen anything like this. It could not be avoided. The old had seen death, had seen carnage of one kind or another, had perpetrated it, but rarely on this scale.

Ezra Pound had stowed his crossbow, as had all the scrappers, and they were milling around, consoling one another. There was little to celebrate in killing other Aux, even the Dammed, especially now.

At the end of a battle, most scrappers wanted to eat, mate and sleep, but there was still work to be done.

The Pack was back together and everyone accounted for, including their dead. Two of the old Aux had passed Randall Flogg on their way back to Mehringdamm and carried him and the child back to Zoo Pack. The two of them and the two dams were taken underground. They were taken down onto Track Seven. No Aux had ever used Track Seven, none but the Dammed.

"Retrieve bolts," said Ezra after he had assigned the burial team. The tone of his utterance seemed strained. His voice was as loud and deep as it always was, but there was regret in it, too.

Their crossbows on their backs, the scrappers began to walk towards the felled Dammed Aux, pulling stilettos from boots and cuffs.

"No," said a voice as an ancient male raised his hand. He looked around, making eye contact with several of the other older Aux standing nearby. "Us, we will do it. Scrappers, you must rest."

Oscar so Wild nodded at the old Aux.

"You, it is a noble thought," he said. "Us, we shot the bolts. Us, we must retrieve them."

"Not noble," said the old male. "Us, we need the scrappers fit. Us, we can't scrap for ourselves. Us, we can do this. You, rest. You, eat. Then, us, we walk."

The old male pulled a blade out of his sleeve and nodded his head vigorously to several other ancients who had heard what he had said and had begun to gather around him. One reached out for the blade that Oscar so Wild was holding, not having one of his own.

"Do it," said Ezra Pound.

So the scrappers rested while the veteran Aux retrieved the scores of bolts that had killed the Dammed. The first few cuts were faltering, but their old hands quickly remembered the skills they had learned on their own battlefields when they had been the scrappers of Zoo Pack. Blades began to flash, and the ancients were soon digging out bolts with a few expert flicks of their wrists.

CHAPTER TWENTY-TWO
TEMPELHOF

THE WALK AROUND had been long, hard and slow.

By the time all the bolts were retrieved and everyone was fed and rested, dusk had fallen.

The Aux were more comfortable in the grey light, but they were also cold and tired. They still had a long walk ahead of them to reach their destination.

The Zoo Pack had abandoned its fiefdom to head east and then south, to visit the Tempelhof Pack.

There was no way to hide their approach. The Pack was too big, too cumbersome and too noisy. There was no opportunity for stealth and they were too tired to attempt it.

The loud bang made at least half of them hit the ice. It was like a thunderclap, and some of the Aux thought the sky was coming down on them.

The Zoo packers knew what rifles were, but few had seen them, and most had only heard shots at a great distance.

The shot was followed by the appearance of two Tempelhof Packers stepping out from cover twenty metres ahead of them in the lee of the station building, rifles at their shoulders aimed at the Zoo Pack. One of the rifles was smoking from the shot fired.

Ezra Pound was the only Aux standing, and even he had ducked, his instincts taking over when the shot was fired.

Slowly he straightened, his eyes never leaving the trail of smoke curling from the barrel of the rifle.

He unslung his crossbow and held it up at shoulder height, away from his body, to demonstrate that he was no threat. He placed it on the ice and kicked it away. Then he nodded to Oscar so Wild to do the same. Wild was half-standing, braced ready to drop or lunge. His teeth were bared, his brow creased, and he was staring at the rifles.

Edward Leer also stepped up. He was shaking, but he felt the need to instil some confidence in the Pack.

"Me, I am Ezra Pound," said the Alpha dog, his voice too loud and too hard as adrenalin pumped through his body. "Us, we are Zoo Pack. Us, we come to talk. We come to talk of Them."

The Tempelhof Aux on the left swung his rifle, indicating that the Zoo Pack leader should approach.

Ezra Pound turned to his pack.

"You, wait," he told them. "Me, I'll get us underground, skittle-scuttle fast." Then he strode forward, nodding to Oscar so Wild and Edward Leer to join him. They made it no further than the sentries.

The rest of Zoo Pack got back on its feet, gathering in a tight group. They gestured towards the sentries, and their rifles, and murmured among themselves. They knew the weapons were fearsome and deadly. The noise they made only proved it.

"Zoo Pack, we have left our fiefdom. We come to make alliances. There is strength in numbers," he told the sentries. "Zoo Pack, we need to get underground. Us, we have been outside too long."

One of the sentries nodded to the other, who backed away, never lowering his rifle, and disappeared into the station. He returned with a war band of a dozen more Tempelhof Aux, each with a rifle slung over his shoulder.

The Zoo Pack's crossbows were stacked in the Tempelhof station before the Pack was allowed underground. Their blades were also confiscated.

They felt like captives among the Tempelhof, with their strange, horrifying weapons.

Ben Gun and Evelyn War did not hand over their slingshots. The Tempelhof Aux didn't know they were carrying them, and didn't ask for them.

Most of the Zoo Pack felt relieved to be underground again, but it was tinged with fear. The Tempelhof were alien to them. So were their weapons. Even their fiefdom was alien.

The platform they went down onto had flat walls with square corners, and a double set of tracks. It smelled strange, too, hot and dusty, and the light was unnatural. There was no soft yellow glow of firelight, not like the spots of warmth in the service tunnels of the Zoo territory. The lights here were too hard and bright and too white. It was not like home, but it was better than being outside.

The Zoo Pack were crammed onto the platform, guarded by the Aux who had escorted them underground. They took off their outer clothing, talked among themselves, remade their family groups and even settled down to sleep among the bedding they had been wearing for the long trek.

Most of the pups and infants were asleep within minutes of arriving underground, and some of the ancients too. They were exhausted by the long Walk Around and by the rush of their encounter with the Tempelhof sentries.

Some of the Zoo Pack scrappers chose not to sleep. They kept a vigil over the Pack, watching their guards, keeping a constant eye on the rifles they carried with their long barrels and their curved magazines full of bullets instead of bolts.

They were wrong. The rifles were full of wrong.

Ezra Pound, Oscar so Wild and the original six, including the Warschauer war band, Edward Leer and Walter Sickert, were led into Atticus Flinch's command chamber. He was the leader of the Tempelhof Pack, but not a typical Alpha dog. He was tall and lean, but significantly smaller in stature than many of the warriors who sat or stood around the chamber.

When Zoo Pack had been discussing making alliances, it had been argued that the Tempelhof were one of the most advanced of the packs, one of the most sophisticated. They had a complex social structure, and they were Believers. Ezra Pound, with his pragmatic approach, disliked them for it, but it was exactly why they were approaching them now.

Atticus Flinch, the Tempelhof Alpha dog, was a shaman and a Hearer. He was considered superior because of that, not because of any prowess on the battlefield. It was this that made him Alpha dog in a long line of shaman Alpha dogs.

"Him," said Atticus Flinch, pointing at Walter Sickert, who was being held up by Robert Browning. "Him is not one of you."

No introductions or explanations had been made, other than to the sentries outside. The Alpha dog simply seemed to know who and what was important.

"Him is Walter Sickert, Hearer of the Warschauer Pack," said Edward Leer. "Them deader and dead."

"Walter Sickert, you, what did you Hear?" asked Atticus Flinch.

"Me, I Heard the Voice," said Walter Sickert in his musical voice. He looked baffled at Atticus Flinch. He tilted his head at him, a frown cutting his half-formed brow ridge.

"You, what don't you understand?" asked Atticus

Flinch, seeing the pup's confusion. "You, tell me what the Voice said."

"It told me Them were coming, skittle-scuttle fast. Them would scrap, tougher and tough. Them would kill the Warschauer, deader and dead," said Walter Sickert, his words becoming increasingly urgent. "It told me the Warschauer, we should run."

"The Warschauer Pack, them didn't run?" asked Atticus Flinch.

"No, them didn't run."

"Walter Sickert, Hearer, you told them to run?"

"Me, I told them to run," said the pup.

"Warschauer Pack, them still didn't run?" asked Atticus Flinch.

"Them died," said Walter Sickert. "Deader and dead."

"Walter Sickert, did you see Them?"

Walter Sickert still looked confused. His frown had not left his brow and his head was cocked on one side. He looked to Edward Leer for reassurance. Ben Gun saw his discomfort and took his hand.

"Stop asking questions," said Ben, concerned that his friend was becoming agitated.

Atticus Flinch and Ezra Pound both glared at Ben Gun. Walter Sickert went on.

"Me, I ran," he said. "Me, I heard the Voice, and I heard Them whistle. Me, I ran."

"Hearer, you ran to Zoo Pack? How?" asked Atticus Flinch, incredulous.

"Me, I'm Evelyn War," said Evelyn stepping forward. "Oberon War, Hearer of Zoo Pack, him was my father. Me, I found Walter Sickert, me and my war band, we found Walter Sickert. Us, we found the Warschauer Pack, deader and dead. We brought Walter Sickert to Zoo Pack."

While Evelyn was speaking, Walter Sickert got Edward Leer's attention and whispered, "Why is him talking like that?" The tale-teller didn't understand, but there was no time to ask what the pup meant.

"Zoo Pack, our sentries were dying," said Ezra Pound. "Oberon War, him tried to warn us that Them were returning, tougher and tough. Him dead. Now, this pup, him survived Warschauer. Him survived Them. There is strength in numbers. Tempelhof, will you make an alliance with Zoo Pack? Will you get whet with Zoo Pack, tougher and tough?"

"The ice is dying," said Evelyn War. "The Dammed, them were outside. Them were blind, and now them are dead, too. Us, we scrapped with them. Us, we killed them, deader and dead. The Aux, we are dying. Us, we must stand together."

"The Voice, it told me so," said Walter Sickert, looking Atticus Flinch in the eye.

"Zoo Pack, them travel far," said one of the Tempelhof lieutenants. She was a huge Aux called Becky Sharp, a middle-aged dam, who was clearly an experienced scrapper and a senior advisor. Atticus Flinch turned to her.

"Zoo Pack, them give up their fiefdom," said the lieutenant. "Zoo Pack, them serious. Tempelhof, we should be serious."

Another lieutenant took his turn to speak.

"Tempelhof, we trust Hearers, we trust the Voice. We must trust Walter Sickert," he said. "Tempelhof, we must make a pact of alliance. Us, we must stand beside our brother Aux. We must stand against Them."

Atticus Flinch raised a hand to still the hubbub growing around him as the Tempelhof lieutenants began to agree with each other.

"Me, I am the Hearer," said Atticus Flinch. "Me, I Hear the Master's Voice. Me, I am Alpha dog."

Walter Sickert clasped Ben Gun's hand a little harder and Ben Gun looked into his friend's worried face. There was no opportunity to speak in the silence. Atticus Flinch's voice was the only one that would be heard.

"The Masters, them speak through me," said Atticus Flinch. "The Masters, them will decide. Me, I will decide."

Atticus Flinch rose and grasped his staff of office. His lieutenants stood to attention. He walked deliberately, using his staff as a prop, to a metal door set into a corner of the room. He entered with a key that hung from his wrist and locked himself into a tiny booth. The lieutenants did not resume their seats. One of them followed the Alpha dog and stood guard at the door to his booth. The others bowed their heads and began to mumble words that the Zoo Packers could not understand. It was a kind of a chant, one of the many Tempelhof rituals that they had heard of.

Inside the booth, Atticus Flinch leaned his staff against the wall and placed an ancient pair of headphones over his ears. Then he threw a switch on the board in front of him that set a generator roaring. An orange light slowly flickered into life on the display. Suddenly his head was filled with words.

On Tempelhof station platform, there was a sudden high pitched whistle. Lights flashed red at the end of the platform and there was a strange hot smell as the rail tracks went live.

It was as if all the Zoo Pack's worst fears were coming true. Those who were asleep woke up and clambered to their feet, searching for their weapons before they were aware that they weren't still dreaming.

Some panicked when they couldn't find their blades and crossbows. They called out to each other in alarm. The Tempelhof guards raised their weapons, fearful that they had fallen foul of some sort of ambush. Then one of the most seasoned of the Aux fired his rifle down the tunnel to bring them all back to their senses.

The Zoo packers dropped onto their bellies on the platform. All except Thomas Hardy. He was close to the guard who had fired the shot, and as he dropped, he kicked his legs out from under him. The guard landed hard on his back. Thomas Hardy wrenched the rifle out of the guard's hands and began to throttle him with it.

"The whistle," he said. "What is it? Them? Is it Them?"

Suddenly the cold barrel of a rifle was nudging the side of Thomas Hardy's head, and a voice close to his ear was saying, "You, let him up!"

"You, let him go, Thomas Hardy," said Patrick Bateman. "Ezra Pound, him will make this right."

Thomas Hardy lifted the rifle off the guard's neck and threw it off the platform onto the tracks.

There was a loud *crack* as the metal barrel bounced off the live rail. Hot white sparks flew, making the Zoo Packers duck again. They shielded their eyes from the glare, and the infants began to squeal or whimper.

The Tempelhof guard on his back on the platform sat up.

"Atticus Flinch, Alpha dog, him is Hearing the Master's Voice," he said. "How does the Zoo Pack Hearer, him Hear the Voice?"

Atticus Flinch Heard the Master's Voice: *Alt-Tegel, change for S Track 25 – Borsigwerke – Holzhauser Straße – Otisstraße – Scharnweberstraße – Kurt-Schumacher-Platz – Afrikanische Straße – Rehberge – Seestraße – Leopoldplatz, change for U Track 9 – Wedding, change for S Tracks 41 and 42 – Reinickendorfer Straße – Schwartzkopffstraße – Naturkundemuseum – Oranienburger Tor – Friedrichstraße, change for S Tracks 1, 2, 5, 7, 25 and 75 – Französische Straße – Stadtmitte, change for U Track 2 – Kochstraße – Hallesches Tor, change for U Track 1 – Mehringdamm, change for U Track 7 – Platz der Luftbrücke – Paradestraße – Tempelhof, change for S Tracks 41, 42, 45 and*

*46 – Alt-Tempelhof – Kaiserin-Augusta-Straße –
Ullsteinstraße – Westphalweg – Alt-Mariendorf.*

The Master's Voice always said the same words.
Atticus Flinch knew the words were important
because his own pack, Tempelhof, was mentioned.
He knew that his own pack was the most important
of all the packs, because Tempelhof was mentioned
twice by the Master's Voice. He understood why
Mehringdamm was mentioned. The Dammed were
outcast by all the other Aux packs. They were the
devil. Tempelhof were the chosen.

Atticus Flinch could recite the words the Master's
Voice spoke, but still he Heard. He was the Hearer.
He threw the switch on the board and the orange
light went out. Then he threw it back to the 'on'
position and Heard again.

The Zoo Packers on the Tempelhof platform were
startled again as the whistle sounded from Atticus
Flinch's ancient tannoy machinery. The rest was
clicks and pops and white noise. There were no
words. The Tempelhof guards also looked surprised.

"Atticus Flinch, top dog, him Heard twice," said
the Aux lieutenant who had explained Hearing to
the Zoo packers. There was a tone in his voice that
none of the Aux on the platform liked the sound of.

Atticus threw the switch on the board in front of
him to the 'off' position, removed the headphones
from his ears, placed them carefully on their hook
and turned to unlock the door to his sacred place.

He did not speak until he had locked the door
behind him and he and the Aux guarding the booth

had both retaken their seats. There was silence in the chamber.

"Zoo Pack, you can sleep at Tempelhof. You are our brothers. You can rest and eat. You can get warm and dry. Then, Zoo Pack, you must leave," said Atticus Flinch. "There will be no alliance. Us, we must part as friends, but there will be no strength in numbers."

"What about Them?" asked Evelyn War. "What about Walter Sickert? Him heard the Master's Voice."

Atticus Flinch cast his gaze on Evelyn War and stared her down. He was not used to insubordination. He did not need to speak to his lieutenants or even gesture his intentions. Two Aux strode over to Evelyn War and took her by the wrists while the Alpha dog was still looking deep into her eyes. She dared to stare back.

"What did the Voice, him say?" she asked.

Robert Browning, Oscar so Wild and Dorothy Barker were on their feet to defend Evelyn. Ezra Pound also rose, stepping between her and Atticus Flinch, breaking their eye contact.

Atticus Flinch stood, and the Alpha dogs faced each other.

Nobody noticed Ben Gun loading his slingshot. He had whipped his arm and was about to loose a stone straight at the head of one of the lieutenants manhandling Evelyn when Walter Sickert spoke, his melodic tones filling the room.

"Zoo Pack, we must leave this place. Us, we must

leave Tempelhof. We must leave Tempelhof Pack. There is no Hearer here. Atticus Flinch, him does not have the ear or the voice of a Hearer."

The stone in Ben's slingshot fell useless to the floor, and the strong hands around Evelyn's wrists loosened their grips.

Walter Sickert was gaining in strength, and with that strength his voice was growing. The Aux were compelled by it, all of them.

The Aux of Zoo Pack had had barely enough time to eat and dry off, and despite being underground they had taken no comfort in their surroundings. They found themselves back outside in the darkest hours before dawn.

They felt mostly relief. Relief and exhaustion.

Their hopes had been set on the Tempelhof Pack, and those hopes were dashed. With every drop of water that fell from every tree and every rooftop and skidded and slid down every wall, the threat of Them grew closer.

Every time the sun rose, hotter and stronger than it had risen before in generations of memories, the threat grew closer.

Deprived of hope, they had to find a new plan, a new Aux Pack to pin new hopes on. Then they had to walk, and walking meant getting whet.

CHAPTER TWENTY-THREE
HALF A TALE

"NORTH," SAID WALTER Sickert as the Zoo Pack sheathed its blades and slung its crossbows.

"Why?" asked Robert Browning.

Ben Gun stepped in. He had not left Walter Sickert's side, except during the battle against the Dammed, since he had first met him in the service tunnel at Warschauer. He was not just his friend. He believed every word the Hearer spoke. He was compelled by his voice.

"Us, we must follow the road most travelled," said Ben Gun. "Us, we must retrace our steps. It is safest. It is fastest."

"Us, we will travel north," said Ezra Pound, so that the entire Pack could hear him. "To the Hacker Pack."

"The Hacker Pack, them have no Hearer," said Evelyn War.

"Them don't need a Hearer," said Ezra Pound. "Us, we have a Hearer. Them will hear his words, and them will make an alliance with us. Them are the best friends we have. The Warschauer, them are gone, deader and dead. Us, we will make an alliance with the Hacker, tougher and tough.

"North," he said again, his stentorian tones filling the air, the steam of his breath billowing out in a cloud over the heads of his followers.

Zoo Pack retraced its steps along Mehringdamm, and the sun rose on another day. The buildings of the broad thoroughfare loomed on either side of them and the cross-streets and alleyways threaded away into shadows. The roofs showed their many colours and the faces of the buildings continued to emerge under the heat of the sun. The dripping was almost continuous, and puddles were forming on the surface of the ice. The world was changing fast.

The Aux adapted quickly. Those who did not own eyeshades had become used to pulling at their caps to cover their eyes. Or they knew just how to wrap their head cloths to allow the right amount of light to penetrate, giving them the best chance of seeing without being blinded by the sun.

They knew how often to tap the ice out of the springs and chains in their boots, and they knew how to adjust the blankets around their shoulders so they didn't shrug them off, trip over them or leave ends trailing on the wet ice.

They knew what to watch and listen for in the landscape of the city. They could feel the rumble of an ice fall before it came, and easily avoided several avalanches, hugging the ground in the middle of the road when the roofs shed their coverings. They learned to pace themselves and help each other along.

The second day's walk was easier than the first, despite the Pack being tired from their adventures of the day before. It was easier despite their lack of sleep and sustenance, and despite their disappointments.

The pups and infants adapted the fastest, but some of the ancients became remarkably spry and inventive, remembering and reliving their glory days.

One old Aux, a dam with only one arm, saw a rodent half way up a tree. It was a fat little ball of dense fur, scrubbing away at the bark of a branch with its teeth.

She pulled a knife from her belt, squinted down its length and threw it, skewering the creature and knocking it from its perch. She sent one of the pups to collect it, promising a portion as a ration later in the day. She hadn't thrown a blade like that for upwards of a dozen seasons. She didn't even know that she still could.

There was no avoiding the cold, dead bodies of the Dammed on the road through Mehringdamm. They looked utterly untouched, exactly as they had when the Zoo Pack had left them on the ice, the cuts in their pallid flesh marking where their bolts had hit their targets.

The Zoo Packers felt no regret, no remorse. Berlin was full of Aux Packs. The Dammed had negotiated with none of them, had traded with none of them, and had been accepted by none of them.

The day passed without incident as Zoo Pack continued to follow Mehringdamm for as far as it would take them. As dusk fell, two solid days outside began to take a serious toll on the youngest and oldest of the Zoo Pack.

"Us, we need to get Zoo Pack underground," Dorothy Barker told Robert Browning. "You must speak to Ezra Pound, tougher and tough."

The Pack had slowed down dramatically over the last two hours before the light had begun to fade. They were covering almost no distance. The cold was setting in and some of the infants were showing signs of hypothermia. They were stumbling, irritable and struggling to speak.

Mehringdamm was far behind them, and, despite Track Seven being clear of the Dammed, no one would have ventured below ground at any of its stations. Track Six was closed beyond Hallesches Tor, sealed off by the Dammed to preserve their fiefdom. If Zoo Pack could only make it as far as Kochstrasse, they could risk dropping down onto Track Six.

"You, scout ahead," said Ezra Pound when Robert Browning approached him. "Zoo Pack will not lose Aux to the Time of Ice. You, take the pup, Ben

Gun, him is sharp of ear and clear of head. You, go underground. Find a safe place."

They were close to Hacker Pack territory, only a few kilometres south of Hackescher Markt, but it could take several more hours to cover the distance. If fate was against them, as time was, the entire Pack could be wiped out in those few kilometres. The alliance must wait for another dawn, another day of bright sunshine and wet ice.

The ice beneath Ben Gun's and Robert Browning's feet showed no marks. No Aux had walked this route for a long time. No Aux ever used the wider streets and thoroughfares in the city, so it was not surprising; what was surprising was the lack of animal tracks.

"No creatures, no rodents come here," said Ben Gun, peering at the clean, smooth ice beneath his feet and the scratches he made on the virgin surface with his sprung boots.

"Nothing," agreed Robert Browning.

They heard nothing and saw nothing as they moved towards Kochstrasse. The station was derelict and decrepit, a ruin with no roof and two walls missing. The entrance and routes down to the platform beneath were exposed to the elements.

Ben Gun took a moment to listen, but heard only the echoes of falling water droplets. Water falling into water.

When they descended onto the platform, it was awash with dirty water. It was unfit for permanent habitation, but as they ventured further along

Track Six the pair of Aux found dry service tunnels where the Zoo Pack could rest and wait for morning.

No Pack had wanted to live so close to the Dammed, none had wanted to be tainted by them. Kochstrasse had not been used since the Mehringdamm Pack had staked its claim to Track Seven, longer ago than anyone could remember. The place had an eerie, deserted feeling. It smelled stale, of old grease and older rust. Ben Gun was unnerved by the atmosphere.

"This place, is it safe?" he asked Robert Browning.

"You, do you hear anything?" asked Browning in return. "Do you hear an echo? You, do you hear a whistle?"

Ben Gun cocked an ear and concentrated. He wanted to say 'yes', but he heard nothing but the ping and plash of water falling onto stone and water falling into water.

"Me, I hear nothing," said Ben Gun.

"Then this place is safe," said Robert Browning.

The service tunnels of Track Six at Kochstrasse felt much safer to Ben Gun when they were full of the Zoo Pack.

There were no amenities below ground at Kochstrasse, but the mood among the Zoo Pack was buoyant nevertheless. They felt safe in the confines of the curving walls and the low, black ceilings.

Pairs of sentries were posted for short watches close to the Pack, who were all gathered in two adjacent service tunnels. No one was left alone.

Everyone shared rations and blankets, and all was soon still and quiet.

"Tale-teller, you tell us a tale," said Ezra Pound, his voice filling the narrow tunnel.

"Gene the Hackman, top dog, him done the great Walk Around," began Edward Leer. "Not for him the darkness, not for him the cold, not for him the Time of Ice. Gene the Hackman, him got whet. Gene the Hackman, him got whet and walked the Earth, and him killed Them."

"Tale-teller, is this an old legend? Us, have we heard this tale before?" asked Ben Gun.

Some of the other Aux tutted or sighed, and one or two called out for quiet or shushed Ben Gun, or hissed at him.

Edward Leer simply cast a wry smile in the pup's direction. He did not answer his question.

"Gene the Hackman, him crossed the land bridge into Auxtralia. The Masters, them lived in the crumbling places there, before them went to sleep. Before Them ate up the World," continued Edward Leer. "Auxtralia was full of the crumbling places and full of Them. All kinds of Them. All kinds of Them Gene, him had not seen before.

"It was hard for Gene. Gene, him ran and Gene, him hid, but Them had Gene's scent. Everywhere him went, Them followed. Gene, him got whet and him hacked and him slashed, tougher and tough. Him killed Them, deader and dead. All kinds of Them. And that was the scrapping, day after day."

"It is a new tale," Ben Gun whispered to Walter

Sickert. One or two of the Aux groaned at his interruption, but most of them were intent on the story, hanging on every word.

"Gene the Hackman, him didn't need the Urgings," said Edward Leer. "Him didn't need the Urgings, because him was the Hackman, truer and true. Him knew how to scrap. Him had killed more Them than any Aux. Him was no omega dog, him was a rogue dog with Alpha blood.

"Gene the Hackman, him scrapped with every kind of Them in the crumbling places, tougher and tough, and him survived.

"Then, it happened. Then, Gene the Hackman, him heard the Voice. Him got the call of the wild."

The silence that had fallen while Edward Leer told his story continued for several seconds after it had ended.

"What?" asked Ben Gun, finally.

Edward Leer tilted his head at the pup.

"You, why have you stopped, tale-teller?" asked Ben Gun. "That is no tale."

"That is the end of the story," said Edward Leer. "That is all the legend I learned. Me, I have nothing more."

"But –" began Ben Gun, but his protests were cut off abruptly by Walter Sickert.

"It is enough," said the Hearer. His musical voice filled the service tunnel and echoed out of it. "The tale is enough."

CHAPTER TWENTY-FOUR
NOISES OUTSIDE

THERE WERE NO sounds in the night. The Aux no longer regarded the constant ping and plash of dripping water as threatening. They were part of the everyday landscape of their lives, and no longer disturbed them.

Sentries were changed every two hours, and everyone was able to sleep. A fug of almost too much warmth filled the service tunnels they occupied, and blankets and pelts were tossed aside as bodies rolled in slumber. The air was no longer filled with the steam of dozens of exhaling bodies as the temperature rose above freezing.

Ben Gun was the first to wake to noises from outside.

Then others quickly awoke around him, and the sentries began to gather to report.

Fierce sounds of battle were filtering down from above ground.

"Aux," said Ezra Pound immediately on hearing the fighting.

"Us, do we join battle?" asked Oscar so Wild.

Ezra Pound looked around at his pack. His scrappers were already dressed in outside clothes and were arming, but some of them were newly called, green, and there was no alliance yet. Almost a third of the Pack were infant pups and ancients.

"Us, we are Zoo Pack," said Ezra Pound. "We are scrappers, tougher and tough." Then he hesitated.

"The Hacker Pack," said Evelyn War. "The alliance. There is strength in numbers. Us, we cannot scrap now."

A hush fell over the Zoo Pack.

"Us, we could evade the battle," said Ben Gun. "Us, we could walk Track Six north."

"Underground, it is not safe," said one of the lieutenants.

Ben Gun shrugged.

"Us, we were safe underground all night," said Oscar so Wild.

The sounds from above ground grew louder. The battle raged. Aux were dying.

"Outside, it is not safe," said Ezra Pound. "We walk underground."

All of the Zoo packers had prepared to venture above ground, and it was easier to wear their outside clothes, blankets and pelts than it was to carry them.

For the first time, it was less comfortable underground than it was outside. The Aux loosened and unfastened as many layers of clothes as they were able and slung blankets and pelts over their shoulders. They removed caps and gloves and shoved them into pockets and belts, but still they were clammy with the sweat of too many clothes and too much activity.

Travelling should have been faster underground. It was not.

The pups whined and the ancients' breathing suffered.

Food rations were not a problem, but even with the brackish dripping water there was not enough to quench the Zoo Pack's thirst.

The scrappers kept to the head of the group and the rear.

There was still a constant fear of hearing the whistle of Them. If they were caught underground, there would be no escape.

They listened, but it was hard to hear anything above the noise the Zoo Pack made with the metal in their boots and the stones beneath their feet. Every footfall sent up a cacophony of echoes, and there were dozens of overlapping footfalls every second.

There was talk of removing the alterations from the boots, but the Zoo Pack would be out on the ice again at the first opportunity. Being stationary for long periods was just too dangerous. Even with the metal gone, the stones would still create enough sound to drown out any echoes.

Tension grew and paranoia began to set in. Someone called for a halt every minute or two. Adrenalin pumped, with no means of satisfaction or escape.

Pups began to bicker, and a brawl broke out between three adolescents that ended with one of them being boxed soundly around the ears by one of the scrapper dams. She hit him too hard and he was unconscious for several seconds. He came to, confused and bleeding from his ear. He became another invalid, reliant on the rest of the Pack.

Robert Browning and Ben Gun went ahead to scout Stadtmitte. Before they had even reached the platform, they found horror.

Every few metres there were signs of fighting. There were sprays of blood on the walls and chunks of leather and cloth littered the ground where armour and clothing had been sliced and rent from bodies. The tunnel smelled of death. Browning picked up a broken blade with a smear of old blood on its hilt.

There was no way to know if this had been a scrap between Aux or an attack by Them. Them left no bodies. The Aux tended to their dead. Either way, no corpses would remain in the tunnels.

"Two days or three," he said.

They approached the platform cautiously, weapons drawn.

Ben Gun listened. He heard something.

"Noises," he said, turning to Browning.

Browning cocked an ear, but heard nothing. He turned to face north along Track Six.

"You, did you hear the whistle? Did you hear Them?" asked Browning.

Ben Gun listened more intently.

They both heard something, but it was coming down from outside.

"Scrapping," said Robert Browning.

"This place, is it safe to pass here?" asked Ben Gun.

"You, listen," said Robert Browning, and he began to walk north up Track Six, picking his way through the debris left by the scrapping. He walked for two or three hundred metres while Ben Gun listened.

The pup heard nothing until Browning returned.

"You, what do you hear?" asked Browning.

"Nothing," said the pup. "You, what did you see?"

"The track, it is safe," said Browning.

The two looked at each other. Robert Browning had to make a decision: whether it was wiser to suffer the discomfort of the tunnels and risk hearing the whistle, or to venture above ground and possibly walk onto a battleground.

The sound of an Aux roaring in pain came to them faintly from far above their heads.

"Us, we walk Track Six," said Robert Browning.

Tension and paranoia grew into fear and panic as Zoo Pack passed through Stadtmitte.

"Zoo Pack, us tougher and tough," said Ezra Pound, gravely. "Zoo Pack, us scrappers." His voice filled Track Six. "Zoo Pack, us will walk and Zoo

Pack, us will stand together. Zoo Pack, us will make alliances, and get whet."

For the first time, Evelyn War understood why Ezra Pound was Alpha dog. The packers around her began to straighten their backs and hold their heads a little higher. They began to walk a little faster. Even the infants stopped whining. Some of the younger pups got in step with one another and began to march doggedly in ranks at the centre of the Pack.

Ezra Pound instilled confidence. Confidence was what Zoo Pack needed.

"Us, we are safe," said Walter Sickert, his melodic tones in stark contrast to Ezra Pound's strong, low voice. "Us, we meet Hacker Pack at Friedrichstrasse."

The Zoo Pack stopped for nothing. Aux were sent ahead to scout service tunnels and to listen. They were sent to check platforms and to monitor sounds from outside.

There were always sounds. Outside was a battleground. Outside the Aux were scrapping some unknowable foe. Underground, there had been battles too. At every platform there were signs of conflict. Blood sprays smeared every surface, a bolt was found embedded in a wall, and two or three more broken blades turned up on the track.

Oscar so Wild retrieved a bandolier almost full of good crossbow bolts and slung it around his body. They never found a single corpse.

A crossbow bolt hit the wall centimetres from Dorothy Barker's shoulder. She was crouching close to the tunnel wall, moving with as much stealth as she could towards the platform at Friedrichstrasse. Alan Stiletto was moving with equal caution along the opposite side of the tunnel.

They were within twenty metres of the end of the platform. A number of bodies lay on it, covered in blankets. They did not know until the bolt hit whether the bodies were corpses or not.

Dorothy Barker ducked and breathed hard. She shouted, knowing that the second bolt would not miss her.

"Zoo Pack!" she said. "Friends! Allies!"

The bodies under the blankets began to stir. A moment later, Dorothy could clearly see half a dozen crossbows pointing in her direction. She was dead if they wanted her dead.

"Me, I'm standing up," she said. "Us, we're both standing up." She pointed to where Alan Stiletto was crouching against the opposite wall. She was confident that they hadn't spotted him yet in the shadows, but she wanted to show that she was being honest with them.

The Aux on the platform looked twitchy. She didn't want to make them even more paranoid and risk an attack.

Dorothy Barker stood slowly, her crossbow held at arm's length away from her body. She had removed the bolt. Alan Stiletto did likewise.

Someone on the platform stood, still aiming her crossbow. It was a large dam Aux.

"Zoo Pack?" she asked.

"Dorothy Barker, Zoo Pack," said Dorothy. "You, listen," she said. "Zoo Pack, all of us, walk all-away around to Hacker Pack. Us, we walk all-away around to talk."

The faint echo of the rumble and scrape of footfalls could be heard in the distance down Track Six.

The Aux dam gestured to a scrapper still on his belly, his crossbow aimed. The Aux stood, never giving up his aim, and then backed away before disappearing into one of the service tunnels.

There followed a pause, then several brief calls that reverberated around the space, filling the platform and tunnels.

Dorothy Barker reflected that the Zoo Pack would also hear the call. She turned to face back down the tunnel. When the echoes from the call had receded, she listened again for the rumbles of the Zoo Pack's footfalls.

The Track Six tunnel was silent.

Zoo Pack had stopped. When she turned back to face the platform, it was full of Hacker scrappers, armed and ready for action. Some of them were obviously carrying new injuries, with dressed wounds as well as scabs and bruises on full view. They only added to their fierce appearance.

A huge Aux with a long, healing blade wound on his face stepped forward, flanked by two lieutenants. He was their leader, Alpha dog.

"Ezra Pound, him is still Alpha dog of Zoo Pack?" he asked.

"Ezra Pound, him is Alpha dog," said Dorothy

Parker. "Him leads Zoo Pack to you. Him tougher and tough."

"Him got the bone for it, to scrap Holeman Hunt. Him got the bone to take Hacker Pack?" asked the Alpha dog.

"Warschauer Pack, them gone, deader and dead," said Dorothy Barker. "Dammed Pack, them gone, deader and dead. Ezra Pound, him wants an alliance with Holeman Hunt. There is strength in numbers."

Holeman Hunt looked hard at Dorothy Barker. The Alpha dog's shoulders dropped slightly, as if he was exhausted. Then he filled his chest and stood tall. He turned to the Aux on his left and said, "You, bring Zoo Pack in. You, bring Ezra Pound in. Me, I will talk with Zoo Pack Alpha dog."

"Me, I'll bring them," said Dorothy Barker. She gestured at Alan Stiletto to join her at the centre of the tunnel. She was determined that there would be no more bloodshed.

They slung their crossbows over their backs, slipped their bolts into their bandoliers and began to return down the track towards Zoo Pack, with a score of crossbows aimed at their backs.

Zoo Pack heard the Hacker Pack call.

All Aux packs had calls, but each pack's calls were unique. There was no way to know what the call meant as it reached the ears of the Zoo Pack scrappers walking a dozen metres ahead of the main Pack. There was no way to know whether Dorothy Barker and Alan Stiletto were safe. Zoo Pack stopped and waited. There was no turning back.

The Zoo Pack scrappers fell into ranks across the width of the tunnel, armed and ready. The rest of the Pack took shelter as best it could behind them.

They could hear the Hacker Aux walking south down Track Six towards them. At least a dozen of them, possibly two dozen. Soon they could see their grey shapes moving against the still grey of the tunnel walls and the paler grey of the track.

"Me, I'm going to shout my name," said Dorothy Barker over her shoulder.

"You, shout nothing else," said the Hacker lieutenant immediately behind her.

"Dorothy Barker!" shouted Dorothy.

The tunnel filled with her name and its echoes. It sounded strange to her.

"It's her, Dorothy," said Robert Browning in the front rank of the Zoo Pack scrappers.

No one answered. Silence must be maintained. Robert Browning should not have spoken. All but the paranoid and the truly sceptical were relieved, however. Dorothy was at too great a distance, and the echoes overlapped too much for them to be able to discern whether it was her voice that had spoken, but it was her name. There was no reason for any Aux to call out Dorothy's name for any ill purpose.

The grey shapes grew closer in the gloom.

At about twenty metres distance, crossbows raised and aimed on both sides, Ezra Pound stepped through the ranks of his scrappers.

"Me, I am Ezra Pound," he said. "Alpha dog, leader of Zoo Pack. Come to make alliance with

Holeman Hunt. You, Hacker Pack, shoot or stand down."

Dorothy Barker began to walk towards Ezra Pound, who gestured to his scrappers to lower their weapons. The Zoo Packers looked to one another, confused, unwilling to give up their arms.

It was Oscar so Wild and Robert Browning who dropped their crossbows first. Others began to follow suit.

"Hacker Pack scrappers, them have come to bring Zoo Pack to Friedrichstrasse," said Dorothy Barker. "Holeman Hunt, him will speak with Ezra Pound."

Many of the Hacker Pack scrappers had also lowered their weapons. All but a few diehard Aux lieutenants, who dropped their crossbows to chest height, but continued to aim them at Zoo Pack.

"Walter Sickert, you were right, again," said Ben Gun to his friend.

"Me, I am never right," said Walter Sickert. "Me, I only Hear the Voice."

The Hacker packers spread out to line the tunnel, surrounding the Zoo Pack on all sides to escort them back to Friedrichstrasse.

The Zoo pack scrappers also spread themselves among their more vulnerable pack members, and by the time they had reached the station, many of them had managed to exchange information with some of the Hackers.

Word began to spread through the Zoo Pack about the noises they had heard outside.

CHAPTER TWENTY-FIVE
HACKER PACK ALLIANCE

THE HACKER PACK had one of the largest fiefdoms in Berlin. Based at Hackerscher Markt, it spread to Friedrichstrasse and beyond. Stadtmitte was at its periphery.

Zoo Pack had heard fighting outside on Hacker territory. The most powerful Aux Pack in the north of Berlin was under threat.

The greeting between Ezra Pound and Holeman Hunt was a friendly, familiar one. They clenched forearms and banged their vast chests together like brothers, when they met on the platform at Friedrichstrasse. Zoo Pack weapons were not confiscated, and many of the Hackers had gathered to greet them.

The atmosphere was serious, though. It was clear that the Hacker Pack was suffering.

Ezra Pound put one huge hand around Holeman Hunt's neck and looked at the fresh scar on the Alpha dog's face.

"Holeman Hunt, you have been scrapping?"

"The Rathaus Pack, them have turned. Them have gone to the wild. Them have turned savage," said the Alpha dog by way of an answer.

"Rathaus Pack, them scrap outside?" asked Ezra Pound.

"Rathaus Pack, them scrap everywhere," said Holeman Hunt. "The Hacker Pack fiefdom, it grows small."

"Zoo Pack, we have no fiefdom," said Ezra Pound.

"You, my brother, you are welcome here," said Holeman Hunt.

With Hackescher Markt abandoned, Friedrichstrasse had become the Hacker Pack's base. It was crowded and many of the amenities were improvised, but a command centre had been set up. Ezra Pound was invited to join Holeman Hunt and his lieutenants to discuss the problems the new order was throwing up.

"Me, I have lieutenants, too," said Ezra Pound. "Them have much to say."

The room was small and too full of Aux. They sat and stood in close proximity, close enough to touch. The Hackers cast baffled glances over Ezra Pound's lieutenants. They did not understand the presence of the two pups, including an invalid, or of the two low-status dams, or the old male. They did not understand why there were only two Aux lieutenants in the party.

"Us, why should we listen to Ezra Pound?" a Hacker lieutenant asked Holeman Hunt. "Zoo Pack has no fiefdom, and no lieutenants," he jeered, gesturing at Pound's entourage.

"Me, I have what you need," said Ezra Pound. "Me, I have the bravest, truest Pack. Me, I have a Hearer. Me, I have a Believer. Me, I have a tale-teller who tells tales never before told."

Ezra Pound spoke in the voice he used to rally his scrappers. He spoke with conviction.

"Me, I have the truth."

He looked at Walter Sickert.

"You, speak," he said.

"The ice, it is dying," said Walter Sickert.

His voice had a visible effect on the people around him. The Zoo Pack had grown a little used to it, but the Warschauer Pack's Hearer was a shock to the Hacker Aux. One of them buckled at the knees and had to steady himself.

"The ice, it is dying and Them live. The Warschauer Pack, them did not believe. The Warschauer Pack, them are gone, deader and dead. Killed by Them. The whistles in the tunnels, underground, them warn us of Them. There is strength in numbers. The Aux, we must stand against Them. The Aux, we must listen to the old legends. The Time of Ice, it is over. The Aux, we will live again. The Aux, we will breathe again. First the Aux, we must make alliances, tougher and tough. The Aux, we must stand together against Them, tougher and tough."

Holeman Hunt stood. He waited for Walter Sickert

to finish what he was saying, but his impatience was clear.

"The Rathaus Pack," he said. "Them scrap with us. Them wound and kill the Hacker Pack. Gene the Hackman, him kept Them off the Lawn. Gene the Hackman, him got whet. Gene the Hackman, him was tougher and tough. Gene the Hackman, him killed Them."

"Us, we are Gene the Hackman," said Walter Sickert, slowly, one word at a time.

Holeman Hunt could not refute the Hearer's claims. The force of his words and the tone in which he spoke them meant more than anything the Alpha dog could say, but his situation was more immediate, more pressing. Them weren't killing the Hacker Pack, the Rathaus were.

Holeman Hunt stood at the centre of the command chamber for long moments. He could think of nothing to say. All he could do was plead.

"You, Hearer, does the Voice say nothing of the Rathaus?"

"Them are on the lawn," said Walter Sickert. "The Aux, we must keep Them off the Lawn."

Holeman Hunt didn't speak again for several long seconds.

It was one of his lieutenants who spoke for him.

"The Rathaus, them scrap with us. The Rathaus, them kill and maim us. The Rathaus, them threaten our fiefdom. Us, why do we listen to a pup?"

Walter Sickert bowed his head and did not speak. He had said all that he had to say.

Ezra Pound stood up next to Holeman Hunt.

"Them can wait," he said. "Hacker Pack, you make an alliance with Zoo Pack, tougher and tough. Make an alliance with Zoo Pack and Zoo Pack, we make an alliance with Hacker Pack."

The two Aux embraced again, grasping forearms and banging chests. The deal was done.

"Hacker Pack, what do you need?" asked Ezra Pound.

CHAPTER TWENTY-SIX
RATHAUS

Zoo Pack and Hacker Pack joined forces. Every scrapper who was fit, who could bear arms, who could stand and fight, was called to the cause.

The pups called by Ezra Pound at the evacuation of Old Zoo were invited to volunteer for duty, and many of them did, hardened by their long walk and by what they had witnessed on their travels.

Dozens, scores of scrappers dressed in their outside clothes, wrapped their head cloths, filled their bandoliers and donned their eyeshades. They emerged outside at dawn, spreading across the Hacker territory from Friedrichstrasse, Stadtmitte, and Französische Strasse. Underground, war bands gathered at sentry points around the periphery of the Hacker Pack fiefdom.

They heard the first howls before the sun had begun to rise.

The Rathaus Pack territory occupied the city far to the west. They were not neighbours of the Hacker Pack. They had travelled great distances to do battle with them.

The Rathaus had traditionally been scavengers, less organised than other Aux packs, wilder and less rational. They had also always been in awe of the city packs. There had always been skirmishes at the territorial borders, but the more organised, more sophisticated packs that lived closer to the centre of Berlin had always held sway, had always been in control.

In the past days and weeks, the Rathaus had become increasingly desperate. The Hacker Pack did not know why. The Rathaus Pack had become marauders. They had adopted guerrilla tactics, attacking Hackers at any opportunity, ambushing them for no obvious reason. Their fighting style had become more than simple forays. There was desperation in every move they made.

Oscar so Wild, Dorothy Barker and Ben Gun went outside at Friedrichstrasse with thirty scrappers, a mixture of Hacker and Zoo packers. They formed a front defending the station and the route back below ground, and they waited, ready to fight on their own terms.

They heard the Rathaus, heard their howls. There was no language left in their calls.

"Them, they are the same as the Aux in Kreuzberg,"

said Dorothy Barker. "Them, they have lost their senses."

"Them should be easier to kill, then," said Oscar so Wild.

"For them, it is kill or die," said Dorothy Barker.

Word spread among the gathered Aux. There must be no mistakes. There must be no mercy. No scrapper must be in any doubt about the pathetic Aux they would come up against. The Rathaus meant to kill them, and so they must kill the Rathaus.

The first crossbow bolt was loosed before the order was given. One of the younger scrappers of Zoo Pack, Richard Dadd, untried and nervous, shot his crossbow too soon. He was not a pup, not called at the evacuation, but as cocky as he was among his peers, he had never seen anything like this.

He had never seen an Aux on all fours. He had never seen anything so ragged, never seen the whites of an enemy Aux's eyes, and he could not help himself.

The shot was good. It pierced the Rathaus dog's throat and travelled into its thorax, ravaging its lungs and slicing into its heart.

Nevertheless, it was too soon.

It alerted the Rathaus to the dangers of an ambush.

For some of the Rathaus dogs, it was already too late. They were committed. They hurtled towards the enemy, teeth bared.

Some barrelled forwards on all fours with blades between those teeth, ready to engage with blades and teeth and claws. Ready to tear and bite, to slice and hack at the foe. Some wielded catapults, some throwing axes. None had crossbows.

The keen pup had been right to get his shot in first.

"Fire!" bellowed Dorothy Barker.

Six of the Rathaus packers were down within seconds of the dam shouting the order, dead or wounded. More bolts were loosed and more Rathaus dogs fell.

They kept coming. They had homed in on their targets and nothing would stop them from attacking.

It was a slaughter, a demoralising slaughter of fellow Aux that the combined force of the Hacker and Zoo Packs took no pleasure in.

Then a Rathaus Packer made it to the defensive line. It took its throwing axe in its hand and whipped it the last three or four metres through the air.

The Zoo Packer, Thomas Hardy, ducked sideways, avoiding the fatal blow, but the blade hit him solidly in the shoulder, shredding his great coat and jacket and embedding itself in the joint, disabling his left arm. He dropped his crossbow with a pained yelp, and drew a blade from his left cuff in time to engage with the Rathaus dog.

The feral Aux came in low and hard, its dripping maw wide and howling. It knocked the Zoo packer over, but his blade was already raised and the weight of the attacking Rathauser slammed the stiletto hard into its gut. Thomas Hardy had only to twist and wrench hard.

The feral Aux was eviscerated on top of him, spilling its hot guts onto his belly and legs. Hardy backed away fast, struggling to get out from under his kill with his disabled shoulder.

Ben Gun whipped his slingshot and felled two Rathaus Aux, although not fatally. They had to be finished off by the Hacker Aux standing next to him. They made a good team. Ben Gun slowed the enemy down, and his Hacker sidekick picked them off.

The feral Aux kept getting closer, though, and soon Ben Gun and his new friend were both making kills. Ben made two direct hits in a row, embedding his stones in the eyes of two feral marauders. His companion killed one Rathauser outright with a bolt to the chest, and felled another.

The Aux howled and thrashed on the ground, blood squirting from the wound high in its thigh. The Hacker fumbled his reload, and the injured Rathauser suffered for too long.

A Zoo Pack dam, Jenny A-Gutter, made the kill shot, but missed the Rathaus Packer stalking in on her right. She took two blade strikes to her lower leg, to the calf muscle and to the tendon behind her knee.

Jenny A-Gutter was down. The Rathaus showed her no mercy, and without time to draw a blade, she was driven to beating it around the head with her crossbow. A lucky blow knocked the Rathaus unconscious.

The dam took great pleasure in loading the crossbow and shooting the Aux in the head at point blank range from her position sitting on the ground next to it.

Jenny could not stand, so found good cover half-buried in rubble at the corner of a derelict building. She spent the rest of the battle on her belly, shooting her crossbow at anything that came within range. Her anger was vicious, and she fatally wounded two more Rathaus Aux. She did not care to waste a second bolt on either of them to put them out of their misery.

Their howls and yelps of anguish filled the air for several minutes as she continued to aim and shoot at their pack mates.

Further down the line, things were less clear cut. The Rathaus Pack penetrated en masse, and the skirmish was much messier. What should have been a simple, one-sided bow fight turned into a close combat struggle between more than a dozen Aux on each side.

The Rathausers bit, clawed and growled. Their blade strikes were erratic and hard to read. The more disciplined Zoo Pack and Hacker scrappers struggled in the melée.

They would strike out with a blade only to find that the Rathaus had resorted to lunging on all fours, tearing with their claws, their blades between their teeth. They would find themselves on their backs, pounced on by feral Rathaus Aux, no better than dogs, biting into them, savaging them with teeth and claws.

One Hacker died that way, his throat torn out by a Rathaus dam, that gloried too long over its victory. The Hacker's whelp brother, horrified by the brutality of the death, pulled the Rathaus dam's head back hard and slit its throat as it crouched over its kill.

As blood spurted from the wound and gurgled in its last breath, he was rewarded with a blade in his back, piercing low down between his ribs. The wound was not fatal, but if a Zoo Packer had not intervened, the next one would have been.

The last three Rathausers finally slunk away from the skirmish, badly wounded, unable to fight against the combined forces of the Hacker and Zoo Pack scrappers. They had lost three of their own, but the narrow crossroads was littered with the bodies of almost a dozen of the mangy Rathaus dogs.

Similar battles took place above and below ground right across Hacker territory. A conflict would be over, the howling and yelping of the feral Aux would cease, the air would still, and quiet would descend.

The Zoo Pack and Hacker scrappers would regroup. They would tend to their dead and wounded, and for a short time they would believe that was the scrapping of that day.

But the feral Aux kept coming. The Hacker and Zoo Pack scrappers kept fighting and kept killing the foe.

As dusk finally fell there was nothing left to kill. The last of the Rathaus Pack could no longer fight. They crawled or skulked away, wounded and dying. They would not fight another day.

As they headed below ground at Friedrichstrasse, Ben Gun heard howling in the surrounding streets.

The last remains of the Rathaus Pack were sending out feeble calls to one another.

He turned to the Hacker who had been his constant companion throughout the fighting.

"Why?" he asked.

"Me, I do not know what you ask," said the Hacker, unwrapping his head cloth as they made their way back to the platform.

"The Rathaus Pack, why do they fight? Why now? Why here?" asked Ben Gun.

"The Zoo Pack, you know so much. Ben Gun, you tell me," said the Hacker, peeling off his great coat and tossing it over his arm.

They were engulfed in the warmth of scores of bodies packed into a few hundred metres of tunnels, close to Friedrichstrasse station platform. Ben Gun was eager to find his Zoo Pack friends. Then all he wanted to do was eat and rest.

The Hacker Pack had become used to living at close quarters with each other since their fiefdom had been reduced. Even Holeman Hunt did not claim a single cell, but lived in his command room, surrounded by his lieutenants. Hacker Pack had been in a constant state of readiness for war with the Rathaus Pack for weeks, and their living conditions reflected that.

Zoo Pack found accommodations where they could, which meant sleeping rough in the service tunnels in close proximity with the Hackers. They were all tired from the day's scrapping. They had all made strong bonds with the Aux they had stood beside and fought with.

Ben Gun looked for Walter Sickert as soon as he hit the platform. Then he went in search of Evelyn War. He found her in one of the anterooms, having a flesh wound dressed.

"You, are you injured?" asked Ben Gun, his eyes wide, the blood draining from his face.

"It was foolish, a tear, nothing," said Evelyn War, rolling down her trouser leg over the dressing on her shin and pulling on her boot. "The Rathaus, them are gone."

"Why did them attack?" asked Ben Gun. "Does Holeman Hunt, him know why the Rathaus attacked?"

"Why is any of this happening?" asked Evelyn War. "Why is the Warschauer Pack, them gone, deader and dead? Why were the Dammed, them blind? Why were them outside? Why did the Tempelfhof Pack, them turn us away? Why did Zoo Pack, us leave our fiefdom?"

"Why?" said Ben Gun.

He hesitated, but only for a moment. Then he reached out to grab Evelyn War's hand and started dragging her out of the ante-room.

"Us, we must speak with Ezra Pound. Us, we must speak with Holeman Hunt," said Ben Gun. There was urgency in his voice and his eyes were suddenly bright. "Us, we must find Oscar so Wild, and Dorothy Barker and Edward Leer and Walter Sickert."

CHAPTER TWENTY-SEVEN
PLANNING

"ME, I KNOW where Them are," said Ben Gun.

He did not wait for everyone in the command chamber to sit. He blurted out the news without preamble, without thinking. He was smiling wildly and his eyes glistened.

"The Voice, even it does not tell me where Them are," said Walter Sickert.

Holeman Hunt sat down suddenly. Walter Sickert's melodic voice still unnerved all of the Hacker Pack, and some of the Zoo Pack. It was compelling. It was as if the Master's Voice spoke through him.

"Hacker Pack, them have not heard Them," said Ben Gun. "Hacker Pack, them have not heard Them whistle in the tunnels. Tempelhof Pack, them turned us away. Atticus Flinch, him turned us away. Him claimed to be a Hearer, but him had no fear of Them. Tempelhof Pack, them heard no whistles in the tunnels."

"Atticus Flinch, him no Hearer," said Walter Sickert.

"No," said Ben Gun. "Walter Sickert, him the Hearer."

Then he continued.

"Rathaus, them heard the whistle. Rathaus, them feared Them. Rathaus, them scrapped outside. Rathaus, them walked all-away around to come here. Rathaus, them knew something."

"Rathaus Pack, them feral dogs," said Holeman Hunt. "Rathaus them kill Hacker. Them kill Zoo Pack."

"Why?" asked Ben Gun.

"Rathaus, them dead," said Ezra Pound. He was growing impatient. "Why does not matter."

"Warschauer Pack, them territory Track One," said Ben Gun.

"Warschauer Pack, them gone," said Oscar so Wild, "deader and dead."

"Dammed Pack, them territory Track Seven," said Ben Gun.

"Dammed Pack, them mad. Them scrapped outside, blind," said Evelyn War. "Dammed Pack, them deader and dead."

"Zoo Pack, us territory Track Two," said Ben Gun.

"Zoo Pack, us got no fiefdom," said Robert Browning.

"Rathaus, them territory west end Track Two and west end Track Seven," said Ben Gun, triumphant.

There was silence in the room.

"That is why Rathaus Pack scrap with Hacker Pack," said Ben Gun. He realised that he was going to have to explain further what was already clear in his mind. "Rathaus Pack, them had a Hearer. Them knew about Them."

There was sudden uproar in the command chamber. Dorothy Barker stood up to protest, and one or two of the Hacker lieutenants did likewise. They were all talking over each other, challenging the idea that the basest, most feral Aux pack could have a Hearer among them.

"Ben Gun, him is right," said Walter Sickert. The noise died down, and, gradually, those who were standing began to sit, although none had lost their indignation. "A Hearer is just a Hearer. Any Aux, him can be a Hearer. Atticus Flinch, him was clever. Him had muscles in his head. The Tempelhof, them sophisticated, them superior. Still, them sent us away. Them know nothing."

Walter Sickert looked at Ben Gun and gestured for him to continue.

"Tempelhof Pack, Atticus Flinch, him turned us away. Tempelhof Pack, them heard no whistles. Them lost no sentries. Tempelhof Pack, them territory Track Six –"

"Hacker Pack fiefdom Track Six," said Holeman Hunt.

"Rathaus Pack, them were trying to get to Track

Six," said Ben Gun. "Them were trying to run from Them. Rathaus Pack, them had a Hearer. Him knew to run from Track Two. Him knew to run from Track Seven. Him knew Track Six was safe."

"Rathaus Pack, them could have made an alliance," said Oscar so Wild.

"Rathaus Pack, them didn't know how," said Evelyn War. "Rathaus Pack, them were desperate."

"The Dammed, them were desperate, too," said Walter Sickert.

"Us, we know where Them are," said Ben Gun.

"No," said Ezra Pound. "Us, we know where Them have been."

"Us, can we discover where Them will go next?" asked Holeman Hunt. "Us, can we ambush Them?"

For two hours the Hackers and the Zoo Pack in the command chamber pored over the map. The dirt was cleaned off it, but what was underneath was difficult to decipher. The heavy plastic was scuffed and scratched. Although the print appeared to be intact, it was difficult to read through the centuries of wear and tear.

The Aux could only recognise the parts of station names that were familiar to them from regular use of the places they knew well; they did know all the tracks by number. The map itself bore only a passing resemblance to the real tunnels, or to the city of Berlin outside.

"Walter Sickert, you? Doesn't the Voice tell you anything?" asked Ezra Pound in frustration after he had spent long hours studying the map.

"The Voice, it tells me what I tell you," said Walter Sickert.

"Track Nine," said Robert Browning. "Me, I think Them will use Track Nine."

"Why?" asked Holeman Hunt.

"Me, I don't know," said Robert Browning.

"Because Track Six is safe," said Dorothy Barker.

"Because Them like to be underground," said Evelyn War.

"You, you trade with Hansa Pack?" asked Ezra Pound, looking thoughtfully into Holeman Hunt's wounded face. Hunt's jaw tightened and the scab on his face puckered.

"Track Nine," said Holeman Hunt. "Track Nine and we make an alliance with Hansa Pack."

CHAPTER TWENTY-EIGHT
TRACK NINE

THE WAR BAND picked for the foray onto Track Nine and into Hansa Pack territory were the strongest and fittest scrappers at Friedrichstrasse.

Many of them were Zoo Pack; the Hacker Pack had been fighting the Rathaus Pack for too long and most had injuries of one kind or another. Those who did not were tired and had been living in less than ideal conditions for weeks. They needed rest and food. It would boost their morale to feel normal for a spell.

One or two of the lieutenants and a few of the most able beta dogs and dams, including Evelyn War, refused to be left behind. They were declared fit.

Ben Gun was excused duty. He protested loudly and long – it had been his idea, after all – but Ezra

Pound was firm on the matter. Ben was surprised how relieved he felt when he realised that he would be able to remain in the relative safety of the Hacker fiefdom with his friend Walter Sickert.

Dorothy Barker was fit. She had not suffered so much as a pinprick since the fight with her own pack dams back at Old Zoo, and those bruises had healed. She was growing in stature as a scrapper with every battle she joined, and she relished the task ahead of her.

Oscar so Wild was passed fit, but Robert Browning had taken a heavy blow during the battle against the Rathausers. The rib he had cracked in his fight with Wild after the massacre at Warschauer was causing him some pain.

A party of twenty Aux was finally assembled, with Ezra Pound at its head. It included fourteen Zoo Pack and six Hacker scrappers.

Them could make two sentries disappear, but not twenty scrappers, armed and hunting Them down.

Having been selected, the twenty scrappers were led to a room at the end of one of the service tunnels, several hundred metres north along the track.

Dorothy touched the arm of the huge Aux walking alongside her. He had his head down, concentrating. He looked up at her.

"Armoury," he said by way of an explanation.

The Zoo Pack didn't use an armoury. They carried and cared for their own weapons.

The room was divided into two. The left-hand side was piled with metal boxes stacked on their sides with the lids removed, acting as shelves. The whole place smelled of rust, and the grease that protected the weapons from corroding.

The right-hand side of the room was full of racks of weapons. Dorothy assumed that they were weapons, because there were blades and crossbows of various kinds, but there were other things that she did not recognise. Things with tanks, feed lines, nozzles and tubes. There were no rifles.

Dorothy concentrated first on the left as the Hacker Aux and the Zoo Pack scrappers they had buddied up with headed for the weapons. Evelyn was quick to join her.

Immediately on their left were the smallest garments, including gloves, hats, gauntlets and boots. Further along they found vests, jackets and coats, and then pelts.

There were more boxes stacked beyond them. They began to lift familiar things out of the boxes, the sort of leather armour that the Zoo Pack sometimes wore. Then they found harder, heavier things.

Dorothy Barker held up a protective vest and knocked on it with her knuckles, making a sharp rapping sound.

"That, it's strong," said Evelyn. "Blades, them won't cut that."

"This, it's heavy, too," said Dorothy, weighing the armour in her hand. "The Hacker, them have good body armour, better than the Zoo Pack."

Dorothy Barker did not know what Them were, but she was afraid. They were all afraid. Them were legend. Gene the Hackman, the great Aux scrapper, had got whet, had killed Them, deader and dead, but Gene the Hackman was a legend, too.

Dorothy Barker stripped down to her shirt and trousers and found body armour that fit tightly around her torso. Evelyn did the same, and they both added elbow and knee guards.

They looked for jackets to fit closely over the top. Dorothy found a long brown leather jacket that fit snugly over her hips and fastened across her body, right up to her throat. She felt good in it. Safe. Evelyn found a looser jacket in heavy quilted nylon.

They also rummaged around among the headgear, and Dorothy found a close-fitting leather cap. It had no peak, but it had a reinforced skull cap in its lining that would protect her head. Evelyn found a bowl-shaped hard shell cap with a peak.

Satisfied, Dorothy Barker and Evelyn War left the armoury. They were comfortable with their own weapons. They knew the grips and weights of their blades, and how to sight their crossbows for precise targeting.

All of Zoo Pack left the armoury with a change of clothes and with new armour. Some were almost unrecognisable.

The biggest beta dog, Frank Brangwin, emerged in a long leather apron, blackened with grease and scarred with scorch marks. He was wearing gauntlets and a black headpiece that came down over his face, with a blue glass panel across his eyes. He also had a pair of metal cylinder tanks on his back.

It was one of the weapons that Dorothy had seen on the racks in the armoury. She didn't know what it was. She hoped he knew what he was doing.

The Hacker scrappers looked much as they usually did, but one of the big dams was also dressed in a leather apron with a tank array on her back. She had lifted the visor of her mask and reached over to do the same for Frank Brangwin. He smiled sheepishly at her, and Dorothy smirked at Evelyn.

"Me, I hope Frank Brangwin, him knows how to use that weapon," said Evelyn.

"Me, I hope his crush on that Hacker dam doesn't get us all into trouble," said Dorothy Barker.

The jog from Friedrichstrasse to Leopoldplatz was an easy one. It was a little over four kilometres of tracks and tunnels, and the scrappers were comfortable. They were armed and ready. They were also confident that Track Six was safe. The Hearer had said so.

They made the distance in a little over thirty minutes.

Leopoldplatz was quiet. Oscar so Wild and a Zoo Pack dam called Singer Sargent scouted the platform. They also ventured some way towards outside, but they saw and heard nothing. The remainder of the war band then waited while the two Aux descended to the Track Nine platform

Wild and Sargent stood on the platform for two or three seconds, listening intently. Nothing.

Oscar so Wild nodded, and they dropped down onto the track. They waited for another two or three seconds. At his second nod, they began to walk away from each other along the track.

Singer Sargent walked the short length of Track Nine towards its terminus. The track was derelict and had never been used. She heard nothing but the ping and plash of falling water.

Singer Sargent turned back to Oscar so Wild, and shook her head. He shook his in return and they both jogged back to the platform.

A few moments later, twenty Aux scrappers were making their way along Track Nine towards Hansaplatz.

Progress on Track Nine was slow. They were stalking. They were on unknown ground, hunting down an unknown foe. Hunting a monster of legends.

They changed formation regularly so that fresh ears and eyes were always to the fore, but Frank Brangwin or his new mate Vanessa Hell always held a flank, him on the left, her on the right. One backed off as the other stepped forward.

Ezra Pound remained solid in the second rank, always in a position to lead. There was no talking, and orders were given with gestures, although there was little need for them. Check and cover procedures were adopted for service tunnels and for blind curves along the track.

Listening was the key. Listening was always the key.

Every twenty metres or so, the war band stopped to listen. As experienced as all the scrappers were,

there was little they could do about the gravel
beneath their feet. They moved slowly on their
soft-soled boots, but forty Aux feet would always
make some sound on the loose stones. Stopping and
checking was the only way to know for sure that
they didn't miss a whistle or its echo if it came.

Amrumer Strasse was only seven hundred metres
from Leopoldplatz, but it took the twenty Aux
almost two hours to reach the station. They were
still three kilometres from Hansaplatz, and two
from the periphery of Hansa Pack territory. They
were in no man's land.

Half of the war band rested on the platform. Two
pairs of two walked the track in each direction and
took up four sentry positions. Oscar so Wild and
Singer Sargent scouted the route outside.

Nothing.

Ten minutes later, they were back in formation,
walking the track, heading to the next station, eight
hundred metres and another two hours further
away.

There was no evidence that Them had been
above ground. The Dammed and the Rathaus Pack
had been driven out of the tunnels by Them. The
Dammed had gone blind and died at the hands of
the Zoo Pack. The Rathaus had grown ever more
feral and died at the hands of the new alliance. The
Warschauer had perished underground in their own
fiefdom.

No one had heard a whistle outside. No one had
seen a footprint, or other marks in the ice. No

one had gone missing outside. Everyone had been accounted for at the end of every battle fought in the open.

Them were in the tunnels. The tunnels were cold, had always been cold, but never as cold as outside. The tunnels had always shown the breath of the Aux, but not now. Where the Aux gathered, the warmth of their bodies drove the temperature up above zero. Where the Aux gathered, they shed their clothes, unused to the heat. The Time of Ice had ended underground before it had ended outside.

Them had survived the Time of Ice. Them had survived hundreds of years of hibernation. Now Them were waking up, and Them were waking up underground.

The war band walked the track, stopping regularly to listen, changing formation as they walked, ever watchful.

They checked service tunnels, but they saw nothing and they heard nothing. They hadn't spoken a single word to each other for four hours. The only sounds were the crunch of gravel and stones shifting beneath the soles of their boots, the faint rustle of the two heavily armed Aux's leather aprons and the ping and plash of falling water.

There was no sign of Them. There was no blood and no fresh wounds in the walls of the tunnels. There were no recently broken blades or bent crossbows. There was no rent cloth. There were no bodies.

There were never any bodies.

The war band stopped at the Track Nine platform at Westhafen. They remained diligent. They set up sentries on the track while most of the Aux took a short rest on the platform. Dorothy Barker and a Hacker called Austin Spar checked the station beyond the platform and listened for sounds outside.

All was clear.

The four-hour trek had been exhausting, so Ezra Pound gestured that, since they had the all-clear, the war band should extend the halt to take some rations onboard.

Some Aux preferred not to eat on the hunt; they liked to travel light. Others disliked the distraction of hunger. Evelyn couldn't eat. All took the time to drink, taking advantage of the camelbacks carried by four of the scrappers. Sentries were switched out and twenty minutes passed.

Finally, when ration packs had been stowed, Ezra Pound gave the order with a flick of his hand, and the war band assembled on the track for the next leg of the long walk.

CHAPTER TWENTY-NINE
THEM

THE SOUND, WHEN it came, was not a whistle, or the echo of a whistle. The sound, when it came, was a long hard shriek. It was like an Aux dam dying at whelping time, but louder and angrier.

The Them that made it wasn't getting ready to die.

The Them that made the sound was getting ready to kill.

They had had no warning. They had not heard the hard, scratching *tiktiktik* sound of chitin on the metal track; or the sounds of bone-hard claws on gravel; or any other sounds.

Half the Aux stopped dead, immobilised by terror. One of the Hackers stumbled as his vision blurred, and the blood drained from his extremities.

There was no one to catch him. His hand spasmed

as he began to shake, and he shot a bolt from his crossbow into the thigh of the Aux in front of him. The injured Zoo Packer faltered, but the bolt had gone straight through the muscle of his leg, missing the bone. Angered, he growled low.

He was one of the lucky ones. The pain and shock made him raise his crossbow. Then, seeing what he saw, seeing the size of the Them and the horror of it, he turned and ran.

The Them was hanging high in the ceiling of the tunnel when it screeched, swinging its head as it screamed its battle cry out over the heads of its enemies.

The *tiktiktik* sounds of hard shell against gravel and metal came only as the Them dropped down onto Track Nine to attack the Aux.

Even crouching on the tracks, the Them was taller than two Aux. Its thorax was like a great barrel tapering to a narrow waist, suspended over a hard ball of an abdomen. The four long, jointed forelimbs that swung from its torso ended in curved, barbed blades. Its bulbous head stretching forwards on a scrawny neck had four bulging wide set eyes and a vast round mouth. The lowest segments of its rear legs were heavy and ended in huge clawed feet. Its hard, bony shell was a vivid green colour, unlike anything the Aux had ever seen. They lived in the dark below ground and in a world of ice and frost and snow above. The shock of orange roofs and red brick walls in the thaw was nothing compared to the iridescence of the Them's glossy carapace.

It reared onto its hind legs, doubling its height, filling the tunnel in front of the horrified Aux.

Ezra Pound was the first with his crossbow up. He got the first shot in. He did not hesitate, he did not blink. He could not blink; his mouth was wide open in an almighty roar that could not be heard even by those closest to him over the echoes of the monster's shriek. He loaded a second bolt, and a third. He kept shooting, and kept howling.

Nothing penetrated. Ezra Pound's well-aimed bolts ricocheted off the carapace of the Them and fell away, harmless.

William and Peter Blade, brothers and seasoned Zoo Pack scrappers died in the same moment as a vast, hooked chitin blade swept through them, a great, barbed forelimb, speckled in lurid shades of glowing green.

Ezra Pound ducked low and fired almost vertically, aiming for the only flesh he could see. It was where the screeches were coming from, red and raw, but it was like no mouth the Alpha dog had ever seen: a great, dripping hole, lined with concentric circles of spiny dentition. His next bolt disappeared into the great maw, and its shriek was strangled as the circles of teeth seemed to fold inwards.

The flailing arms never stopped swinging. Arthur Rimbaud, who had scrapped for Zoo Pack for several seasons, and was strong and solid, but had never shown any great talent with blade or crossbow, was swept up by one of the Them's claws when it could not penetrate his borrowed body armour.

He thrashed and wailed as he was manhandled towards the creature's head. Finally, with nothing left to lose, he fired his crossbow one-handed into what should have been the Them's face.

The bolt hit something soft and penetrated, probably an eye. The angered Them tossed its head and cried out again, giving Ezra Pound a target to aim at. His bolt made contact with the back of Arthur Rimbaud's head as the Them fed him into its wide open mouth. It was a merciful death.

Those scrappers that were paralysed with fear were easy targets. They were laid waste to in seconds, picked off and hacked to pieces by the Them. The rest scattered.

Some hugged the tunnel walls, shooting their crossbows at the Them's impenetrable bony shell, when they could hit their target at all. The Them moved faster than fast. Skittle-scuttle fast. Its cutting limbs were a blur of luminous green, and its thorax swung and twisted with every move of those four terrifying scythes.

One or two of the lieutenants shouted orders that nobody could hear above the shrieks of the beast, and Ezra Pound kept up a constant howl of menace and outrage.

Dorothy Barker and Evelyn War both made it to the tunnel wall. They kept loading and shooting their crossbows, hoping that something would hit and if it hit that it might penetrate. All the time they stuck together, shoulder to shoulder. They never lost contact with the reassuring touch of another Aux as they backed away from the fight.

Westhafen station and outside were only seconds away. Neither Dorothy nor Evelyn wanted to run, not yet. They had been in this together since Warschauer.

Vanessa Hell had been towards the rear of the group when the Them had shrieked its first appalling scream. She had been one of the first to run.

Frank Brangwin, on the left flank, was right in front of the Them when it dropped out of the tunnel ceiling. He fumbled with the nozzle of his weapon, twisted to adjust something on the tank when he couldn't make it fire, struggled, panicked and fell hard on his back.

There was a strong smell of gasoline as one of the old tanks split beneath him. Struggling frantically to right himself and deploy his weapon, Brangwin didn't see death coming.

He died instantly as his head was crudely severed from his body, fresh blood adding to the grease and scorch marks on his leather apron

Oscar so Wild had been towards the rear of the war band when the screech had gone out, and he'd been passed by the first runners. He did not stop them.

He broke formation and made for the tunnel wall to his right, his crossbow aimed. His first shot missed. He fumbled loading a second bolt, but his aim was true. It ricocheted off the Them. He didn't know what part of the monster's body he'd hit, but he saw the bolt fly off and hit the tunnel wall opposite.

Then he saw Ezra Pound crouching right in front of the Them. Oscar so Wild's hands were shaking. It took him twice as long as it should to load a third bolt into his crossbow. He didn't dare shoot it, because he didn't know if his hands would manage to load a fourth.

Oscar so Wild sidled up the tunnel, his back tight to the wall, until he was level with Ezra Pound.

"Alpha dog," he called, but he could not hear his own voice above the raging scream of the Them. Ezra Pound was intent on the battle, shooting and reloading his crossbow and shooting again. It was futile. Oscar so Wild could see that it was futile.

Scant metres from him, Somerset Mourn, a Zoo Pack dam that he knew well, whom he had served in war bands with for many seasons, was sliced in three before his eyes.

She was divided from the right hip to the left shoulder. Her left arm hit the ground first, then her torso, with the right arm attached. Her legs looked as though they would remain standing indefinitely, but they followed a short while after.

Ezra Pound kept firing, and the Them kept swinging. Oscar so Wild's fear left him. He felt suddenly very calm for a moment. Then he was filled with rage. His leader, the Alpha dog Ezra Pound, was squatting in a tunnel filled with the bloody corpses of his scrappers, facing down the Them; and it was futile.

Oscar so Wild suddenly couldn't stand the sight of it, the thought of it. He dropped his crossbow and reached for his blades. He took two long strides into the centre of the tunnel beside Ezra Pound, the double blades – one in each hand – held wide from his body.

Oscar so Wild roared.

"Get whet!"

A wry smile ghosted across Ezra Pound's face as he heard the battle cry over the echoes of the Them's squeal.

Oscar so Wild swung his blades at the Them's hind limbs, which clung to the rails by its curved yellow talons. He ducked clear of chitin blades, and aimed for the joints, hoping to find some weakness.

Oscar so Wild's blades hit hard green shell and did not penetrate, but the force of the blows made the limbs jerk. The Them's swinging, killing arms flailed and it became more erratic.

The Them shrieked in frustration, its scything blades slowing as it steadied itself.

Ezra Pound was finally able to get off his knees. He shot another bolt into the Them's screaming maw, and began to move to his left. He had no scrappers left to defend, no battle left to fight.

Oscar so Wild swung one blade and then the other, aiming both at the joint in the Them's right hind limb. Shards of speckled shell sprayed from the wound he finally managed to inflict, and the joint buckled.

Oscar so Wild saw his chance and began to run.

He did not look over his shoulder, but hoped that the Alpha dog was doing the same. He could see Evelyn War ahead of him. She was the only Aux left alive in the tunnel. She still had her crossbow raised. She had stayed and she had seen everything.

In one last ditch effort before he retreated, Ezra Pound slung his crossbow over his shoulder and pulled his own blade as he saw the Them lurch towards him, injured. He swung the blade only once. It glanced off one of the Them's curved forelimbs, and the momentum drove the blade down hard onto the track rail, sending sparks flying.

There was a sudden *WHOOMP* as the spilled gasoline from Frank Brangwin's weapon lit on fire, and Ezra Pound was enveloped in the blaze. He staggered for a moment.

VABOOM! The tunnel was filled with light and noise as the second tank on Frank Brangwin's back exploded violently.

Oscar so Wild flew at Evelyn as she dropped her crossbow, taking her down with him onto the track as the tank exploded. The blast was at his back, hitting him hard, and bowling them both over. He landed on top of Evelyn between the rails.

He managed to clamber off her and help her to her feet as she doubled over, coughing. She'd been winded by the sudden weight of Wild's body falling on top of her

Oscar so Wild wanted to see Ezra Pound walking out of the flames, but he knew it could never happen.

It was impossible to see anything in the glare of the intense fire. Evelyn saw nothing as she clutched her hands to her face against the bright flares of the explosion, but they both heard one last penetrating shriek. It was different from before; this was not a battle cry, but the sound a creature made when it was doomed and dying.

Oscar so Wild pulled his eyeshades from his pocket, and he stood and watched. He felt he owed it to Ezra Pound.

He could hardly discern the body of the Alpha dog, no more than a pathetic mound to one side of the tracks in the tunnel. The Them, wreathed in flames, bucked and tossed its body. It threw back its head and screeched.

The last echoes of the explosion overlapped with the shrill scream of the Them's death throes, and then the scream took over, reverberating through the tunnel.

Finally, the Them fell, toppling headlong, nothing but a stinking ball of flames, black smoke billowing from it.

The smell was like nothing Evelyn War had ever known, sour and acrid. The Them did not burn with the sweet smell of meat, but with the smell of charring claws and hair.

Both Aux pushed their head cloths closer into their noses and mouths to keep the stench at bay. Wild took one last look down the tunnel to be sure that the Them had perished. The last of the echoes abated and then he put an arm around

Evelyn, her head still on her chest, and led her up and outside.

Evelyn War never thought that she would mourn the death of the Zoo Pack leader, but her view of him had changed on the long Walk Around. Today, she had also seen his bravery in the tunnels.

CHAPTER THIRTY
DECIMATED

ONLY SIX OF the original twenty remained.

They were dazed shellshocked, and some of them were injured. The landscape was broad and flat, aside from a few derelict buildings. It was the site of the old overground railway station; somewhere below the ice sat the old tracks.

The Aux could see and hear for hundreds of metres in all directions. There was no threat outside. It was cold, and they were not dressed for it. They could not remain above ground for long. They stood or paced, remaining in a tight group, but no one stood guard. No one took charge.

Vanessa Hell was inconsolable. She could not believe that she had run, that she had left Frank Brangwin behind. She did not want to believe that he was dead, and she blamed herself. Dorothy Barker blamed her too.

They all heard the explosion.

"Ezra Pound, him deader and dead," said Dorothy Barker. It was a statement of fact, to no one in particular. "Evelyn War, her dead too, and Oscar so Wild."

"Alpha dog, him tougher and tough," said one of the other Zoo Packers, indignant. But they all knew there was no hope for the Zoo Pack leader and his lieutenant, or for Evelyn War, who had been the beginning of everything.

"Holeman Hunt, him Alpha dog now," said Vanessa Hell.

Dorothy Barker made a sound that bordered on disgust, but no one questioned it. It was not the time.

The six Aux turned at the sound, but none of them raised a weapon. They should have been on high alert, but they were tired and shocked. They were more curious than guarded.

Oscar so Wild and Evelyn War emerged from the station.

Dorothy Barker took a dozen long strides towards them.

"Ezra Pound?" asked Dorothy.

Oscar so Wild shook his head. Dorothy Barker threw a hard punch at the lieutenant's shoulder. Then she looked sternly at him. She did not apologise for the attack, and he did not expect her to.

She put an arm around Evelyn War.

"Me, I'm glad to see you," she said. "You both."

"Yes," said Wild.

"The Them, it is dead," said Evelyn.

"Are there more?" asked Dorothy Barker.

Oscar so Wild shrugged.

"There will always be more of Them," said Evelyn War.

They were still looking at one another, standing no more than a metre apart. The rest of the remnant of the war band had remained standing at a distance. They did not want to hear, or could not bear to.

Dorothy Barker glanced at Evelyn War and lowered her voice so that there was less risk of the others hearing her.

"There are no more of Them," she said. "Us, we have to believe there are no more. Us, we cannot stay outside. We have to walk all-away around the tunnels."

"To Hansa Pack?" asked Oscar Wild. "Or back to Hacker Pack?"

Dorothy Barker shook her head. She would have no part in that decision.

Oscar so Wild looked at Evelyn War. Their eyes locked for a moment.

"Oscar so Wild, you Alpha dog now," said Evelyn.

The lieutenant looked over his shoulder at the ragtag group of Aux that remained from the original war band. Only eight of them, including himself, and no leader but himself. They could not kill the Them when they were fresh and there were almost three times as many.

"Us, we walk to Friedrichstrasse," he said, "faster and fast. Us, we talk to the Hearer. Us, we talk to Holeman Hunt."

Oscar so Wild puffed out his chest and made himself look as big as he could. He set his face, glanced once between Evelyn and Dorothy at the other scrappers, and then, holding his head high, he walked towards the shabby group of Aux.

"The Them, it is dead," he said. His voice was steady, confident, rising from his chest. He had to lead these seven Aux back through the tunnels of Track Nine. He had to give them the confidence to go back underground. "Ezra Pound, Alpha dog, him gave his life. Us, we will return to Hacker Pack, regroup and return."

He stood before the huddled group, Dorothy Barker and Evelyn at either shoulder.

"You, ready your weapons," he bellowed.

One or two blinked at him and the rest stared. Oscar so Wild growled low, as if about to unleash a torrent of rage upon them.

All Aux scrappers had known the wrath of a seasoned, embittered lieutenant at some point in their training, and they all remembered it now. They readied their weapons; one or two fumbled, but recovered. They were all armed with loaded crossbows or blades within a second or two.

Vanessa Hell had the nozzle of her flame thrower clutched in both hands, the visor of her mask in place.

"You," said Oscar so Wild, pointing at the big Aux dam, "bring up the rear."

Oscar so Wild turned to lead the way back down onto Track Nine, Dorothy Barker and Evelyn War beside him. The remaining five Aux kept a respectful distance, half a dozen paces behind their new leader.

"Why her?" Dorothy Barker asked Oscar so Wild. "Her, she ran, she got Frank Brangwin, him killed."

"Fire," said Wild. "The Them is killed by fire. Blades and fire."

Dorothy Barker slung her crossbow over her back and pulled her stilettos.

"Are there more?" asked Dorothy Barker again.

"Yes," said Evelyn War. "There will always be more Them."

CHAPTER THIRTY-ONE
RETREAT

THEY DID NOT stalk. They did not listen for the whistle or the echo of a whistle. An echo of a whistle meant nothing. Silence meant nothing. Them could be anywhere at any time. Them were in the tunnels of Track Nine.

"Us, we move fast," said Oscar so Wild as the war band dropped down onto the track at the Westhafen platform. They did not check and cover. They did not walk the track to listen. They did not hunt. They were in retreat.

They kept formation three abreast, with Vanessa Hell to the rear. Oscar so Wild took the centre position in the first rank. Dorothy Barker took the left flank and Evelyn War the right, in the second rank.

Many more Zoo Pack had been lost to the Them than Hackers; they had stood for longer against the beast. Conan Doyle, who had been shot through the leg, was the slowest of the Aux, but he had bound his leg and was fit and strong.

He managed to move well, but with an awkward gait. He walked on Wild's left and kept up a good pace. Vanessa Hell and Frank Brangwin, with their cumbersome clothing and the weight of their weapons, had set the war band's pace for the jog down Track Six on the way out.

Hell was almost as slow as Doyle, particularly with the extra weight of fear, guilt and grief that she was carrying. The two of them set the pace back to Leopoldplatz.

No consideration was given to the noise they made. No one cared how much scraping and kicking Doyle did with his wounded leg, or how much clanging Hell's tanks made. It didn't matter. Speed mattered.

They made good time, urging one another on. They staggered to a near-halt only once, bunching up in the tunnel when Conan Doyle's leg spasmed and kicked out from under him. Oscar so Wild ducked down, put a shoulder under the Aux's arm and lifted him back to his feet in one swift movement. They loped along together for a hundred metres or so before Doyle picked up speed again, and was able to continue unassisted.

Adrenaline drove them. They made the kilometre and a half back to Leopoldplatz in less than twenty minutes.

The climb up to Track Six was a relief. Vanessa Hell and Conan Doyle walked side by side in the centre of the Pack as they took a slightly slower pace along Track Six towards Friedrichstrasse.

They were the two weakest members of the war band. One of the two other Hackers, a male called Richard Gall, took Vanessa Hell's weapon and headgear from her and brought up the rear with his other packmate.

Vanessa Hell had not stopped sobbing since they left Westhafen. She began keening once they had been safely on track for a few minutes. Doyle tried to console her, but he was tired and his leg ached. Dorothy became increasingly irritated with the dam.

"You, you'll lure the Them back with your mating call," she said over her shoulder.

Vanessa Hell cried out in alarm.

Oscar so Wild glared at Dorothy, and said, "The Them, it is dead. It burned up on Track Nine. Track Six, it is safe."

"There will be more Them," said Conan Doyle, "tougher and tough."

Evelyn glanced at the wounded Aux, but said nothing.

No one else spoke for the hour it took for the eight Aux to make their way back to Friedrichstrasse.

They were brought in by the sentries posted to meet them. Word was sent ahead of their imminent arrival, and the always busy platform thronged with Aux as the war band made its way up the track towards it.

There were whispers and gasps as they came into view. Soon the gathered Aux were wondering at how few had returned, and how wretched they appeared to be.

Holeman Hunt stood on the tracks to greet the returning heroes. He already knew how decimated the war band was from his sentries' reports. He also knew that Ezra Pound was not among them.

Holeman Hunt embraced Oscar so Wild. He clenched his forearm and bumped chests with him. He formally recognised the authority of the lieutenant in front of his own pack, and in front of Zoo Pack. He recognised him as Alpha dog, as an equal.

"Oscar so Wild, you Alpha dog, now," he said.

"Ezra Pound, him is dead," said Oscar so Wild. "Zoo Pack, we have no fiefdom. Zoo Pack, we have no Alpha dog. Zoo Pack, we have no name. Us, we are all Hacker Pack now."

Silence fell among the Aux, Zoo Pack and Hacker alike as they took in the lieutenant's meaning.

Oscar so Wild stepped out of Holeman Hunt's embrace and nodded at his new leader. He looked over his shoulder at Dorothy Barker and Evelyn War, who also nodded at Holeman Hunt.

Holeman Hunt frowned.

"Us, we can discuss this further," he said. "The Them, is it dead?"

"It is dead," said Oscar so Wild.

"Then it is over," said Holeman Hunt.

The throng of Aux let out a celebratory whoop and a cheer. Some wept for the fallen, but they would be celebrated in the tales of the future. They would not be lost to oblivion. The Aux gathered on the platform started to talk among themselves of retrieving the bodies and of celebrating. It was over.

"It is not over," Walter Sickert's eerie voice echoed around the tunnel, and the crowd fell silent once more.

"Them are many," he said. "Us, we know now what Them are and how Them die.

"Now it begins."

CHAPTER THIRTY-TWO
BLADES AND FIRE

LONG HOURS WERE spent discussing Them and the threat they posed. Them could not be ignored. Killing one was not enough.

"There is strength in numbers," said Walter Sickert.

"My father, him said that, too," said Evelyn War. "Us, we must make alliances. The Aux, we must stand together."

"Tempelhof Pack, them turned us away," said Oscar so Wild. "Them have territory on Track Six. Tempelhof Pack, them are safe."

"Atticus Flinch, him despised Ezra Pound, Alpha dog," said Robert Browning. "Tempelhof, them might make alliance with Holeman Hunt."

"No," said Walter Sickert. "Atticus Flinch, him no Hearer. Him no Alpha dog."

"Hansa Pack," said Holeman Hunt. "Us, we make an alliance with Hansa Pack."

"Them, their territory is Track Nine," said Dorothy Barker.

"Us, we killed the Them," said Holeman Hunt. "Us, we can kill more Them."

"That, it was a fluke," said Oscar so Wild. "The Them, it killed twelve Aux. The Aux, them didn't get whet."

"Oscar so Wild, you got whet," said Dorothy Barker. "Ezra Pound, him got whet."

"No," said the lieutenant.

"Oscar so Wild, you got whet, you felled the Them," said Evelyn War.

The dams had seen it. They had not run. They had retreated, because they had no choice, but they had not run scared. And even when Dorothy had left, Evelyn had stayed.

"Me, I saw it. Me, I saw your blade fell the Them. Me, I saw Ezra Pound, him raise his blade."

"You, what else did you see?" asked Oscar so Wild.

"Nothing," said Dorothy Barker, her head dropping in shame. "Me, I turned away. Me, I believed in Ezra Pound, Alpha dog. Me, I saw the Them felled. Me, I thought the Them, him was killed, deader and dead."

"The fire, it killed the Them," said Evelyn War.

"Then us, we take fire," said Holeman Hunt.

"Better to fight Them outside," said Walter Sickert. "Gene the Hackman, him got whet and him killed Them, deader and dead. Him killed Them outside."

"Them are underground," said Oscar so Wild. "Them are only underground."

"Us, we cannot escape Them in the tunnels," said Dorothy Barker. "Them are fast, skittle-scuttle fast. Us, we cannot scatter. Us, we cannot hide. Us, we cannot take cover in the tunnels."

They had wrestled with the problem for hours and no one had anything new to say. Edward Leer had listened. He was used to being listened to – he was the tale-teller – but he had listened. When no one had anything left to say, he began.

"Gene the Hackman, top dog, him done the great Walk Around," he said. "Not for him the darkness, not for him the cold, not for him the Time of Ice. Gene the Hackman, him got whet. Gene the Hackman, him got whet and walked the Earth, and him killed Them.

"Two-Feet-Walk-on-the-Ground, him ran the World. Him big fella. Them hated him very much. Two-Feet-Walk-on-the-Ground, him make Gene the Hackman to keep Them off his lawn and him sleep long time. Two-Feet-Walk-on-the-Ground, him the Master. Gene the Hackman, him keep Them off the lawn while the Master sleep long time.

"Them got together, tighter and tight. And Gene the Hackman, him Heard his Master's Voice and him got whet and him killed Them. Him clever; him had muscles in his head. Him knew the one thing always drew Them quickest. Him built fires and

Them come. Him pulled his two great blades and him swung and him hacked and him scrapped and him killed Them, deader and dead.

"Gene the Hackman, him heard the Master's Voice and him felt the Urgings. Gene the Hackman, him led the Pack on the Walk Around, and him kept the lawn clean of Them."

"Blades and fire," said Oscar so Wild.

"The best blades and the deadliest fire," said Holeman Hunt.

"Them like the fire," said Walter Sickert.

"Then us, we use it to catch them and we use it to kill them," said Oscar so Wild. "Zoo Pack, we avenge Ezra Pound, Alpha dog's death."

Dorothy Barker clenched her fist and punched the air, ferociously.

"And us, we make an alliance with Hansa Pack," said Evelyn War.

Dorothy Barker loosened the fist and put her arm around her pack sister, squeezing her shoulder.

"Us, we make an alliance, tougher and tough," she said. "There is strength in numbers."

"Me, I can do fire," said Ben Gun. He had said little throughout the meeting, except to back up Walter Sickert or to agree with Evelyn War. He was loyal, and would remain loyal, whatever the cost.

Holeman Hunt laughed at the pup. Everyone had always laughed at Ben Gun. He didn't care. Evelyn War, Robert Browning and Dorothy Barker didn't care either. They had scrapped with Ben Gun. They appreciated the value of his ideas. He understood how to listen and he understood how things worked.

"Let the pup, him speak," said Evelyn War.

Holeman Hunt glanced at the Zoo Pack dam.

"Let him speak," said Oscar so Wild, quietly.

"You, speak," said Holeman Hunt. Ezra Pound was dead, but the alliance was solid; it meant more now than ever.

The Hacker Pack Alpha dog did not want to be responsible for dozens more Aux in conditions that were already difficult. He did not want one of his own lieutenants to get the bone to challenge him, or one of Zoo Pack's. Better to respect Oscar so Wild. Better Oscar so Wild should be Alpha dog and Zoo Pack should remain.

"Me, I have my slingshot," said Ben Gun. "Me, I can make a fire wherever you want it. Me, I can shoot a spark into your fuel and light any fire at a distance."

"Ben Gun, him is right," said Evelyn.

The next two hours were spent devising a plan.

At the same time the Hacker lieutenant John Steel was sent to rouse Zoo Pack scrappers. They would need training with the flame weapons.

The armoury was opened and whetstones prepared. All blades would be honed.

Blades and fire. The Them would be killed by blades and fire, deader and dead.

CHAPTER THIRTY-THREE
TWO WAR BANDS

TWO WAR BANDS left Friedrichstrasse before first light.

A large force, mostly of Zoo Pack scrappers, left overland for Hansaplatz. The Zoo Pack had experience of the outside. They were confident on the slick ice and better understood the changing nature of the city. They knew how it felt and sounded. They understood the threat of the ice falls and how to predict them, and they understood the movements of the rodents. They had encountered the Dammed and had overcome them.

The Hackers had fought the Rathaus. They had retreated below ground and had reduced their territory, but they had not gone the long Walk Around. They had not been outside, except to do battle.

The war band, forty strong, headed south for Hansaplatz. They hoped to find the Hansa Pack, to join forces with them, to make an alliance.

Robert Browning led the expedition. He took two of Holeman Hunt's lieutenants with him, including John Steel.

Evelyn War insisted that she accompany him. Walter Sickert was not fit for another long trek outside, and the war band needed to move fast. So Evelyn War wanted to represent her father. She was the best choice.

"Robert Browning, you take Evelyn War," said Holeman Hunt after a long discussion. "You make the long Walk Around to Hansa Pack."

The rest of the scrappers would return to the tunnels.

It was a classic pincer movement. The Aux would flush out the Them, drive them above ground and hope to do battle with them outside.

The Aux would die. They knew they would die in the tunnels if they failed. They knew they would die in the tunnels if they succeeded. Death was inevitable. Death had always been inevitable for the Aux scrappers.

Every scrapper, Zoo Pack and Hacker, carried gasoline. Every scrapper that walked the long Walk Around and every scrapper that walked the tunnels.

When every flame weapon tank was full and strapped to an Aux back, camelbacks that weren't needed for water supplies were filled with gasoline.

When they were all full, jerry cans and water bottles were filled with gasoline.

They were strapped to backs, hung around shoulders and attached to belts. Every scrapper had a supply of gasoline somewhere on his body. The biggest, strongest scrappers carried the most, but everyone carried at least three litres of the fuel, including Ben Gun.

"Me, I made a big promise," said Ben Gun, sitting in one of the service tunnels where the light was good, a large bottle of gasoline, and wadding, tinder and sinew in piles at his side. He was toying with pieces of felt as he sat next to Evelyn.

"You's a scrapper, tougher and tough," said Evelyn War.

She took hold of his chin in her hand and turned his face towards her, looking him fiercely in his yellow eyes. "You's the best Aux with a sling shot, truer and true."

"How?" asked Ben holding out a handful of felt and tinder to Evelyn.

"Me, I will help," said Evelyn.

They tried different methods of making the little missiles, testing them as they went along. Finally one of Evelyn's little balls lit with a bright flame that didn't fizzle out.

Ben and Evelyn spent an hour making projectiles. Dry, flammable wadding was scarce and highly prized, so their supply of it was limited. They supplemented it with felt and sawdust to make firm little parcels of tinder. They soaked them in gasoline, rolling them and tying them tight. Then Ben carefully stored them in a waxed pouch so that they wouldn't dry out.

Ben Gun spent another hour making a fireproof slingshot. The flame-retardant fabric was inflexible and unforgiving, unlike the leather he was used to. It wasn't subtle and didn't flex in his hands or with the movement of his arm.

Evelyn watched, and then took the slingshot from him. She untied the strings of fabric from the pouch and began to weave them into cords. She tried two or three different ways to weave the cord, but nothing gave Ben the accuracy he needed. On her third try, she realised that if she twisted threads of the fabric and then plaited them loosely, she would gain more stretch in the cord. Ben tried the slingshot again.

With another hour's practice, Ben Gun was getting within five centimetres of his target every time he slung a stone. It was close enough.

Evelyn snickered with glee.

Holeman Hunt had given him a sparking mechanism, a flint with a metal wheel that fit neatly in his hand. He lit a spark under one of his projectiles, cradled in his slingshot, then whipped his arm and aimed. It hit the fifteen-centimetre square of felt he was targeting, and a small blaze erupted that lasted for four or five seconds until the fuel in the missile was used up and the felt burnt to embers.

"Ouch!" he cried. He sucked his scorched fingers idly as he watched the little fire, mesmerised.

Gloves... He needed gloves.

Ben Gun thought about it and wondered whether he could fire his slingshot accurately with gloved hands. Then he remembered the Dammed. He remembered the exhilaration he had felt. He had been wearing gloves outside.

He turned to Evelyn War

"Me, I'm ready," he said.

Every able-bodied Aux had a role to play.

The injured and the infants remained at Friedrichstrasse, but everyone who was mobile, everyone who could don outside clothes and fix metal to his boots, any Aux who could survive outside for a few hours had a job to do.

They were divided into groups, according to fitness. The most able would travel the furthest and endure the most. The least able would travel only as far as Track Six took them to Leopoldplatz.

Hansaplatz was four kilometres away, and it would take more than two hours for them to march down the tracks. They had hand carts and barrows for the gasoline, and they had a gut full of determination.

The rest would travel outside from Leopoldplatz to Amrumer, Westhafen, Birkenstrasse and Turmstrasse. Some would have to travel four kilometres underground, then another three kilometres outside. It would take time and effort.

Only six Aux were chosen for the Turmstrasse war band. All had one or both arms missing and could not wield weapons. They didn't need to; they needed strong legs to walk on and strong backs to haul fuel. It was enough for them.

Long after Robert Browning's war band had left Friedrichstrasse for the long Walk Around to Hansplatz, long after the veteran Aux had been deployed, Holeman Hunt and Oscar so Wild took their three dozen Aux for the jog along Track Six to Leopoldplatz.

They dropped down to Track Nine, and began their journey south towards Hansa territory. They did not expect to make it there without encountering Them.

They were most at risk. The Them had attacked without warning. There had been no whistle and no echo. It had hidden in the ceiling space of the tunnel, and had kept silence until it had shrieked its horrendous battle cry, and then it had descended among them.

It had slaughtered the Aux without mercy.

Their crossbow bolts had not penetrated its carapace. Only Oscar so Wild's blades had made any impact on it. Only an accident had saved them, an accident that had killed the Zoo Pack leader.

Twelve Aux had died because of the Them. Twelve Aux that had been hunting the Them had been killed by their prey.

Oscar so Wild took his position front and centre with a Hacker Pack scrapper on either side of him. Each wore a protective apron and a visor. Each carried the tanks of a fire thrower on his back.

They jogged with the flame nozzles held waist-high in both hands in front of them. They were armed and ready. Still Oscar so Wild didn't trust them. They had not seen what he had seen. He was glad that he had made sure his blades were honed.

Holeman Hunt took the flank in the second row. He, too, carried blades. Every row after that consisted of a pair of Aux, hugging the tunnel walls. Each pair had one Aux carrying a flame weapon and one carrying blades. The formation should allow them to surround any single Them that attacked, so that they could counterattack from all sides.

That was one plan.

CHAPTER THIRTY-FOUR
HANSA PACK

ROBERT BROWNING'S WAR band arrived at Hansaplatz at the end of a long Walk Around. The journey had been without incident. Some of the Hackers had been aghast at the scenes they had passed through, at the streets and buildings.

They were wary of travelling the broad thoroughfares that were anathema to them, but they did as they were ordered. Progress was fast. The scrappers grew in confidence as time passed and they encountered no threats, from feral Aux or from anything else.

Even the cold did not penetrate as it once had.

Hansa Pack sentries picked up the war band, but seemed relieved to see them, especially John Steel, who was familiar to them. They were immediately invited underground.

"John Steel, you are welcome," said Makewar Thackeray, Alpha dog of the Hansa Pack. "Me, I know why you are here. Hansa Pack, we have lost Aux. Hansa Pack, we hear echoes in the tunnels. Hansa Pack tale-teller, him tells old myths."

"Them," said Evelyn War, stepping forward to introduce herself.

Hansa Pack had been trading and bartering with Hacker Pack for generations. They were on friendly terms. They often found mates among each other's packs.

It was not difficult for Makewar Thackeray to throw in his lot with his old friend John Steel and pledge an alliance to Holeman Hunt and the Hackers.

He was one of the youngest of the pack leaders. He was strong and keen, but he was not too proud to take advice from a more experienced Alpha dog like Holeman Hunt. Negotiations were completed in an hour.

"Where did the sentries, them disappear?" asked Evelyn War. "When?"

"For three days," said Makewar Thackeray. "First at Güntzelstrasse. Hansa Pack, we keep a sentry there, because of the Dammed. The Dammed, them have gone quiet these last days."

"The Dammed, them are gone, deader and dead," said Robert Browning.

Makewar Thackeray frowned in surprised.

"Them killed the Dammed?" asked one of his lieutenants. "The Dammed, them were fierce, tougher and tough."

"No," said Browning. "Zoo Pack, we killed the Dammed. Outside. The Dammed, them were blinded outside, them were desperate, them were running from Them. Us, we killed the Dammed, tougher and tough."

A gasp went up in the command chamber at Hansaplatz. The Dammed were among the most dangerous and most feral of the Aux. No Aux Pack went up against the Dammed, or the Rathaus, but the Zoo Pack had done it and they had triumphed.

"Where else?" asked John Steel, getting Makewar Thackeray back on track.

"Westhafen," said the Alpha dog. "Two Hansa scrappers, them disappeared at Westhafen."

"We killed the Them at Westhafen, deader and dead," said Robert Browning. "Ezra Pound, tougher and tough, him died killing the Them."

"Ezra Pound, him a legend," said Makewar Thackeray. "Him like Gene the Hackman."

There was silence in the command chamber for a moment as the Aux bowed their heads.

"Two war bands," said John Steel. "Us, we must make two war bands. Us, we must walk Track Nine to Guntzelstrasse."

"What about the plan?" asked Evelyn War.

"John Steel, him is right," said Robert Browning. "Us, we must send a kill team to Guntzelstrasse and us, we must send a war band to walk Track Nine to Leopoldplatz."

"Us, we cannot halve the war band," said Evelyn War. "Us, we are not enough."

"Us, we will walk the track to Guntzelstrasse," said Makewar Thackeray. "Us, we will take care of our own."

Hansa Pack did not have flame weapons, but they were experts with blades, particularly halberds and long-handled axes. They took great pride in their weapons, in the quality of their blades and the sharpness of their edges. Nevertheless, John Steel insisted that he hand over two of their own fire throwers and instruct half a dozen of the Hansa in their use.

"It is time," said Evelyn, urgently, once the weapons were handed over, and John Steel had gone over the instructions three times. "Us, we must leave."

All along Track Nine, the veteran Aux of Zoo Pack were getting into place above ground, laying pools of gasoline.

They had been given instructions and were careful to follow them where the ground allowed. It was not always possible; sometimes too much water had pooled or the ground was too high. But they found enough places to spread the gasoline safely and to mark the deposits. When their task was complete, they began their long Walk Around back to Friedrichstrasse. It was cold and wet. They were not used to the conditions outside.

Many of the old Aux had not been above ground since before the Time of Ice had begun to die. Many of the old Aux did not recognise landmarks that had once been familiar to them. They were not allowed to use their own rat-runs and the narrow streets where they were most comfortable.

The trees were bare and strange-looking, not frosted with veils of ice. The ice beneath their feet shone with a slick layer of water. The sun was too bright in a sky that was too blue and too pale. It was all very troubling.

Most of the Aux were too proud to show their fear. Some felt no fear, reserving it for Them. A few felt no fear because death held no terror for them; they were old and they had lived a life. If their time had come to die then violent death was the Aux way. There was no shame or sadness in it.

All but two of the veterans, one male and one dam, made it back to Friedrichstrasse. Those two died of cold and old age, because they had run out of life. The others carried their bodies back to the Hackers' fiefdom.

CHAPTER THIRTY-FIVE
FIRE

"There!" called the lookout.

Several Aux in both war bands on Track Nine were designated as look outs. It was their job to scour high up in the arched tunnel walls and ceilings for Them.

Any anomaly, any sign of movement was to be signalled. Each lookout was teamed up with an Aux carrying a flame weapon, with its nozzle set to the narrowest stream. Every anomaly was flamed with a spike of fire.

The lookouts called regularly. The tunnels were old and ragged: moss grew in clumps, mineral deposits had formed and there were holes, breaks and cracks in the original structure. The flames soon lit them, exposing them for what they were, and the war bands moved on.

It was all good practice. The scrappers became adept at taking cover against the tunnel walls, at readying their arms and steadying their nerves.

The lookouts got better at anticipating what was a growth of vegetation or a cluster of crystals or a fissure in the old materials of the tunnels. Gradually, they called out less and less.

As the lookout called, the fire thrower with him shot a flame up into the ceiling of the tunnel. The rest of the war band scattered.

The Them shrieked, expanding its mouth into a gaping hole ringed with circles of dirty fangs. It dropped onto the tracks, and its dirty yellow claws squealed against the rails as it gripped them, ready to swing. The dying light of the flames danced over its lurid green speckled shell.

Holeman Hunt was already surging forwards, wielding his blades, his battle cry on his lips.

"Get whet!" he roared.

His words were echoed by the battle cries of other scrappers as they followed suit, though all the Aux words were lost in the deafening scream of the Them.

A fire thrower shot a narrow bolt of flames above the Them's head. He did not want to risk injuring the Aux or blinding them with the light of the fire, but he had a weapon and he would use it.

The Them twisted its head, mesmerised by the flames, and Holeman Hunt's blades hit home, hacking at the monster's barbed forearms.

Hard green shell flew free, spraying into the tunnel wall. One hit Holeman Hunt in the cheek and hot blood began to drip onto his coat. He continued to swing. The cracking of his blades against the Them's bony armour filled his ears until the next hideous shriek took over.

Oscar so Wild was beside Holeman Hunt, slicing his blades into the Them's swinging dappled forelimbs, taking advantage of the distraction that the fire thrower had set up. Another trail of flames passed overhead, and then another stream crossed it.

The Them lurched towards the flames, twisting its luminescent body to follow their progress high above it. It screamed again as its lower right forelimb was severed at the joint, clanging onto the rail in front of its grasping claw.

It swung its head down to attack Holeman Hunt, but the Alpha dog saw it coming.

He sliced a blade hard across the Them's face, though it was hardly a face at all, just two pairs of wide-set, bulging magenta eyes and the great hole of a maw. He managed to hack several teeth free of the circular jaw, before the head pulled away.

More scrappers attacked the Them from behind. A leg joint began to buckle, and another forelimb soon dangled from its joint. Fire throwers continued to weave patterns of flames high in the tunnel ceiling over their heads.

The Them was under siege. It swung its scything, barbed forelimbs in earnest.

The first scrapper went down, a low, scooping strike taking out his legs below his body armour. He bled out in moments, both his femoral arteries sliced through.

A second Aux was decapitated. His body dropped in the path of a third, who stumbled and died on his face when a barbed chitin limb drove down through his back, penetrating his armour.

The Them lifted the body a metre off the ground as it tried to retract its limb, the barbs tearing through the flesh before the Aux corpse dropped back onto the tracks.

The tight circle of Aux, attacking with blades, was surrounded by a circle of Aux with fire throwers. Scrappers were dying.

"Blades retreat," shouted Dorothy.

No one heard.

Dorothy threw up her arms, raising her blades above her head, and stepped back between the fire throwers at her shoulders. She nudged the one on her left to light up, hoping that others would see what she intended.

She kept shouting, but still no one heard. She ducked between the next two fire throwers and grabbed the next blade scrapper by his coat, pulling on him, manhandling him out of the rank.

She raised her own weapons again, this time banging them together. Nothing.

The Aux dam beside Oscar so Wild was breathing hard. She swung her two curved blades as one across her body, back and forth in a steady rhythm. It was a blunt technique that the Zoo Pack did not employ, and it was no match for the Them.

The creature cut the blades from the dam in one strike, amputating both her arms at the elbows. It sliced again, this time across her gut. She was dead before she hit the ground. The fire throwers behind her filled the gap she left.

Daniel DeFoe saw his chance. The Aux were dying and he had a fire thrower nozzle in his hands. He could kill it. He aimed at the body mass of the Them. With the nozzle on the narrowest setting, holding his hands steady, he let off a stream of flames.

He knew the risk he was taking. He knew that the flames would wash back into the Aux. He knew that the Aux would be blinded by the light and would not be able to see to fight, to wield their own weapons against the Them.

The Aux were dying anyway. One death was the same as another. He could save many more Aux by killing the Them.

Oscar so Wild felt the heat of the flames as they crashed off the Them's carapace. He screwed his eyes shut and stepped hastily backwards, hoping that he was stepping into a space, onto firm ground.

He put out a hand to grasp hold of Holeman Hunt, not entirely confident that the Hacker Alpha would have the sense to follow his lead.

On the other side of the circle, Dorothy Barker was still trying to pull blade scrappers out of the battle so that the fire throwers could do their work. So that they could kill the Them.

Flames began to penetrate hard shell. The smell of burning bony armour, like scorched hair and claw, began to fill the air. Acrid black smoke rose from the Them's charring carapace as it changed colour from the hideous green to blue to purple.

The beast flung its arms around in one final attempt to take out some of its attackers, and one of its great curved forelimbs sliced into Dorothy Barker.

The hard, bony spike entered her side through her borrowed jacket, only millimetres below the line of her body armour. Her arms had been raised and her body exposed from the waist up as her armour shifted with her movement. The spike would probably have penetrated anyway, even if the curved blade would not. The spike emerged on the far side of her navel, protruding several centimetres.

All the remaining scrappers still alive had retreated behind the circle of fire throwers. They covered their faces or hurriedly put on eyeshades so that they could watch the Them die.

Daniel DeFoe had done most of the hard work.

Some of the other fire throwers chose to preserve their stocks of gasoline. The next to attack kept a steady stream of flames aimed at the monster's head and a third pumped fire into its back.

The Them's dying screech was unlike anything the Aux had ever heard. It was as unlike its battle cry as it could be and still be an animalistic scream. It did not thrash as it died. It crumpled like an ancient purple skeleton held together by cobwebs.

It stank and it smoked. It was as hot as hell, but at least it had stopped making its hideous wailing noise.

And that was the scrapping of that hour.

CHAPTER THIRTY-SIX
INJURED

"GET... THIS... DAMNED... thing... out... of... me," growled Dorothy Barker, between gasps, holding the Them's curving forelimb in her hands where it entered her body. She tried to pull it out of her flesh.

Oscar so Wild had hacked the limb free of the blazing Them and carried Dorothy clear at the end of the scrap.

He stood over her. One of the dams walked towards them, tugging a flask out of her waistband and pulling the stopper out.

"Drink or pour?" she asked Dorothy, holding the flask close to the injured Aux's body.

Dorothy growled at the dam and grabbed the flask from her. She took a long slug of the filthy tasting alcohol, coughed and then poured a generous quantity over the entrance and exit wounds in her side and stomach.

"Good," said the dam.

"Now," said Dorothy.

The dam, Gertrude Harms, reached for Dorothy's hand, but Dorothy slapped her away. Oscar so Wild was holding the chitin limb in both hands, ready to pull.

"You," said Dorothy, "brace. Put a boot against my ribs."

Oscar so Wild did as he was told.

Dorothy wrapped both her hands around Wild's ankle so that her body was firm when he removed the thing that was sticking out of her. It was barbed, and her flesh would tear.

She took two long breaths. She could already feel the alcohol taking hold of her.

"Now," she said again.

Dorothy Barker did not scream. She was unconscious before the blade was all the way out of her. She remained unconscious while the wounds were cleaned and dressed.

"You, leave me," she said when she came round.

"Us, we are in the middle of a tunnel," said Holeman Hunt. "Us, we will leave you outside at Westhafen, safer and safer."

"And cold," said Dorothy Barker.

She tried to stand, but her injuries and the alcohol she had drunk made her unsteady on her legs.

Oscar so Wild put a shoulder under one arm,

Gertrude Harms put a shoulder under the other, and together they lifted Dorothy to her feet.

"Me, I hear something," said a voice from the gathered war band.

"Leave me," said Dorothy again.

"An echo of an echo," said Holeman Hunt. "Us, we have time."

While Dorothy was being tended to, the rest of the war band had gathered its dead into a service tunnel twenty metres back down the track. The Them would not have them.

One of the Aux, a younger beta male, brought back a felt jacket that one of the dead had been wearing. It was miraculously free of blood. He tossed it to Wild with a nod. They would look after their own, and Dorothy Barker would need the extra warmth.

They moved on, as before, slowed down by Dorothy Barker. They had lost a total of half a dozen Aux scrappers. It was only half what they had lost to the first Them. It was a small victory.

The whistle echoed through the tunnels, but never seemed to grow closer. It was unnerving. It sounded nothing like the shrieks that the Them made at close range, not the battle cry, nor the death throes.

Holeman Hunt led the band from the front, his face bloodied from his encounter with the Them.

Ten minutes later they reached Westhafen. Eight of the Aux scouted the station and the platform. Then Dorothy Barker, helped by Gertrude Harms, made her way outside.

The dam had been assigned to look after her,

regardless of the fact that Dorothy couldn't stand her. She was determined to make it back to Friedrichstrasse alive. She was dammed if she was going to die with only this odious Aux for company.

The station complex at Westhafen was dotted with what looked like little flags. It was an almost comical sight. Rags had been torn and tied to stakes driven into the ground to mark the pools of gasoline set by the veterans. They formed a misshapen ring covering several hundred square metres of rough ground, with pools dotted where the terrain allowed.

Gertrude Harms half-carried Dorothy Barker, cold and pale, to one of the derelict buildings. They found an internal room on the ground floor that was almost intact, with four walls and a ceiling.

Dorothy huddled in a corner of it, drawing her knees as close to her chest as her injury would allow. She covered herself in the big felt jacket. It was as much as she could do to keep as warm as possible.

"Hey!" she said as Gertrude pulled off her cap. She'd wanted to cry out, but the word was little more than a whisper and barely a protest. Gertrude Harms rearranged Dorothy's head cloth before swapping headgear with her, giving the injured Aux her own fur cap instead of the leather one she'd been wearing. It would be much warmer.

Dorothy Barker did not have the energy to thank her. She was tired, terribly tired. Someone had already put on her eyeshades against the bright blue light of the day, and she closed her eyes behind them onto blackness. She would sleep or she would die; she didn't care which.

Gertrude Harms left Dorothy Barker to scout the area and check the gasoline pools. Two had drained off. The ice was too porous or too wet in places to sustain the pools.

Everything was wet. The pings and plashes that they had all become used to had given way to the sounds of moving water.

Gertrude Harms stopped to listen to the gentle gurgling of narrow streams forming and running away, and to the whisper of thaw water pouring down the stone and brick faces of buildings.

They were not unlike the sounds that water made being poured for drinking or washing, but they were constant and not made by Aux hands.

She turned back to her task of surveying the puddles of gasoline. Most of them were still intact. She bent to remove the flags where there was no gasoline on the surface. She stood up to survey the landscape. The circle looked good. The plan just might work.

Gertrude returned to Dorothy Barker once her task was complete. She sat close to her, wrapping her arms around the injured dam. It was cold, and she could do nothing but try to maintain their warmth until someone came for them. She didn't know how long that would be. She wondered if anyone would ever come, as she listened to the odd gurgle and whisper of flowing water.

CHAPTER THIRTY-SEVEN
GÜNTZELSTRASSE

MAKEWAR THACKERAY LED his own war band to Guntzelstrasse. He took his best Hansa beta dogs, twelve males and eight dams. They were his most experienced lieutenants, his most able scrappers, truer and true. He would stand beside any of them in any battle. If the Them was the toughest foe, tougher and tough, he would bring his best.

They heard the whistles echo along Track Nine as they passed Spichernstrasse at a steady jog. Some of them had heard it before and nodded to those who had not in confirmation. As it tracked back and forth and around and around, they could not tell where it was coming from. They assumed it was coming from ahead of them. From the foe they expected to meet at Güntzelstrasse.

Stephen Bone, the nozzle of his weapon wide open, triggered his fire thrower the moment the shriek began to sound in his ears. The horrendous scream drowned out all thought of him doing anything else, kicking his instincts into overdrive.

He was in the second rank of Aux jogging towards Güntzelstrasse, so the scrapper to his left in front of him was hit by the flames, and bowled over. He rolled between the rails, beating at his clothes, pounding at the flames to put them out, but his hands and face were scorched.

The flames hit the Them. Bright flares of red and yellow heat spread across its glossy green thorax, head and speckled limbs as it swung frantically to defend itself.

The Aux on the ground was lucky. The spike of one monstrous, barbed limb grazed over his back twice, tearing his jacket and gouging two long scratches in his skin, but producing nothing more than a trickle of blood from each.

They were superficial wounds, less serious than the burns to his face and hands. His burning clothes now smothered, the Aux scoured the ground around him for the weapon he'd dropped when he'd hit the rails and got back to his feet.

Half a dozen of the Aux scrappers had been blinded by the light of the flames as they hit the Them and washed off its hard-shelled thorax. Blinded by the flames and by the luminescence of the Them's yellowish green carapace. They'd ducked or scrambled backwards, grabbing for eyeshades.

Two of them had been scythed down by the Them, cutting and hacking at anything in its path. One lost an arm, the other was sliced diagonally through her torso down to her hip.

The Them's cutting limb stuck there for several seconds, giving the other Aux a short reprieve before it pulled itself free. The corpse fell limply to the ground.

The second fire thrower already had his visor in place when the first triggered his weapon. He joined battle almost immediately, with a narrower, more penetrating burst of flames aimed at the Them's head.

The creature bucked and weaved so much it was hard for the Aux to maintain a lock on his target, with so little experience of his weapon.

The rest of the war band began to regroup behind the fire throwers, and the second male opened up his nozzle for a bigger target area.

The Them would not die. It raged and swung, cutting the air and leaving long scratches in the walls of the tunnel when it did not find its prey. It's bony shell gradually changing colour, transforming from green to turquoise to a rich blue.

The fire throwers backed up, staying outside its range. With the nozzles open, the flames were cooler, although the spread was greater.

The Them's carapace smelled foul as it smouldered and turned purple. The creature continued to swing and flail, but it did not die.

Stephen Bone's tanks emptied first. The gout of

flame sputtered and drooped. The tank coughed and the flame went out.

Bone stepped back, shaking the hose of his weapon. He had not thought about time; blades had no time limits. His battle was over. Moments later the other fire thrower died.

The smoking Them shrieked wildly, raising its four upper limbs in a ghastly waving salute. Its yellow claws screeched on the rails as it propelled its way towards the Aux.

The other scrappers were ready with their blades.

The Hansa Pack carried long-handled weapons with curved, double heads. They took great pride in the quality of their steel and in how well it could be honed.

The charred purple chitin of the Them's shell had grown brittle with the heat. Makewar Thackeray made a long, clean cut in the Them's thorax. Then he sliced into one of its forelimbs.

The Them shrieked again, its hard, high-pitched scream. It sounded like fear and frustration, and the Aux were galvanised by the change in tone.

With scrappers to either side of him, and more beyond them, Makewar Thackeray continued to swing and strike with his halberd. The Them struck back.

It splintered one axe handle, sending the head spinning into the tunnel wall. With the same limb, it drove a spike down behind the collar bone of the Aux who had been wielding it, deep into his chest.

He went down first on his knees, and when the

barbed limb was pulled out, fell sideways, his throat bubbling with bright red blood from his punctured lung.

He was the last Aux of Hansa Pack to die.

The lieutenants scrapping in the tunnel beyond Spichernstrasse were the finest in Hansa Pack for a reason.

Every time the Them swung a limb, it was met by a strike from a blade. When the two met, the Aux blade won the day. The honed steel sent chitin flying or made a clean cut, or even severed a limb.

When axes and halberds weren't parrying, they were slicing and hacking into the Them's discoloured body and head as it lurched and screeched.

Its death was inevitable. When it came, the Them crashed to the rails, spraying gravel in all directions.

Makewar Thackeray looked down on the monstrous corpse in disgust.

"That is the scrapping for this day," he said. "Us, we gather the dead. Us, we return to Hansa Pack."

"Then?" asked Stephen Bone.

"Then?" asked the Alpha dog. "Then, us, we prepare for more battles. Us, we made a pact. Us, we made an alliance. Them will not kill us deader and dead. There is strength in numbers. Us, we will fight."

The Aux war band rested for a moment or two. As they gathered their dead and turned for home, they heard the whistle and its echoes. It was not coming from Güntzelstrasse.

"More of Them," said one of the lieutenants.

"Them, there will always be more of Them," said Makewar Thackeray. "There is strength in numbers."

CHAPTER THIRTY-EIGHT
A CLEAN KILL

"Them," said Evelyn War as the whistles rang around the tunnels.

Everyone in the war band knew that the foe was on Track Nine, but Evelyn couldn't help giving voice to the knowledge. The sounds had begun almost as soon as they had left the Hansa Pack. The echoes overlapped and seemed to be coming from more than one direction.

"Hansa Pack, them can fight Them?" asked Evelyn War. "Them can kill Them?"

"Makewar Thackeray, him Alpha dog," said John Steel, "him tougher and tough. Him truer and true. Hansa Pack, them will kill or die."

"There is strength in numbers," said Evelyn War, almost under her breath, as if trying to reassure herself.

Ben Gun fist-bumped Evelyn's upper arm.

"Evelyn War, tougher and tough," he said to her.

"Ben Gun, him have muscles in his head," said Evelyn War, looking down on the pup and smiling slightly. She breathed a little deeper as she jogged down the tunnel beside the young Aux. She began to feel calmer.

This was what her father wanted. If she died today, in this foreign tunnel, she had achieved what her father had wanted. She had kept her word to him. Zoo Pack had made alliances with Hacker Pack and Hansa Pack. There was strength in numbers. They were fighting Them.

The whistles and their echoes repeated around the tunnels, deadened by the sounds of three dozen pairs of soft boots jogging on gravel.

She concentrated on the crunch of the overlapping footfalls. Her feeling of calm increased. Then she remembered all the anger she had felt over the last few weeks. She remembered the stilettos in her boots and the crossbow on her back.

She breathed in so that she could feel the pressure of the bandoliers crisscrossing her body. The crossbow bolts were useless, but their presence reassured her anyway. The pebbles in her cuffs, pressing against her wrists, reassured her, too.

Evelyn War remembered the plan. She was satisfied.

Robert Browning's war band walked the first kilometre to Turmstrasse without incident. There were only the whistles, and the lookouts calling when they saw anomalies. They followed the same procedures as Holeman Hunt's war band walking in from Leopoldplatz.

Neither war band knew where they would meet or when. Neither knew how many Them they would encounter in the tunnels along the way. How many they would have to kill and how many casualties they would take in the scraps.

The service tunnel at Turmstrasse was dark and narrow, and closed at one end. Its greasy black walls were more reflective than the dull black walls of the larger tunnels, and the small amount of light reflected unevenly off its surfaces. Evelyn War hated service tunnels.

As always, the cover and check procedure was carried out. The Aux saw nothing.

They turned their backs on the service tunnel and continued to jog along the track the last dozen metres to the platform. There were more service tunnels and the platform still to check. Robert Browning had also selected two pairs of Aux to scout outside the station.

The war band broke ranks when the Them exited the service tunnel they had just checked a dozen metres behind them. They heard the screech of its claws on the rails.

A lookout shouted, and a fire thrower shot a burst of fire back down the tunnel, lighting up the Them.

It was an imposing figure lit up in the orange glow of the flames. Its thorax was long and tapered, speckled yellow and green, and its head a bulbous form resting on a long, narrow neck. It opened its mouth to wail, forming a hole half the size of its head, raw and hollow, with its concentric rings of jagged dentition.

Its limbs throbbed as the flame pulsed. They were jointed, with narrow upper arms and great curving forearms like barbed scythe blades ending in impossibly sharp points where the colour concentrated in a lurid luminous green. The upper hind limbs were narrow, too, but the lower limbs were bulky, ending in flat, clawed feet that clung to the track rails.

The rails screeched as the Them ran its yellow claws along them, walking towards the flames, drawn to the heat.

Three more Aux with flame weapons joined the first. The four walked tight abreast in the tunnel, towards the Them. They set the nozzles of their fire throwers to the narrowest, hottest stream and killed the flames until they were close.

The tunnel went black.

Almost within range of the Them, the four fire throwers hit the triggers on their weapons in unison. Four streams of flames hit the Them's body virtually simultaneously.

It screamed in pain as its hard shell rapidly changed colour through a range of greens and blues to purple. Then it began to blacken and smouldered. The chitin flared red, burning through to the flesh beneath. The monster thrashed its forelimbs, but they were useless. The Them could do nothing but back away from its death.

The four Aux followed.

Heated from within, a boiling cauldron of flesh, the thorax carapace could contain the pressure no longer. It exploded in a shower of purple chitin shrapnel and half-cooked organs. Ichor sprayed the tunnel walls as the Them expired.

The Them crashed onto Track Nine, oddly intact, but for its exploded torso.

The Aux who had begun the firefight released the trigger on his weapon, and waited while the other three Aux cut their own fire throwers. Then he waited another moment or two before approaching the Them.

He nudged a forelimb. He picked up a piece of purple shrapnel the size of an axe blade, orange ichor running and dripping from it. He wiped the worst of the stinking muck onto his leather apron and shoved the souvenir into his belt.

Then he took a stride to the head of the Them, still intact. He kicked it once, hard, with his soft-soled boot. The bulbous mass rocked and wobbled. The Aux spat in one of the Them's lazy bulging, magenta eyes, already turning milky in death, and walked away.

That was the scrapping. That was the cleanest kill. No Aux died.

The four Aux walked back to the platform, all the adrenaline of the firefight leached from their bloodstreams. They sat in a row on the edge of the platform for a moment, the other Aux gathering around them. They were praised and congratulated. They were hailed as the heroes of the hour.

Then it was back to business. Their tanks were replenished. Their nozzles were checked and cleaned. Their triggers and flints were tested.

It was less than ten minutes before Robert Browning's war band was back on the tracks, back on the long walk along Track Nine towards the next station at Birkenstrasse.

Still the whistles did not stop, nor their echoes.

CHAPTER THIRTY-NINE
PINCER MOVEMENT

THE TONE OF the whistles changed. The pitch changed. There was menace and anguish in it suddenly, as Holeman Hunt's war band travelled south along Track Nine from Westhafen.

"Listen," said one of the Aux.

They stopped en masse in the tunnel, their feet falling still on the gravel. All that remained was the soft sound of their breathing.

The whistle had changed. Something was happening further down the tunnel.

"Them," said Oscar so Wild. "Them are attacking."

"No," said Holeman Hunt.

"Scrappers, them are attacking Them."

The screeching echoes, broken and desperate,

continued for a minute or maybe two as the gathered war band listened.

Then, as suddenly as they had begun, they stopped. The strange tone of the sounds stopped and the echoes died away. Then they began again, a keening in the tunnels, a breathy whistle all around them. Things were changing.

"Is it dead?" asked one of the Aux. "The Them, is it deader and dead?"

"Yes," said Holeman Hunt.

"And how many Aux, them dead with it?" asked another voice, low and bitter.

Oscar so Wild turned on the war band.

"Us, we are Aux, tougher and tough. Us, we are Aux, truer and true," he said. "Us, we are faster and fast. Us, we are braver and brave. Us, we stand in alliance. Us, we stand together."

Holeman Hunt put his hand on the lieutenant's shoulder.

"Oscar so Wild, Alpha dog, him is right," he said. "You, scrap like an Aux or whine like a pup." He glared at the Hacker Aux. "Have you got the bone for it, Fred Walker?"

Fred Walker puffed out his chest. He was a young beta dog, and he was afraid. He didn't want to show it. He had spoken out of turn, and out of fear. He needed to rally.

"Me, I scrap like an Aux," said Walker, taking hold of the nozzle of his fire thrower and pulling down the visor of his mask as if to prove his point.

Holeman Hunt fist-bumped the male in the chest

and strode back to his position at the head of the pack.

The keening echoes continued to sound all around them, bouncing off the tunnel walls as they made their way towards Birkenstrasse.

They had travelled only a couple of hundred metres when quiet descended again. They stopped, suspicious. Silence was their enemy as much as the whistles were, as much as the shrieking of the Them was as it dropped out of the ceiling.

Holeman Hunt signalled to the fire thrower to his left, who sent up a long, arcing beam of flames into the ceiling of the tunnel for several metres ahead of them. There was nothing. The whole tunnel lit up with the red and orange glow of the flames, but they could see nothing ahead of them.

The quiet unnerved the war band more than the whistles and echoes had.

They continued down the track at a much slower pace. Weapons drawn, they stalked the tunnel, hugging the walls away from the mass of gravel that gave away their every footfall.

The fire throwers faced into the tunnels towards the front of the war band, the Aux carrying bladed weapons kept further back, weapons drawn. They made slow progress for another twenty or thirty metres.

"There."

The call came from halfway down the pack.

An answering gout of flames shot into the ceiling space of the tunnel.

Nothing.

The Aux who had made the call pulled the fire thrower into the tunnel and pointed.

"There!" he shouted again, pointing dead ahead. The flame shot low between the ranks of Aux pressed flat against the tunnel walls.

The Them was not high in the ceiling space; it was on the tracks ten metres in front of them, ready.

Behind it was another pair of Them. Behind that, the shadows of more.

Holeman Hunt stepped into the tunnel and waved his arm.

"Flames!" he called.

The word was cut off by the shriek of three, or four, or half a dozen Them as they emitted their battle cry in unison.

It didn't matter, the call had gone out. The scrappers knew what they must do.

The fire throwers stood shoulder to shoulder across the tunnel. When an Aux's gasoline supplies ran low, he stepped back to refuel and another fire thrower took his place.

The Them surged towards the heat and light of the streaming fires until the flames lit them up and made their carapaces glow yellow and green.

Their heads swung back and forth, their cutting limbs slicing and hacking at the air, but they could not reach their targets. They backed up in the glow of the flames, wailing and howling their joy and their rage, their carapaces dancing with colour as the heat of the flames ebbed and flowed.

Robert Browning's war band, approaching along Track Nine from the opposite direction, was engulfed in a cacophony of noise. They were overwhelmed by the cries of half a dozen Them and were wrong-footed for a moment. Then they saw firelight in the tunnel ahead. The pincer movement was in effect. They were no more than a hundred and fifty or two hundred metres from Holeman Hunt and his party.

The Birkenstrasse station lay between them.

Robert Browning gave the signal, and the war band jogged another hundred metres. They knew they could not be heard, but the scrappers' hearts began to pound with anticipation. The pack moved faster and fast, with a purpose.

A second signal brought the fire throwers to the fore.

Evelyn War fist-bumped Ben Gun on his bicep. The pup cringed slightly. The dam didn't know her own strength, in the thrill of imminent battle.

For the first time, Ben Gun felt his hands shake as he put his finger through the loop in his slingshot. He took several short steps up to Robert Browning and tapped him on the shoulder.

Robert Browning looked down. Ben's wide eyes told him everything he needed to know, even before the pup raised his hand and waved: they should move forwards. They weren't close enough. Ben Gun was not confident that he could make the shot.

John Steel stepped up on the other side of the pup. He put his hand on Ben Gun's shoulder, looked over his head at Robert Browning and frowned. Robert Browning glared back. The message was clear. Ben Gun could do this. Browning trusted him. It would happen.

Robert Browning lifted his arm high in the air, making the signal for the war band to move forwards. They jogged another fifty metres.

Holeman Hunt's war band had been pressing the Them, and Browning's Aux were within twenty metres of their targets. They were right on top of Birkenstrasse station. The plan had to work. It had to work first time.

The air in the tunnel of Track Nine vibrated with the shrieks of the Them as they backed slowly away from the flames.

Them longed to attack the Aux, who were out of reach beyond the deadly flames. But more than that, Them revelled and basked in the heat and light the fire afforded Them. There was a price to pay for bliss.

Ben Gun felt the heavy weight of a huge Aux hand on his shoulder. He looked down at it and then up into John Steel's face. His eyes darted across to Robert Browning as he reached into his waxed pouch for the first of the little balls of fuel that were such a crucial part of the plan.

Then he felt pressure on his head. He whipped around.

Evelyn War was right there with him.

John Steel was suddenly gone, and Evelyn War was at his side instead. She dropped in her knees to come down to the pup's level. Ben Gun looked into the dam's eyes for a second.

He saw everything there that he needed to see. They were friends. She trusted him. If she could have said something, over the battle cries of Them, she would.

It didn't matter, he had listened to every word she had spoken since they had first met, whether she had known it or not. Every word she had spoken was ringing in his mind. Every word Walter Sickert had spoken was there, too, urging him to do his job, to be the most important Aux in the scrap.

The tale-teller's voice in his head told him that he would become a legend, that tales would be told of Ben Gun for generations, that every pup would hear those stories a hundred-hundred times.

Ben Gun filled his lungs deeply. He rolled the little metal wheel of his sparking mechanism with his thumb and felt the flint engage. The spark lit the ball of fuel nestled in the fireproof slingshot. The rest was instinct.

Ben Gun heard the nozzle of the weapon in the hands of the scrapper next to him open. He heard a drip of fuel fall to the ground at the Aux's feet. The fire thrower, a Hacker called Damien Hurts, thumbed the trigger without igniting the spark.

Lighting the fire was Ben Gun's job. Except Ben couldn't have heard those things with all the noise in the tunnel. He must have imagined them.

Ben Gun saw the arc of liquid fuel as it flowed through the air down the tunnel. He saw where the gasoline landed and pooled ten or a dozen metres distant, to the left of the tunnel.

He whipped his arm and loosed the sling. He watched the trajectory of the little ball of fire as it flew through the air towards the pool of gasoline against the wall of the tunnel.

The Aux war band did not see the flaming projectile hit the fuel, but they saw the surge of flames as the gasoline lit. Part of the tunnel floor was filled with flames, which climbed the wall where the gasoline had sprayed.

Ben Gun loaded a second fuel pellet and lit it. Damien Hurts triggered his nozzle once more and sprayed the right hand side of the tunnel with more gasoline. Ben Gun whipped his arm and let loose his projectile. He hit his target again. More flames filled the tunnel.

Evelyn War grasped his shoulder in triumph, and then urged Ben forwards as the pack moved towards their prey.

Two fire throwers stood ready, one on either side of Ben Gun. They were fully loaded and ready to go. Two of the best Aux fire throwers in the Hacker Pack, two of the most reliable, with the best aim.

Holeman Hunt was within twenty metres of them. He and his war band were dangerously close. They wanted no casualties on their own side. Accidents were not an option.

Them were the target. Herding Them was the objective.

Flames flickered and flashed across the bodies of

Them on both sides. They were surrounded by fire. Despite their thrashing and lurching, both factions of the Aux counted five foes. Five of Them!

Killing one had been tough. Tougher and tough!

Killing five!

Damien Hurts, staying close to Ben Gun, triggered a short burst of fuel into the gaggle of Them. It splashed and splattered, landing in a puddle in their midst.

Ben Gun had loaded his slingshot, and was about to light his missile when he hesitated. He looked into the dark mask of the fire thrower, but could not see the Aux's eyes. Damien Hurts shrugged.

Ben Gun thumbed his sparking mechanism and lit the missile in his slingshot. He looked hard at the Them, the light from the flames strobing over their bodies.

He whipped his arm and let the missile loose. It flew high into the ceiling of the tunnel, looking like a tiny comet as it passed over the heads of Them.

Ben Gun watched its trajectory. Out of the corner of his eye, he thought he saw one of Them watching it too, arching its neck to get a good look at the little ball of fire.

It landed, and a sheet of flames rose into the air between Them. Flames darted from one to another as the splashes of gasoline that had landed on Them and rolled over their hard-shelled bodies lit up. The flames burst, and burned out quickly, leaving flashes of blue on their glossy green chitin.

Them began to scamper and lurch in a tight circle,

not knowing where to go or how to escape the flames.

Holeman Hunt's war band had closed in, keeping up a barrage of flames. One fire thrower switched out for another, and then another, as fuel supplies began to dwindle. They could not get any closer. It was up to Ben Gun.

Damien Hurts took his cue and sent up another arc of gasoline, puddling it among Them. Ben Gun lit another missile and loosed it. Another wall of flames rose in their midst.

Them shrieked and keened. Their heads lurched. They swayed and scythed their luminescent limbs.

A wail went up from one of Them as it was skewered by the spiked limb of its neighbour. It swung a speckled limb in retaliation, and an answering screech filled the tunnel.

The Aux fire thrower sent up another arc of gasoline, and another.

Ben Gun lit the puddles.

Them began to huddle together.

Them had no choice but to move towards the platform of Birkenstrasse station.

Ben Gun felt another firm squeeze to the back of his neck. Evelyn War was right there with him, willing him to succeed.

Robert Browning's war band followed Them. They walked through the wall of fire that Damien Hurts and Ben Gun had built. It had begun to die away; there was room for the Aux to pass between the fires, single file.

As they passed through, the puddle fires began to die away too.

Holeman Hunt's fire throwers kept flames at Them's backs. Damien Hurts triggered his weapon and rained gasoline over Them's heads in puddles. Ben Gun lobbed his torch missiles into the puddles. Them lurched onwards, up onto the platform and through the station.

Holeman Hunt's war band was able to track around Them as the space opened up, sending flames into the gaggle of Them, herding Them, steering their movements.

Them had become confused. It was too bright and cold as they got closer to the outside. Them were increasingly mesmerised by the warmth of the flames.

The Them that had been injured by its mate kept lower to the ground, angrier, wailing more readily. It ducked its blue head out between the flames, looking for a means of escape, keen to attack, hurting and spiteful.

It struck out twice, but to no avail; Holeman Hunt's Aux scrappers had room to manoeuvre, to keep out of its reach. They also had the fire power to drive the Them back into the gaggle.

At last, it sprang out between two puddles of flaming gasoline and swung a scything blade at Ben Gun. The pup was short and light. He ducked fast, hitting the ground on his belly.

Ben grabbed Evelyn's hand and took her with him, but the Aux to her right, another dam, was caught in the curve of its hot, blue forelimb. She was carved in two just below her armpits. One arm was severed across the bicep and her chest was opened.

The war band was close-packed, and the corpse of the dam fell hard against the Aux standing next to her. He ducked his head, taking her weight. As he lowered her to the ground, a second strike came in, but Damien Hurts had reset his weapon. Fire came out of the nozzle of his fire thrower instead of liquid gasoline.

He fired high to avoid a splash-back. He managed to hit the Them in the head, nevertheless, driving it back into the gaggle.

Little by little, Them were driven out of the station, onto the open ground outside.

Them were getting angry and Them were getting desperate. Their cries and shrieks were getting increasingly alarming. At least, outside, the sounds could dissipate more easily.

The streets outside the station were empty. Noise rattled around the buildings that surrounded them, but nothing like the continuous echoes that filled the tunnels below ground.

Them did not seem to suffer in the sunlight as the Aux did. They did shrink from the cold. They lifted their clawed hind feet from the ice in jerking movements, as if walking on hot coals and their lower limbs turned from green to yellow to grey. Their breath steamed in great billowing clouds. They puckered their wide, round mouths to contain the heat of their respiration so that only thin streams remained. Their movements slowed.

Ben Gun looked around. He saw the flags dotted at intervals in an oval shape in the broad street. Holeman Hunt and Robert Browning had seen it too, and the fire throwers. All their efforts were put into driving Them into position within the battlefield marked out by the flags.

As soon as they were inside the area, Ben Gun began to snap off his flaming projectiles, ring-fencing the combat zone. Them would not escape. The Aux would kill or be killed on this battlefield.

More than half the fuel the Aux had carried along Track Nine from Leopoldplatz and Hansaplatz had been used. The supply was limited by what the Aux could carry. The flame weapons' tanks had been refilled several times, and many of the Aux were carrying empty jerry cans and camelbacks. There was nowhere to refill them.

Three more minutes and the circle of fire was complete, but it would not last forever. The pools of gasoline were generous, and had been laid down carefully, but they, too, were limited by what fuel had been barrowed and carried to the site by the veteran Aux. No one could predict where Them would be found, so the gasoline had been spread out over several sites.

The Aux war bands had to kill Them, and they had to do it fast.

Holeman Hunt and Robert Browning both gave the signal at the same time. More than sixty Aux spread in a wide circle around the five Them.

The fire throwers stepped forwards to attack on

all sides with hot narrow blasts of fire, aimed at their thoraxes.

The cold air and the bigger distances counted against the Aux. The fire throwers were more effective in the confines of the tunnels. They braced themselves and strode towards the gaggle, one step at a time, a tight circle of Aux. Their faces shielded, big shapes in long, leather aprons, they looked almost as monstrous as Them.

Them spread as the heat from the flame weapons dissipated around Them. All the blue had gone from their hard shells and they were dull and green. The bright sun and the blue sky gave Them the false sense of an unreal warmth. Only the ice beneath their clawed feet seemed to bother Them at all. But that only made Them move more quickly, skittering across the surface skittle-scuttle fast, *tiktiktik, tiktik*. Their claws dug into the ice, giving them grip, holding them steady.

The Aux were at a disadvantage once more. The fire throwers had no time to weave metal into the soles of their boots, though most of the blade scrappers had rotated to the rear of their groups to prepare for coming outside.

Them ducked and wove. Them surged into the flames and then retreated.

One of Them lurched forward, screaming, its head low, teeth bared. Its lower forelimb hooked under a hose and cut through it, and fuel gushed out of the feeder line.

Realising what was happening, the Aux holding

the nozzle, which was now attached to nothing, threw her arms up in horror. Her body was thrown into the air as the flames all around ignited the fuel, and her newly filled tanks exploded on her back, killing her instantly.

Her body flew several metres through the air and landed full in the chest of one of Them, turning it instantly blue and glossy. The startled creature was bowled over and sat down heavily. It recovered quickly, taking most of the Aux's arm into its hideous maw as compensation, biting it off and chewing it down.

Damien Hurts had left Ben Gun's side to join the battle. He tried to back out of the attacking line when his fuel ran dry, but he was too late.

One of Them saw the last drizzle of fire splutter out of the scrapper's nozzle and dived towards him. The squeal of its claws on the ice was almost more devastating to Hurts's senses than its shriek of delight as it brought down two curving limbs from on high.

The Them cut diagonally across Damien Hurts's body, slicing through from shoulder to hip on one side and from armpit to knee on the other.

The Them cut through the straps of the tank harness as it carved, and the apparatus fell away in one piece, without a scratch on it.

Damien Hurts's body was in more pieces than anyone cared to count.

There were more than two dozen fire throwers and only five of Them, but the conditions were poor.

The battlefield was too big. Them thrived too easily under the heat of the sun. Them had too much ease of movement outside the confines of the tunnels.

Every time a fire thrower got close to a Them, the Them attacked. Them scythed and sliced and hacked. The flames bounced off their hard shells, spraying blue speckles among the green, and spread thinly through the cold air.

The Aux were dying.

CHAPTER FORTY
REINFORCEMENTS

"BLADES!" SHOUTED HOLEMAN Hunt, despairing of watching his fire throwers falling.

Aux from Zoo Pack and from Hacker Pack waded into the battle, standing shoulder to shoulder with the fire throwers, doing what they knew how to do. They were scrappers.

Ben Gun watched Evelyn War pick her target and join the melée. She attached herself to one of the oldest fire throwers, an Aux called Robert Graves. He'd been at the forefront of every action. He was still standing, still fighting, still adjusting his nozzle and spreading his flames. Flames that travelled shorter distances in the cold air outside, that glowed less brightly against the bright blue sky. Flames that hit chitin with less heat and less force than before.

Ben Gun was a pup. He was not a scrapper. He had been called, because they had all been called, but he was the only pup on the battlefield. He was there because he was good with a slingshot and because Evelyn War believed in him... because he was Walter Sickert's friend.

He was the Hearer's friend.

He was the stuff of legends.

Ben Gun had lit all the fires that he could light. The fire throwers were not setting new puddles for him, and the veterans, who had set the pools at the perimeter of the battlefield, were all gone. All the fuel was gone. There was nothing left for him to do.

Ben Gun looked up from the edge of the battlefield as one of Them let out another deafening screech.

Them were lesser outside too.

The pup looked up. All he could see was a great, gaping maw, and rings of jagged teeth.

Without realising what he was doing, Ben Gun reached for his waxed pouch. He plunged his hand inside. He had made a lot of the little fuel soaked missiles. There were more than he would need. He had made sure of it.

He took one of the tightly wrapped little balls out of the pouch and placed it in his sling. He took the sparking device out of his pocket and thumbed it against the missile. It lit up, a bright little ball of fire.

Ben Gun, his eyes fixed on the wide open maw of the screaming Them, whipped his arm and loosed his missile.

He heard the low growling cry of an Aux, and a large male body in a grey felt great coat crossed his line of sight.

The next thing Ben Gun saw was a stream of smoke escaping from the tight pucker of the Them's pursed mouth.

He had hit his target. The bulbous head of the Them began to discolour. Blue patches began to appear among the yellow and green speckles. It gave a strange, choking cough. It began to wave its barbed forelimbs in a frantic, disorganised dance, and its head began to bob and swing.

The frenetic motion of the Them's limbs caught an Aux scrapper off-guard. The beta male tried to parry the spike that was driving towards him, but his blade was not firm enough in his hand, and it was easily knocked away.

He ducked, but in doing so he only gave the Them a better target. The spike that might have missed the Aux's neck drove straight through his heart, killing him instantly.

Ben Gun felt his knees buckle beneath him. He had killed one of his own.

The Them opened its mouth and coughed out the fuel pellet.

It shrieked again, throwing its head back and clawing at the sky with all four of its forelimbs.

Ben Gun saw the ruin of the inside of its maw.

Instinctively, he lit and aimed a second fuel missile. He whipped his arm and loosed the little ball of fire. Once more his aim was good.

This time, Ben Gun saw the pucker closing around the ball of fire. He saw the hard shell of the Them's head turning purple and burning from the inside out. He saw the Them's head explode. Its magenta eyes bulged scarlet and popped, and ichor sprayed, bright orange streaks against the blue sky.

Then he saw the Them's arms swinging. He saw the Them's forelimbs, turning bright blue, scything back and forth, cutting down yet another Aux... and another. He saw Aux bodies broken and bleeding, maimed before his very eyes.

The Them's head had exploded, and still it would not die.

Evelyn War flashed in front of him with Robert Browning at her side, both with a blade in each hand. She had her long stilettos and he had two double-blades.

She thrust and he swung. The two Aux scrappers carved away at the Them. They cut away at its hind limbs, ducking and weaving, trying desperately to avoid the deadly barbed blades raining down from above. Ben Gun let loose another missile and another, and another. His little balls of fire found the cracks in the Them's chitin, found the meat beneath the bone. He cooked its body the same way he had cooked its head.

It took three of the Aux to kill the Them.

Finally it fell.

Half of the fire throwers were dead and a dozen of the blade scrappers, too. There was no way to retreat and nowhere to retreat to.

Only one of Them was dead. Its body lay on the battlefield, twisted and broken, but it was not enough.

It spurred the Aux on.

Ben Gun moved around the circle.

The fires set by the veterans had all but died away. He looked for targets. He looked for Them to open their mouths. But Them were fighting the Aux, and there was no fire left to draw their attention, for Them to wail their pleasure at.

The rumble of footsteps, the pounding on the ice and the low growl of a fresh war cry came from Birkenstrasse station.

Them did not falter or turn to see what new threat was upon Them, and the Aux were too busy defending themselves.

Another scrapper was taken down, speared through the gut by a piercing limb, and another, near decapitated, his carotid spilling his blood in great, red gouts onto the ice.

Only Ben Gun's head turned to see the arrival of the Hansa Pack onto the field of battle.

Makewar Thackeray was backed by more than two dozen fresh scrappers, all carrying long-handled blades, all fitter than the Zoo packers who had taken the long Walk Around. All stronger than the Hackers, who had been scrapping the Rathaus for weeks.

The ice thrummed with their footfalls as thirty fresh Aux thundered into the melée, swinging their halberds and axes at Them.

Zoo Pack and Hacker Pack scrappers fell back, giving the fresh Hansa Pack scrappers room to wage war. They needed it.

Holeman Hunt and three of his best scrappers had wounded the Them most injured by the fire throwers. The monster had serious fire damage to one side of its thorax and two of its limbs. It was lopsided and awkward.

Holeman Hunt swung his halberd, opening up the Them's carapace, exposing the meat beneath. A second blow, then a third, severed a purple limb. His lieutenant took out a hind leg.

The Them slumped to the ground.

In another two minutes, the four Aux had carved the beast up between them in a mass of broken hard shell, raw meat and ichor.

Two of the Aux took injuries. One took a searing slice down his torso, and a dam had her bicep torn almost clean off by the barbs on the curved blade of one of its intact speckled green limbs. It was a small price to pay.

Only three Them remained.

John Steel and Robert Browning breathed hard on the periphery of the battle for several minutes, watching the Hansa scrappers doing their work.

A tall, lean dam with an axe was torn down metres from them, when the haft of her weapon was splintered by a cleaving blow from the Them she was battling. The heavy, double-headed blade seemed to hover in the air for a moment before turning and finding a swift straight path for her. She tried to evade it, but the blade landed heavily in her back, burying itself between her shoulder blades. She slumped to the ice, killed by her own weapon.

Enraged by the terrible misfortune, both Aux males bellowed, and, weapons drawn, they rejoined battle.

Working beside and inside the Hansa, they added their own blades, attacking hard and low to the Them's hind legs and abdomen. They hooked and jabbed with their shorter blades, fast and repetitive, while the Hansa took care of the body and the great swinging forelimbs of the monster.

The Them's hind legs went first, Browning and Steel hacking the joints to shreds, dropping the beast so that it could neither move nor resist the onslaught of the many weapons.

It took three more Hansa scrappers with it, but it finally died.

The first rifle report crashed through the air like a shock, echoing around the battlefield and overlapping the second.

Then there was a volley of shots.

The air was filled with the sound of gunfire, a sound that many of the Aux had not heard before.

The injured Aux, the exhausted and the useless, hit the ground. At the first opportunity, they turned to see where the terrible noise was coming from.

No one had heard their approach.

No one had expected them.

The Aux of the Tempelhof Pack stood in a single rank at the edge of the battlefield, among the dying flames of the last of the veteran's fires.

They had their rifles at their shoulders and they were firing at the last few Them.

They hit their targets, and their bullets penetrated carapace armour and the hard-shelled limbs alike.

Them jerked and spasmed. Them clawed the air with their barbed forelimbs.

The Aux fighting Them saw wounds appear in Them's armoured bodies. They felt the shrapnel hit their faces and tear their clothes. They saw ichor spraying through the air. They watched, aghast, as they stepped back from their dying foes.

Them lurched, spun and thrashed their barbed blades. Them set up terrible cries and shrieks as the Tempelhof rifles unleashed a second volley.

Two Hansa Pack Aux and a Zoo Packer wheeled, sharply scurrying in all directions away from the Them as its body began to fall towards them, brought down by the second volley of shots from the Tempelhof.

It was dead, finally obliterated.

The last Them tilted its head back and shrieked to the sky as if for mercy before falling to its knees. All of its upper limbs hung loosely at its sides, useless. Its torso was riddled with bullet holes, dripping orange ichor. When its cry was complete, its head fell to its chest. The weight of it carried its body forward and it fell on its face on the ice, spraying a pool of meltwater over the nearest Aux.

The echoes of the volley of shots rang around the battlefield. Then there was silence.

A long, triumphant silence.

CHAPTER FORTY-ONE
KINGDOM

EVELYN WAR WAS the first to volunteer to return for Dorothy Barker, but it was John Steel who went back for her.

She was still alive when he and Gertrude Harms carried her down the tunnel to Birkenstrasse. She was still alive when they arrived home at Friedrichstrasse. She had been unconscious for hours.

The platform at Friedrichstrasse had never seen so many Aux. The place was so warm, with the heat of their bodies, that the majority of the youngest and oldest Aux had given up clothes almost entirely. No fires were lit, and they sat in the darkness, crammed together, to listen to the newest of the tales.

Tales that would become legends.

Becky Sharp spoke for Tempelhof Pack.

"Atticus Flinch, him no Alpha dog. Me Alpha dam," she said.

The Time of Ice was over, and things were changing. Things were changing everywhere, but Tempelhof Pack had seen a big change in a short time. There had never been an Alpha dam in any Aux pack.

Becky Sharp stood on the platform in her full war gear, with a rifle over her shoulder. She stood with the staff of office held lightly in her hand. On the top of the staff sat the charred head of one of Them.

"Zoo Pack, them left and then there was a pop, a bang, a fizz," said Becky Sharp. "The lights, them died, and the Master's Voice, him never spoke again. Atticus Flinch, him no Alpha dog. Him no Hearer. Him afraid."

Becky Sharp lifted her staff and banged it down on the marble platform, hard. The head of the Them moved; its rings of teeth chattering. Some of the pups in the throng gasped and some tittered.

"Them!" exclaimed Becky Sharp. "Us, we found it on the rails, deader and dead. When Atticus Flinch, him Heard the Master's Voice, us, we stay off the rails. The rails, them kill. The rails, them burn."

Becky Sharp lifted the staff and slammed it down onto the platform once more.

"Them was on the rails. Them was deader and dead. The Master's Voice, him deader and dead. Atticus Flinch, him finished. Becky Sharp, me Alpha dam!"

Becky Sharp, Alpha dam of Tempelhof, raised her

voice to a shout. The gathered Aux, carried along with her fervour, cheered and whooped.

When the noise died down, Becky Sharp continued.

"Becky Sharp and Tempelhof lieutenants, us, we decided to make an alliance with Zoo Pack. There is strength in numbers," she said. "Us, we track Zoo Pack. Hacker Pack, them send us to Track Nine. Tempelhof, we kill Them, deader and dead."

Again, Becky Sharp's final statement was delivered with gusto, and, again, the gathered Aux cheered and whooped, applauding the dam with fervour.

"What about us?" asked Ben Gun. "What about Zoo Pack? Us, we walked all-away around. Us, we made alliances. Us, we saved Walter Sickert. Us, we have no fiefdom. Us, we have no Ezra Pound, no Alpha dog."

Becky Sharp's brow ridge furrow deeply as she looked down on the Zoo Pack pup. The Them's head on her staff of office quivered.

Holeman Hunt rose and stood on one side of her. Seeing the determination with which he joined the Alpha dam, Makewar Thackeray stood, and took a pace or two to stand on her other side. Hacker Pack and Hansa Pack were old allies, and Makewar Thackeray would further that alliance, especially after what he had seen on the battlefield.

"Zoo Pack, it has an Alpha dog," said Holeman Hunt. "Zoo Pack, it has Oscar so Wild. Zoo Pack, it has a Hearer, it has Walter Sickert. Zoo Pack, it has our promise, it has our respect, it has our friendship. "

There was a long pause.

"This day," Holeman Hunt continued, "this alliance, we ousted Them from Track Nine. Tomorrow, us, we oust Them from Track Two. Tomorrow, us, we take back Zoo Pack fiefdom."

Oscar so Wild stood and gestured for Edward Leer to join him. The Aux of Zoo Pack cheered and pounded their fists on the platform or slapped their hands against their thighs.

"Ezra Pound, him gone, deader and dead. Him a great Alpha dog. Him the stuff of legends, tougher and tough," said Oscar so Wild. The second round of cheers from the Zoo Pack was louder and longer than the first, and the other packers joined in. They all knew what Ezra Pound had done in the tunnels.

"Edward Leer, him our tale-teller. Him told the old legends, him told them smart. Him has muscles in his head," said Oscar so Wild. "Him knew when to listen and him knew when to spin a fable."

Another cheer reverberated around the tunnel and died away.

There was silence.

Edward Leer knew what he must do.

"Gene the Hackman, top dog, him done the great Walk Around," he began. "Not for him the darkness, not for him the cold, not for him the Time of Ice. Gene the Hackman, him got whet. Gene the Hackman, him got whet and walked the Earth, and him killed Them."

He took a breath. The gathered Aux waited in silence for what would come next.